"Memphis . . . darlin'.

"I didn't forget you. To this day, I have yet to walk through an airport without looking for your face, and every time it snows, I remember what it felt like to kiss you."

All movement within her ceased except the heartbeat that was suddenly racing out of control. She looked up at him. Truth was staring her right in the face.

"Cowboy, you take my breath away."

He lowered his head with a groan, and when their lips grazed and then centered, he felt an empty space inside of him closing. His hands shook as he ran them through her hair.

Billie soared. The touch of his hands, the strength of his body, the tenderness of his kiss all served to prove that she was treading deep water with no chance of survival, unless one of them made a quick move.

"Ah, Memphis, you are the best thing I—"

"Don't say it, Matt. Just hold me."

By Sharon Sala

SHARON SALA

Second Chances

HarperTorch
An Imprint of HarperCollinsPublishers

This is a work of fiction. Names, characters, places, and incidents are products of the author's imagination or are used fictitiously and are not to be construed as real. Any resemblance to actual events, locales, organizations, or persons, living or dead, is entirely coincidental.

HARPERTORCH
An Imprint of HarperCollins*Publishers*
10 East 53rd Street
New York, New York 10022-5299

Copyright © 1996 by Sharon Sala
ISBN: 0-06-108327-5

First HarperTorch paperback printing: January 2003
First HarperCollins paperback printing: October 1996

HarperCollins ®, HarperTorch™, and ❦™ are trademarks of HarperCollins Publishers Inc.

Printed in the United States of America

Visit HarperTorch on the World Wide Web at www.harpercollins.com

10 9 8 7 6 5 4

This book is dedicated to the victims who perished in the Oklahoma City bombing that took place at the Alfred P. Murrah Federal Building on April 19, 1995, to the families they left behind, and to the rescue workers who gave those they saved a "second chance" at life.

❧ ❀ ❀ ❀ *Prologue*

"All flights have been grounded until further notice.
We repeat . . . due to the near-blizzard conditions in the
city of Denver, all flights have been grounded at this
time. Contact your ticket counter to . . ."

The announcement coming over the public address
system was no surprise to Matt Holt. He'd been on one
of the last planes to land and considered himself lucky
to be on firm ground now, even if it was blanketed with
several feet of snow with more still falling.

He stood along with other morose travelers who
suddenly found themselves snowbound on New Year's
Eve, staring out the windows of the observation deck
and into the night at the thick, swirling eddies of snow
buffeting the glass. Unlike many of the other travelers
who were bemoaning the celebrations they'd be missing, Matt was lost in thought, remembering the son
he'd just left in Los Angeles, and the satisfaction he
felt in knowing that in a little over three years, Scott
would graduate from UCLA.

He'd given up more than time and money for Scott's
education. It was a long way from Los Angeles to
Matt's ranch outside of Dallas. Their visits were few

and far between, but he didn't care. He'd made a promise to himself on the day Scott was born that his son would not follow the same wild, hell-raising path that he'd taken.

His eyes narrowed in thought. In a short time a new year would be at hand. If he was lucky, it wouldn't be as rocky as the last nineteen had been. Scott hadn't been planned. For that matter, nor had Matt planned on getting married at the age of sixteen, but he was man enough to admit that the need for it was all his fault. For all intents and purposes, his freedom had ended the night he'd gotten Susan Brookhauser pregnant. He'd celebrated his seventeenth birthday by walking the floor with a newborn son, who had a rousing case of colic. Nine years later, a drunk driver had ended what was left of their marriage in exactly fifteen seconds. Three days later Matt buried Susan, took their son by the hand, and went home to feed and water the cows he and Susan had just bought. It was July, and there was a hell of a drought. Grieving would have to wait.

A blast of air suddenly flattened snowflakes against the windows, driving some of the onlookers back away from the view. But Matt never flinched. At the age of thirty-five, a blizzard was nothing next to what he'd already faced and survived.

He shifted his stance, ignoring the other travelers, who were bemoaning their fate at being stranded without their loved ones. He'd never known his parents. Foster homes had been his life until he'd gotten Susan pregnant. Then she and their child had become the first family he'd ever had.

But that was then, and this was now, and there was no one waiting for him who cared whether he came or went except for a couple of hired hands and a thousand head of cattle. Their concern went only as far as paychecks and hay by the ton. With Scott in school halfway across the country, Matt Holt was more or less right back where he'd started in life. Alone.

Matt was not the only snowbound traveler who'd purposefully distanced himself from the moody crowd. Billie Jean Walker was stranded, not only in the Denver airport, but between her past and her future. Like all the other times she'd tried to connect with her father, going home to Memphis for Christmas had been a mistake. She'd known it all the while she was packing to leave the UCLA campus. Twice while waiting for her plane to embark from LAX she'd almost talked herself into spending the time alone in the dorm. There would be other students there who had nowhere to go for the holidays. She could hang out with them. And while she was standing there talking herself out of going, her flight had been called.

Like a puppet under someone else's control, Billie found herself boarding with the other holiday travelers and, hours later, disembarking in Memphis. No one waited for her there with open arms. Even though she hadn't really expected her father to be present, she still felt a brief surge of disappointment. And as soon as she did, she hated herself for being so weak, for wanting something from a man who didn't want her.

A cab driver was the first person who welcomed her to Tennessee. Jarrod Walker was too busy with his latest wife to do more than wave in Billie's direction when she walked into the house where she'd been raised.

Billie took one look at stepmother number six and headed for her room to unpack. It wasn't so much the bountiful breasts and plunging neckline of stepmama's dress that put her off as it was the hard glitter Billie saw in her eyes when they were introduced. If it hadn't been so pathetic, Billie might have laughed. Number six didn't need to feel threatened by the appearance of a daughter. Jarrod Walker had never wanted to be a father.

For years, he'd more or less hated Billie's guts for ever being born. Then insult had been added to injury when his wife had learned of one of his infidelities and, in a fit of depression, had taken her own life, leaving Jarrod with a child . . . and an unwelcome responsibility.

Christmas morning was the fiasco Billie feared it would be. In spite of the time she'd spent choosing her father's gift—a hand-tooled, leather briefcase—he'd barely looked at it before tossing it aside. He had eyes for nothing and no one but his latest wife.

Number six had unwrapped presents for forty-five minutes solid while Jarrod watched with a doting eye. Between every gift, the pair exchanged passionate kisses, with no thought or consideration for Billie's presence. Finally, Billie had taken her single gift from her father, another pair of gloves, and tossed them into the closet with the other twelve pairs he'd bought her over the years, quietly choosing to leave the room before their performance became X-rated.

Christmas dinner was no better. The only comments her father made to her were criticisms or condemnations and were accompanied by six's silly giggles and high-pitched squeals of admiration for his witty repartee.

Days later, Billie boarded a plane to LA with relief, anxious to get back to campus and the holiday parties she knew would be in progress. And she'd almost had it made until a Denver snowstorm changed her plans.

A traveler sitting beside Billie muttered, "This is not the way I planned to spend New Year's Eve."

She nodded. It hadn't been on her agenda either. She'd had visions of finally connecting with the dimpled, broad-shouldered hunk who lived down the hall from her—of being right next to him at the stroke of midnight in an irresistible dress and sweeping him off his feet.

She sighed, shifting restlessly in her seat. Honesty forbade her daydreams to go any farther. If the truth be known, the hunk down the hall didn't know she existed. Although she'd just turned twenty, she felt too tall and inadequate to ever attract anyone like him.

And to add insult to a dreadful day, a familiar ache was beginning to pull at the back of Billie's neck. The long black hair she'd piled high on her head that morning was starting to weigh on her nerves. Were it not for the tangles it got in when she traveled, she would let it down to hang loose.

Bored with the same scenery of bags, coats, and travel-weary faces, she glanced around and, not for the first time, noted the tall, silent cowboy who stood a distance away at the windows overlooking the snow-covered runways.

His sheepskin coat looked huge, and she could only imagine the breadth of shoulders beneath it. That wide-brimmed, black Stetson he was wearing seemed more suited to shade sun than snow, but he wore it with the assurance of a man who fit his skin. Only a brief glimpse now and then of his face had been possible, but what she'd seen of the man she admired, right down to his long-legged Levi's and the black, work-worn boots, slightly turned up at the toes.

She watched him from across the room, imagining in her youthful fantasy that he was a man of secrets and unleashed passion.

And so time passed until it was nearly midnight, and as the hour neared, the waiting area began to come alive. It was as if the travelers had been forced to admit that their chances of getting off the ground on this night were gone. In a fit of merrymaking, some seemed intent on ringing in the new year no matter where they were. One traveler produced a bag of party favors he'd been carrying with him, another a giant bag of popcorn that had been destined for someone else's party. Money was pooled and soft drinks were purchased and passed throughout the gathering crowd. Strangers who'd been sitting next to each other for hours without speaking suddenly struck up conversations.

Unwilling to be left out of the meager festivities, Billie stowed her carry-on bag beneath her seat, piled her coat on top of that, and stood. As she began to move through the crowd, a man thrust a can of soda into her hand. She smiled bashfully, unaware that it transformed her serious features into those of true beauty. On impulse, she took a second can of soda and turned toward the cowboy at the windows. He seemed impervious to the revelry around him, but Billie recognized self-imposed isolation when she saw it. She should. She'd been practicing it all her life.

While she watched him, she began to realize that there was something more compelling about him than the strength he conveyed. Had she stopped to analyze her impulse, she might have known it was his solitary state that drew her. But she didn't hesitate, and because she didn't, the first impulsive thing she'd ever done was destined to change her life forever.

Matt sensed, rather than heard, her approach, as if someone had invaded his space without asking. Instinctively he shifted his absent gaze from the swirling snow outside to the reflection of the woman he saw coming toward him from the rear.

At first, she was nothing more than a tall, dark shadow. It was hard to tell exactly how much woman was concealed beneath the long, bulky sweater she wore, but she had a slow, lanky stride that made his belly draw in an unexpected ache. Just as he was concentrating on slim hips encased in tight denim and telling himself he'd rather be alone, she spoke.

"Would you like something to drink?"

Every thought he had came to a stop as her voice wrapped around his senses. Men called it a bedroom voice—a low, husky drawl that made his toes curl and his breath catch.

He turned, and as he did imagination came to a quick, painful halt. She was so beautiful, and so damned young it made him sick. He took a deep breath and redirected his thoughts to a saner place as she offered him the can of soda.

It was a simple motion. Nothing difficult about accepting a cold drink from a pretty woman, but when he reached for the can and got her fingers instead, once again he lost contact with reality. Her skin was smooth and soft against his work-roughened palm, and it set him to wondering if she felt like that all over. He shuddered, then frowned as he tried to get back to the business at hand, hoping she would blame his reaction to her on the cold can instead.

But when their hands touched, Matt wasn't the only one in a state of sudden confusion. Billie lost her train of thought, while the smile on her lips froze like the snow against the windows. There was a look in his eyes that she'd never before seen on a man's face. A mystery, an intensity in the dark blue gaze that she hadn't bargained for. Several staggering breaths later, she remembered what she'd been about to say.

"I thought you might like to . . ."

She never got to finish what she was saying. He took the can and set it down on the ledge without taking his eyes off her face. Mesmerized, she stood without moving as his hands lifted toward her cheeks. When his fingers sifted through the strands of escaping curls that were falling around her eyes, she caught herself leaning toward his touch and jerked back in shock. Then he grinned, and she felt herself relaxing once more.

He lifted a stray curl from the corner of her eye. "That face is too pretty to hide."

A surge of pure joy made Billie weak at the knees. Embarrassed, she looked away, and when she looked back, found herself locked into a wild, stormy gaze and dealing with another sort of surge. Ashamed of what she was thinking, she pretended interest in the storm and knew that she was blushing.

"Where are you going?"

I wish to hell it was with you. Wisely, Matt kept his wishes to himself.

"Dallas."

She nodded and looked down at the floor.

"I was in Memphis for Christmas vacation. I'm on my way back to California." When she got the nerve to look up, those dark blue eyes were still staring intently. She felt compelled to add, "I'm in college there."

A strange, almost fatalistic smile spread across his face. Billie paused, wondering what was going on inside that mind.

"So is my son."

This time she didn't hide her surprise. "You don't look old enough to have a son in college!"

Regret spread into one big ache. It took everything Matt had to manage a weak grin.

"I got an early start."

When Billie realized what he was implying, she blushed again, and wondered where the composure she'd spent twenty years creating had gone.

They shared a long, silent moment, then the noise of the crowd behind them broke the tension. It was obvious by the loud chanting voices that the countdown to midnight had begun.

"Ten . . . nine . . . eight."

Billie looked up. His eyes were so blue. So compelling. So lonely. She took a deep breath.

"Seven . . . six . . . five."

She bit her lower lip, then took a step forward. Just in case. Hoping—wishing—needing him to want what she was wanting.

"Four . . . three . . . two."

Matt groaned beneath his breath. He saw the invitation in her eyes as well as her body language. So help him God, there wasn't enough strength left in him to deny either of them the obvious.

The merrymakers were in full swing as they shouted, "Happy New Year!"

Matt cupped her face in his hands, then waited. If she didn't want this, now was her chance to move. To his utter joy, she not only stayed but scooted a hairbreadth closer to his chest until he could almost feel the gentle jut of her breasts against the front of his shirt. Almost . . . but not quite.

"Happy New Year, Memphis." He lowered his head.

Until it happened, Billie Jean Walker had no idea she'd been waiting for this moment all of her life. But when his lips touched hers in a soft, undemanding way, she went limp. Just when she was getting used to the feel of him on her, his mouth moved, molding her lips, then centering and sucking the breath from her body and the sanity from her senses.

Billie moaned, then swayed against him as she realized he had swallowed the sound. The pull of their passion was too real to ignore. Sliding her arms around his neck, she clutched the sheepskin collar of his coat for support and leaned into the embrace.

All sound of the party faded. She knew only the man in whose arms she stood. Felt his body only as it reshaped itself to hers. Tasted tears and knew they were her own.

Matt groaned as he came up for air.

Dear Lord, this was more than it should have been, and not nearly enough. The restraint he'd imposed upon himself years ago had just disappeared in a stranger's arms at the stroke of midnight on a lonely New Year's Eve. He wanted this woman in a way he'd never wanted anything before, and it couldn't be. This kiss had to mean nothing more than passing a holiday tradition in a time-honored way.

When he broke contact, Billie couldn't think. All she knew was that she was sorry it was over. There were tears in her eyes as she struggled with words that wouldn't come.

Matt tried to smile as he pressed a fingertip across her swollen lips. "Sssh, don't talk. It will ruin the magic."

Tears spilled down her cheeks in silent misery for the dying moment.

He leaned forward until their foreheads were touching. "Ah, Memphis, you're killing me."

They stood, head to head, their breaths mingling on each other's faces, listening for the sounds of breaking hearts and dying passion. And then, to Billie's surprise, he dug his fingers through the coils of her hair, pulling out every pin he could find.

Billie held her breath, watching in open awe at the wild need on his face. And when her long hair tumbled around his hands and across her shoulders, she shivered.

"Beautiful . . . you are absolutely beautiful." His voice was soft as he traced the path of her lower lip and the moisture he'd left behind. "How can I let you . . . ?"

The question ended before it was over because it wasn't his to ask. Letting her go was not his option because she'd never been his to keep. The pain of that knowledge was more than he could bear, and because he cursed the truth between them, reverted to true nature and took what little she could give before it was too late.

Twice more they shared a kiss that rocked them where they stood. The first wrought fantasies of actually moving beyond a kiss. The second was explosive enough to move beyond fantasy to the truth of what he wanted to do with her.

Billie felt the proof of his need as it pressed hard and urgently against her lower belly. She groaned, clutching at his shoulders as she tried to draw him closer.

Lifting his head with a jerk, he stared intently at her wide dark eyes and she had no way of knowing that he saw more fear and uncertainty on her face than lust. And because he did, it gave him the courage to do what must be done.

With a wry smile and a final, lingering look, he turned, picked up his bag from the floor, slung the strap over his shoulder, and disappeared into the crowd. To her dismay, he never looked back.

Billie was in shock. Long moments passed before she could think to move. Then, when she did, she began to run—forgetting the bag and coat that she'd piled beneath a seat—forgetting that every piece of identification she owned was in her purse beneath the coat—forgetting everything but the need to find the man from Dallas and beg him for more than he'd given her. But she'd reacted too late. He was gone.

Hour after hour and throughout the long night, Billie walked the halls of the airport, searching for a tall cowboy wearing a big black hat and boots that turned up at the toes, praying that any minute she'd turn a corner and see his face and his smile. But when daylight came she was forced to face the facts. In less than two hours she would be boarding a plane bound for California, half a country away. And she didn't even know his name.

She had no way of knowing that Matt Holt had paid a cab driver an exorbitant amount of money to get him out of the airport and to a hotel. He hadn't trusted himself to stay, and he didn't trust her to have enough sense to tell him no.

Determined that their paths not cross again, he'd delayed his own departure a day and a half longer. Even when he'd known for sure that no tall, dark-eyed woman would be waiting, he walked the airport corridors with an emptiness he hadn't expected to feel. As if he'd lost something unexpected and precious that he shouldn't have.

After his flight had taken off, he sat in his seat, staring out of the window and watching the earth from above, trying to concentrate on the work that awaited him back home and the thousand head of cattle always waiting to be fed. But it was no use. He couldn't think past the lump in his throat and the knot in his belly.

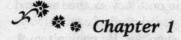 **Chapter 1**

Two and a half years later

Wind whipped in and out the open windows of the dusty black Jeep, shifting collars and hairdos with pushy insistence. But the occupants were long past caring about their appearances. Their entire focus was upon the ranch house just visible in the distance.

It had been a long, hot ride from Los Angeles to Dallas, but their destination was at hand. Summer vacation had arrived, bringing three of the four book-weary students inside the Jeep halfway across the country just to see what made their driver tick.

On the UCLA campus, Scott Holt's slow Texas drawl, along with a quick wit and a ready smile, made him a favorite among the females, as well as the males. And over the years, his amiable attitude and sharp mind had impressed more than one of his professors. With a little over three semesters left to graduation, Scott could almost see the light at the end of his long tunnel of education. But the satisfaction in knowing he was nearly at the end of his degree was nothing to the jolt of pleasure he got in coming home.

"Texas air even smells better," he said, and, in a quick burst of laughter, accelerated. His passengers began grabbing at belongings as they shouted at him to slow down.

Scott looked over his shoulder, grinning when the pretty blonde in the backseat suddenly clutched the seat with one hand and shook the other one at the back of his head.

"What's wrong, Steph?"

Stephanie Hodge rolled her eyes and tried hard to frown, but it was difficult to stay mad at someone as engaging as Scott Holt.

"I'm reminding myself that I'm going to be busy the next time my big brother decides to hang out with cowboys."

"I thought you said you lived just off the highway," Mike Hodge grumbled, bracing himself with a hand against the dashboard. "That rooftop you pointed out is still a good two miles away."

"Four," Scott said, then laughed again. "You're in Texas now, remember? Out here, everything's bigger—even miles."

Both brother and sister groaned, then proceeded to tease their classmate in a good-natured manner while reminding him that they'd get back at him when he returned to California that fall.

As Mike and Stephanie were one-upping each other with sarcastic jokes at his expense, Scott glanced up in the rearview mirror at his other passenger, wondering what expression B.J. was hiding behind her sunglasses today.

Stephanie glanced nervously over at her seatmate. "You okay, Billie?"

Billie nodded and smiled, while longing for the chance to get out and stretch. It seemed like hours since their last stop. She was ready for shade and something cool to drink. Her long legs were straddling a stack of duffel bags, and her bare neck and arms were a berry brown beneath the thin cotton tank top that she wore. She rode with the bumps and thumps as if she were rooted to the spot, while the wind whipping through the windows tried unsuccessfully to undo the long, black braid hanging over her shoulder. Only a few of the shorter strands had escaped the braid and whipped madly around the edges of her eyes, but she didn't seem to notice or care.

Scott shrugged, shifting his gaze to the road ahead. B.J. was an odd one, but he liked her—even admired her. Already into her second year of graduate school, she often acted like the trio's chaperone instead of their equal, although little more than a couple of years separated them in age.

She was the kind of girl he could hang out with when he was between girlfriends, or when there was nothing else to do. She didn't chatter nonstop, or read things into their relationship that weren't there. To be honest, Scott didn't know why they hadn't gone past being friends. He'd even been a little surprised when she'd agreed to come to the ranch along with Mike and Stephanie, but his invitation had been genuine just the same. He sensed a loneliness in B.J. that even a roomful of classmates couldn't breach.

"Is that it?" Mike asked, as a peeling, two-story farmhouse suddenly appeared on their left.

"Nope. That's old Daisy Bedford's place. Doesn't amount to much anymore, but it's hers just the same." Scott laughed to himself, remembering the years of cold war that existed between Daisy and his father. "She's a character. See that window on the second floor, the one that faces south?"

As they moved past the house, the trio turned to look at the upper story while waiting for him to continue.

"Wave at it," he said, and they did so without question.

"I'll bet a dollar to a doughnut that Daisy not only saw you, but knows down to the ketchup stain on Stephanie's shirt what you guys are wearing."

"You're kidding!" Mike said, and pivoted even farther around in his seat. "How?"

"She's got a telescope. Keeps a weather eye on anything within seeing distance, including my dad, and he knows it." He laughed again, as old memories returned. "They've had a running feud for years about it. He's just as bad, though. He does outrageous things in plain view of her window that he knows will tick her off. When she's had enough, she leaves these odd, ominous warnings on the answering machine without leaving her name. It's not that she thinks we don't know who it is, it's just that she doesn't give a damn."

"Warnings as in threats?" Stephanie asked, unable to stop a slight shiver of apprehension as the old, faded farmhouse disappeared from view.

Scott grinned and looked over his shoulder at Stephanie as they settled back into their seats.

"Naw, more like 'I told you so' messages."

Mike laughed. "Wow! What a neighbor."

B.J. was more thoughtful, wondering how a woman alone and advanced in age could handle something so vast as this Texas land. Curiosity compelled her to ask.

"Does she still work her land? I saw machinery in the old barns."

"Nope. Dad said her husband died before I was born. When he and my mother first bought our place, Daisy was on their front porch to welcome them to the area. When Mother was killed, Dad said she came and cleaned our house so that it would be ready for mourners."

B.J. frowned. "So why is she so antagonistic now if she was so helpful before?"

Scott laughed aloud. "I'm not sure, but I think it started when I was around twelve. Dad had this one lady friend who has long since gone by the wayside. Anyway, it had something to do with them skinny-dipping in a stock pond while I was in school. Daisy wears her widow's mantle like a yoke of burden and was pissed at Dad for not doing the same." Scott shrugged. "My parents got married when they were teenagers, and Dad was real young when Mother died. For that matter, he's still quite a hoss. He won't be forty for a couple of years yet."

While B.J. was absorbing Scott's unexpected confidences, they topped a small rise.

Scott suddenly whooped, "We're home!" and

swerved toward the driveway to their left, coming to a sliding stop in front of his house.

Roofed with red Spanish tiles, the brown, adobe walls of the long, U-shaped house, as well as the courtyard in front that was filled with colorful but hardy flowers, was reminiscent of Spanish grandees rather than the Texans who'd come later.

As she tried to imagine a man who had not only raised a child by himself but had prospered, it wasn't envy Billie felt as she stared at the house; it was regret. If only she'd had a father like that.

Stephanie crawled out of the backseat, groaning and stretching at the same time. "Thank goodness we're here. My butt will never be the same."

"That's good news," Mike said, and grinned when she gave him an obligatory swat.

Billie crawled over the bags at her feet and out of the Jeep, stretching one long leg and then the other before arching her back and lifting her arms to the sky. Her braid swung down her back like the pendulum on a clock, and the thin fabric of her tank top clung to her hot, sticky torso like a bodysuit.

The motion was nothing unusual, but both Mike and Scott were instantly struck by the unconscious sensuousness of it . . . and of her. They looked, then quickly looked away, aware that Billie would not welcome what they'd been thinking.

"Leave the bags," Scott said. "We'll get them later. It looks like everyone is down at the barns. Come on, I can't wait for you to meet my dad."

Mike grinned. "Yeah, me either. Personally, I think

you've been stringing us along all these years about his stunts. I'm willing to bet that he's not nearly as big and wild as you claim."

Scott's eyes twinkled. "Just shut up and follow me."

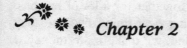 **Chapter 2**

As they walked toward the corrals, Scott couldn't help noticing the culture shock on his friends' faces. It was as if they didn't know which way to look first, although he had to give B.J. credit for appearing more interested than nervous. He knew she wasn't a native Californian, as Mike and Stephanie were, but she *was* from Memphis, which claimed its own kind of big-city living.

The air near the barn was thick with dust and the frantic bawling of cows being separated from their offspring. Add to that the loud, colorful language of the hired help working the cattle, and the scene they walked up on came close to being a three-ring circus.

Mike pointed toward a corral to their left. "What are they doing?"

"Separating cows from their calves."

Stephanie moaned. "But why, Scott? Just listen to them cry."

He grinned. "Cows don't cry, they bawl . . . or, if you tick them off real good . . . they bellow."

She made a face, then shrugged. "Whatever. It still

seems awfully mean. Why don't you just leave them together until the calf grows up?"

"We don't leave them together for a lot of reasons. Cows shouldn't be nursing year-round because they lose too much weight. And, we make more money if we sell the calves before we have to start feeding them out. We don't keep everything we raise. Dad always holds back a few heifers each year to replace the cows too old to breed, but other than that we sell all the new calves. Also, every few years we have to replace our herd bulls. That way we eliminate inbreeding and keep the bloodlines strong."

Mike leaned against the fence, watching the animation on Scott's face, and saw a side of him that he'd never known. Scott Holt might be just shy of a business degree and able to blend with the L.A. in-crowd quite well, but unless Mike missed his guess, Scott would always be a country boy at heart.

While the three continued to talk, none of them noticed that B.J. had climbed a corral fence, taken a seat on the highest rail, and was watching the scene before her in silent fascination. In her mind, the dirt and ruckus was secondary to the strength and skill of the men at work.

And then, in the midst of all of the noise, a new and louder one was suddenly added. A thick cloud of dust began appearing on the rise beyond the barns. They turned to look as a small herd of cattle topped the hill and began heading toward the corrals at a run. Behind them, and at breakneck speed, a man riding a big dirt bike suddenly appeared, weaving in and out around the perimeter of the herd, chasing after stragglers, pushing them onward toward the gates, which were quickly being swung open. The engine revved at a constant, high-pitched whine, as man and machine flew over the ground with little care for obstacles in their path.

Bare-headed except for a red bandanna tied around his forehead, shirtless, and coated with a thin film of dust, he rode the dirt bike with the same effortless skill of a man on a horse. Tight denim accentuated his long legs as he straddled the bike with consummate grace, moving with the motion, yet ever conscious that he was the one in control. As the last of the cattle were herded into the pen, he revved up the bike and popped a wheelie, breaking the intent expression he'd been wearing with a wide, engaging smile.

A couple of the hired hands cheered his devil-may-care attitude, and one tossed his hat in the air, following it with a colorful curse that made Stephanie blush. But blushing was the last thing on Billie's mind. From the moment he'd come over the hill, she'd been in shock. It was all she could manage to grip the fence and try not to fall.

Scott laughed aloud, unaware of B.J.'s reaction. He couldn't have asked for a better display of his father's personality if he'd ordered it.

"Who's that?" Mike asked, watching in open-mouthed awe the big dusty man getting off of the bike.

"That, my friends, is my father. He's a little rough around the edges, but he's pure gold through and through. You're gonna love him."

Brother and sister eyed Scott with renewed respect,

wondering if he was hiding any of these wild, cowboy ways, while Billie momentarily lost the power to talk. Pure, unadulterated panic shot through her, leaving her weak and wondering if she should turn tail and run now, or wait for the other shoe to drop.

One of the men shouted at Matt, pointing toward the foursome at one end of the corrals. "Hey, boss, your boy is home."

Matt turned, a wide smile of delight marking his joy as he saw Scott wave. He started toward him in a long-legged lope.

Scott ran to meet him and was instantly engulfed in a big hug.

"Welcome home!" Matt said, and clapped him roughly on the back, unashamed of the lusty embrace they had just shared.

Scott grinned as he realized the impact his father's appearance would have on them all.

"Damn, but it's good to see you," Matt said, and, in a fit of delight, actually lifted Scott off his feet. When he put him back down, Scott was laughing.

"I used to think that one day I'd get too big for that to happen. Now, I think you'll just have to get too old."

Matt gave his son a go-to-hell look. "Only in your dreams, boy, in your dreams."

Stephanie sidled up between the trio of men to ogle Matt's dusty physique, with no apologies for looking her fill. Scott grinned again, only this time at his dad's discomfiture at being the object of such unbridled attention.

"Gee, Dad, you shouldn't have bothered to dress on

our account," Scott quipped, then laughed aloud when Matt wiped a dirty handprint down the middle of Scott's semiclean T-shirt.

"Don't mess with me, boy. You know I can outdirty you any day of the week."

At this point, Matt decided he'd been looked at long enough, and it was time to officially meet Scott's friends.

"I see you brought company, although I probably won't know how to act." He winked at Stephanie, who promptly blushed and tried to pretend she hadn't been gawking at his half-dressed body. "I haven't talked to anyone but Nate and Charlie and these damned cows in so long that I may have forgotten how."

"Dad, these are my friends, Stephanie Hodge and her brother Mike."

Matt winked at Stephanie again, and smiled at Mike. "I'll wash before I shake your hands. You might not be as forgiving as Scott."

Then Scott realized that one of his visitors was missing.

"Where did B.J. go?"

Mike pointed a distance behind them. "Up there on the fence."

"Come with me, Dad, there's one more I want you to meet."

Scott started toward the corrals, expecting his father to follow. But Matt had taken one look at the long black braid hanging down the middle of the young woman's back and, in spite of the midday heat, had an unexplained chill. When she turned, he realized his premonition had been justified.

Memphis! Sweet Jesus, it's Memphis!

Scott tugged playfully at her hair. "B.J., come down off your perch and meet my dad."

Oh God! Oh dear God! How could this happen? She squinted her eyes, then bit her lip as she swung her legs over and around, dismounting the fence as she would have a horse.

When her feet hit the ground, she looked up. The man beside Scott looked as shocked as she felt.

"Dad, I'd like you to meet my friend, B.J. Walker."

Matt finally moved, but his legs felt like lead. He didn't know what hurt him worse, the fact that Scott was holding her hand, or that she let him.

"Billie," she said, ignoring the surprise on Scott's face as she corrected him. "My name is Billie."

Matt took a deep breath and looked at Scott. He knew this would come out all wrong, but so help him God, he had to know the answer to one question now.

"Are you sleeping with her?"

Scott was so shocked that for a moment he couldn't find the words to answer. His father was notorious for saying what he thought, but even this was extreme.

"I don't think that it's any of your damned business." Then he startled himself, as well as Billie, by putting his arm around her shoulder in a less-than-brotherly embrace.

Billie flinched, then looked at Scott in surprise. Not only was he acting strange, but she'd never heard him use that tone of voice. If she didn't know better, she might think he was acting possessive, and there was nothing in their relationship that warranted such behavior.

"But it's my business, isn't it, Scott," she said sharply, and moved out from under his arm. Her eyes were wide and fixed, her mouth trembling slightly as she looked at Matt. "Scott and I are just friends." Then she added, "I had no idea."

Accepting her explanation at face value, all Matt could do was stare. He knew if he didn't change the direction of this conversation soon, everything was going to fly to pieces, including his relationship with his son. Trying to put a semblance of normalcy back into the conversation, he joked, "If he'd let me know you all were coming, I would have polished my boots."

Mike and Stephanie looked at Matt's bare, dusty chest, the sweat-stained bandanna tied around his forehead, and the body-molding jeans he was wearing. Mike rolled his eyes when he noticed that Stephanie couldn't seem to tear her gaze away from Scott's father.

Matt struck Stephanie as somewhere between the kind of man her mother had warned her about and the kind that you married. In looks, he was drop-dead gorgeous. She poked Scott on the arm and giggled. "You didn't tell us your dad was so witty."

Relieved that the conversation had taken a lighter turn, Scott's mouth tilted in a smaller, but just as wicked, version of his father's cocky grin.

"Oh, he's a charmer when he's on a roll, aren't you, Dad?"

"I don't have to answer that."

Just then a loud round of curses sounded in a nearby corral. Matt turned to look. When he realized what was happening, he made his excuses.

"I'd better get back to work. Scott's going to have to play host and show you where to put your things."

He started to walk away, then turned. He was looking at Scott, but the question was directed at Billie, and she knew it.

"They will be staying . . . won't they?"

Unaware of the underlying meaning to his father's question, Scott assured him they were.

"You bet. I talked them into a whole week on the ranch. Thought I'd show them a little of the real world before they fritter away their summer vacation on frivolous pursuits."

Matt felt weak with relief. Thank God. He had walked away once and regretted that more than anything he'd ever done. Maybe . . . just maybe . . . he'd been given a second chance. And then he remembered the odd look on Scott's face when he'd asked Scott about their relationship and thought again.

Taking her cue from Matt's behavior, Billie looked away as he walked by her, and it was still not enough to break the tension between them. *Why, Matt? Why didn't you say something? Why didn't you tell Scott we'd met before?* The questions were making her crazy, and it didn't seem as if she would get answers anytime soon.

Rocked by the fact that she was actually going to spend the night under the same roof with the man who'd haunted her dreams for over two years, she couldn't think of anything to do or say that wouldn't make her appear a fool. And then Scott called.

"Come on, B.J., or should I say, Billie?"

She lifted her head. The taunt in Scott's voice was just shy of anger, but she wasn't in the mood to explain. He knew her given name. He'd chosen to call her B.J. instead. That was his choice, as it was hers to have Matt Holt know her real name. Besides, it was only fitting that he know her name when he already knew how she tasted. She glared back at Scott, her chin tilting in a "dare to argue with me" posture.

"Nothing has changed except maybe your manners, but I suppose you can call me what you've always called me."

Scott frowned, unsure of why he'd chosen to shift their easy camaraderie, but well aware that he had.

He started toward the house. "Okay, you've met the man. Now I guess we'd better unload the Jeep."

Stephanie slipped her hand under Billie's arm as they followed a few footsteps behind. "Wow! Scott's dad is something, isn't he? Did you see the way he looked at you? I think he likes you."

Billie felt her face getting hot, and it became even worse when she realized that Mike and Scott had overheard Stephanie's remark.

"You're imagining things," she said shortly. "He was just being kind."

Mike grinned, but Scott saw nothing humorous about it at all. He'd seen women make fools of themselves over his father for years, and in all fairness to his dad, Matt had rarely, if ever, done anything about it. But he had to admit, the old man had reacted pretty oddly to B.J. What was worse, Scott didn't think he liked the fact that his dad might be hitting on one of his friends. The more he thought about it, the angrier he got. It didn't seem right, and it damn sure wasn't fair. His dad had his own set of friends. He had no business horning in on any of Scott's.

"Grab your stuff," he ordered when they reached the Jeep.

They reached for their bags, intent on carrying everything in one trip. To Billie's surprise, Scott reached across the seat and took the largest of her bags out of her hands.

"I'll carry that. It looks pretty heavy."

The look on Billie's face was a combination of surprise and disbelief. "Where were you when I carried it, plus these two, down the stairs at my apartment? Sitting out in the street talking to Mike, I believe."

Scott flushed, then glared, but he wouldn't let go of the handle.

"It's no heavier now than it was then," she added, yanking it out of his hands. "Now lead the way and get over whatever it is that's rolling around in your feeble little mind."

Mike whooped. "Boy, she nailed you there, buddy. Come on, show us to the uh . . . bunkhouse."

Because he had no other choice, Scott relented, refusing to ask himself what the hell he was doing. He had no claim on Billie Walker. In fact, he was pretty sure he didn't even want one. What she did was none of his business. But as he led the way into the house, he kept thinking of Billie . . . and his dad . . . and got mad all over again.

It took most of the afternoon before Scott convinced

himself he was making a big deal out of nothing. By suppertime, the friends were back to normal, laughing and teasing in the kitchen as they shared the duties of preparing a meal.

Playfully, Scott flipped water at both the women, who were peeling vegetables to put in with the half-cooked pot roast. Stephanie turned just in time to keep from getting it in her face, then spun and shoved a peeled onion toward his nose.

"Children, children, I think that's enough," Billie said, pretending to scold and sidestepping the water they'd spilled on the floor.

Scott frowned. Somehow she always wound up being the referee in the crowd, but after today he saw her attitude in a different light, and because he was a man, reacted before he thought. His tone of voice was just shy of condescending as he waved a dripping dish-cloth over the floor.

"Excuse us! Miss Walker says we need to behave. It's too bad she doesn't know how to play."

The expression on Billie's face stilled. Criticism was something she'd lived with all of her life, and some-thing to which she thought she was accustomed, but she'd never had to endure it from people she consid-ered her friends.

Billie lifted her chin, daring Scott to continue. When he looked away, she turned back to the sink and started washing the potatoes they'd peeled, glad to have some-thing to do with her shaking hands. She scrubbed at them furiously, trying to ignore a knot of pain in her chest that was rolling and tightening with every breath that she took. To her dismay, the knot gave a yank, sending tears to her eyes that had nothing to do with the onions Stephanie had peeled.

The moment he'd said it, Scott knew that he'd hurt her feelings. Even Mike and Stephanie were giving him funny looks.

Once again, he'd been the one to inject discord into the group. *What the hell's wrong with me*, he wondered. The stiff set to Billie's shoulders made him feel even worse.

"Look, B.J., I didn't mean that the way it sounded."

Billie knew she couldn't answer, and she wouldn't turn around and let him see her tears, so she shrugged her acceptance while the water ran cold between her fingers. A long moment of uneasy silence hung between the four friends when the back door suddenly opened with a thump. They turned to look.

Matt blew into the room along with a gust of wind and dust.

Ignoring the fact that his clothes were wet and his boots were caked with mud, he took a deep breath and smiled.

"Something sure smells good."

They watched in silent fascination as he bent over. His soft, nearly undetectable groan was the only sound to be heard as first one boot, then the other, dropped near the door.

And then Billie gasped.

Scott heard rather than saw her reaction and laid it to the fact that his father was still half-dressed, although to be fair, this time he *was* carrying a shirt in his hands. Once again, jealousy reared its ugly head.

"Damn, Dad. Aren't you dressed yet?"

Matt straightened with a grunt. Grinning, he balled up the shirt and threw it across the room to Scott.

"Hell, boy, I had to give old Daisy Bedford her thrill for the day. Besides, if you can find a way to wear that thing, let me know. I was about to toss it in the trash."

Billie stared past the broad expanse of bare body to the dark, underlying shades of bruising that were just starting to show. Unaware of the water dripping from her elbows and onto the floor, she pointed at his chest.

"He's been hurt."

Scott suddenly focused on the dark band of new bruises along his father's rib cage. Ashamed at what he'd been thinking, he crossed the room to his father's side.

"Good grief, Dad, are you all right? What happened?"

Matt started to laugh, then caught his breath as a painful spasm rippled across his belly.

"Oh hell, that hurt." He tried a grin instead. "Yeah, I'm fine. I just had a little run-in with a stubborn heifer, a pond, and a fence."

Stephanie was appalled that he could be so blasé about such horrible injuries. "Maybe you should see a doctor."

Matt grinned. "Honey, the last time I saw a doctor was over a poker table, and I was winning."

His levity broke up the uneasy silence that had

greeted him, and they all relaxed. Still concerned, Scott accompanied his father out of the room as he went to clean up. Mike tossed his dish towel onto the cabinet and followed, leaving Billie and Stephanie behind.

Billie's eyes were wide, her mouth slightly parted in shock. She couldn't find anything funny about the pain Matt was in, or the fact that Scott seemed bent on making their friendship into something it was not.

Once again, the coincidence of it all was too much for her to absorb, and she turned back to the task at hand. Thinking about potatoes and carrots was easier than letting herself remember how Matt Holt's mouth had fit exactly upon hers. Of how his breath had quickened, of how his hands had gripped, of how he'd coerced a longing from her that she hadn't known how to give back.

Stephanie leaned against the counter and sighed. There was a soft, dreamy quality to her voice that Billie couldn't fault. She knew just how Stephanie felt, and then some.

"He's something, isn't he?"

Billie nodded, and started chopping the vegetables into bite-size pieces. *Something* was not the word she would have used.

"We'd better get these on to cook."

Stephanie had to give one last, exaggerated sigh. "I suppose that you're right," she conceded, and went back to work. By the time the men reappeared, supper was ready.

Billie carried the last bowl to the table and sat between Scott and Stephanie without looking at the man sitting at the head of the table.

"This is a real treat," Matt said, looking around the table and trying not to let his gaze linger too long on the dark-haired beauty to his right. "I rarely have anyone to share a meal with, especially one that looks this good."

"We all helped," Scott said, then slid a hand across Billie's shoulder and squeezed lightly, adding a wink to enforce his actions.

Matt's hopes slid farther into what seemed to be a bottomless pit. Scott claimed he and Billie were just friends, but each time he looked, Scott was either touching her or watching her like a hawk. He might call it friendship, but in Matt's eyes, Scott seemed to want more, and that was all Matt needed to know. He looked away. Even if it killed him—and from the way his heart ached, it very well might—he would never steal from his son.

Billie glared at Scott, then shrugged his hand from her shoulder.

"What?" he muttered, pretending not to understand what she meant.

Billie rolled her eyes. Arguing at the table would serve no purpose but to ruin everyone else's meal. She was at a loss to understand Scott's sudden and unexpected bursts of attention, but if he didn't get a grip, she was going to readjust his attitude whether he liked it or not.

Unable to withstand the enticing odors any longer, Mike picked up his fork. "I'm starved," he said.

They all laughed as Matt passed him the first bowl. "Then dig in, boy."

He didn't hesitate to oblige.

It was somewhere near the end of dessert when Matt changed the tenor of the conversation. He was tired of pretending Billie wasn't at the table. Even if she was his son's girl, the least he could do was try to make the best of a bad situation. It was a good plan, even a fair one. But Matt was lying to himself. He didn't care what the hell she said, he just wanted to hear the sound of her voice.

He laid his fork on his plate, folded his arms across his chest, and tilted his chair until he was balanced and rocking slightly on the two back legs.

"So, Billie . . . Scott is majoring in business, Mike's thing is marine biology and Miss Stephanie is into shopping—aka fashion merchandising. What's your major?"

His husky voice stroked her senses. When she dared to look up, the expression in his eyes shattered the fragile quiet in which she'd been hiding. Panicked by the sudden attention, instead of talking she choked on her last bite of apple cobbler, and grabbed for water to wash it down. Scott thumped her on her back as Stephanie rushed to refill her glass.

Just as she was catching her breath, Scott's hand slid down from her back to her waist. Without missing a beat, she stomped his foot beneath the table.

"Damn," Scott cursed, and moved his hand.

Unaware of the byplay between them, Mike looked up. "Is something wrong?"

Billie glared at Scott, who finally had the grace to look ashamed.

"Foot cramp," he muttered, and rocked back in his chair, unaware that he'd mirrored his father's earlier action.

Matt knew something was going on. The way it looked to him they were having a lovers' spat. This only strengthened his determination to try to forget he'd ever met Billie Walker.

When she could talk without gasping for air, she struggled to remember what they'd been discussing. "I'm sorry, Mr. Holt. What was it you were asking?"

Matt's chair hit the floor on all four legs. He leaned forward. Folding his arms on the table, he tried a smile.

"Matt . . . call me Matt."

She paused for a moment, but it was enough to let Matt know that she was as wary of him as he was of her.

Finally, she nodded. "Matt."

"That's better. Now back to the question. What's your major? Do you graduate soon?"

Scott interrupted. "Oh, she's already in grad school. B.J. is a real computer genius."

Without giving Scott the pleasure of knowing she was annoyed, she answered Matt on her own.

"I majored in computer science and have a little less than a year before I get my master's degree."

Matt smiled, and Billie remembered another time and another smile, and was thankful that she was still sitting down. The darn things had a tendency to make her feel weak.

"That's good. Education is something special. I did well to finish high school, so I'm really proud of Scott for pursuing his goals."

Scott flushed. Once again, he felt like a fool. Here he sat, playing up to a woman who was nothing more than a friend while being jealous of his own father, who adored him.

"Scott is lucky to have a father who cares," Billie said shortly, then wished she'd kept her mouth shut.

There was a flash of understanding in Matt's eyes. It made her realize that she'd unintentionally given away a part of her life she hadn't meant to share. Not even with her closest friends. She didn't want them to know that her father didn't love her, or for that matter, didn't even want her in his life.

"Do your parents live in Memphis, too?" Matt asked, and the minute it was out, wished he could take it back.

Billie looked as shocked as he felt, and they held their breaths, waiting for someone to remark upon his slip. To her dismay, it was Scott who jumped on the fact.

"How did you know where Billie was from?"

Matt shrugged. "I don't know. One of you mentioned it. I forget who."

"My mother's dead," Billie said, not giving Scott time to dig further. "My father still lives in our family home."

Matt's eyes narrowed thoughtfully. There was something about the way Billie tilted her head when she explained that made him think of a boxer offering his best side for a knockout punch.

"He'll probably want our heads for delaying your trip home. Feel free to call him at any time while you're here."

All expression disappeared from Billie's face.

"There's no need to call. He won't care where I am."

Again, Matt caught a longing in her voice that he didn't quite understand, and wished he had the right to pursue it.

"Our folks were glad to get rid of us," Mike said, and made everyone laugh when he went on to explain. "Steph and I live on campus, but we're also less than thirty minutes from home. Mother sees more of us and our dirty laundry than I think she cares to."

Stephanie rolled her eyes. "It's true, but I do my own. Mike just dumps his in the laundry room, kisses Mother on the way out the door, and tells her she's looking prettier every day. She doesn't believe him, but she still does his wash."

"Only because she doesn't like the way I do my own," he retorted.

Scott grinned. "Yeah, I remember one semester everything you wore had a tinge of pink. You were the locker room sweetheart, weren't you?"

Matt laughed aloud, and Billie was struck once again by the sheer magnetism of his face. He was so much man, and even though they were sitting together at a table, he was just as lost to her as he'd been the night he'd walked out of the airport and never looked back.

She swallowed painfully, aware that the knowledge hurt now just as much as it had then. Afraid that she'd make a fool of herself and start crying in front of everyone, she started gathering up dishes.

"Is everyone finished?" she asked.

Matt heard the trembling in her voice and hated that he was the cause of her discomfort. He reached across the table and took the plates from her hands.

"Oh no you don't, you're our guest. It's enough that you and Stephanie helped fix the meal. You aren't doing the dishes, too."

Because they were too close to each other for comfort, Billie didn't argue.

Stephanie grinned. "Scott, not only is your father funny, but he's also wise."

He groaned. "Don't say any more. He's been telling me for years that father knows best. You're only making things worse."

Matt laughed and thumped Scott on the back as they both started toward the kitchen. They were almost to the door when Scott turned.

"Hey, Mike?"

"Hunh?"

"Grab a stack of dirty plates and come on. You're not getting out of this, either."

Mike groaned good-naturedly and did as he was told, leaving Billie and Stephanie alone in the room.

"So . . . what do you want to do?" Stephanie asked.

Find a hole and crawl in. "I don't know. Watch TV, I guess."

"I know where it is," Stephanie said, and led the way out of the dining room, leaving Billie to follow at will.

When Billie heard the men coming back for a second load of dirty dishes, she bolted out of the room, unwilling to be caught in Matt Holt's inquisitive stare.

That night and long after the lights were out and everyone else was in bed, Matt walked the floor, unable to sleep. He kept telling himself that he was just restless, but it wasn't true. He knew where the girls were sleeping. He also knew that it was only one door down from Scott's old room, where he and Mike had bedded down. It wasn't that Matt was thinking of going into Billie's room. It was the fact that Scott might. If that happened, Matt was pretty sure it might be more than he could face.

❊ ❊ ❊ Chapter 3

Everyone sitting around the table looked up from their cereal and juice as the back door flew open. Matt came in, then stopped in the doorway.

"Hey, Scott, go get my checkbook off the dresser. I need to pay the bull hauler, and my boots are caked with cow sh—" He caught himself in time, then grinned. "Sorry, ladies. I nearly forgot myself."

Stephanie giggled, and Mike smiled. He'd already decided that Scott's dad was beyond cool. Billie paused, her spoon halfway to her mouth, and stared at the man who'd just blown into the room. She was beginning to understand that the wild, unruly streak of daring she'd witnessed when he'd ridden the dirt bike was only a glimpse of his real personality. In a way, he was almost larger than life.

While Scott hurried out of the room to do his father's bidding, Billie looked away, afraid to be caught by that cool, intent gaze, yet at the same time, wanting it—and more.

Matt braced himself against both sides of the doorframe with outstretched arms, missing nothing of Billie Walker's nervous expression. When she looked

away, he understood, but at the same time he per-
versely wanted her attention—and more.

He looked at Mike. "What's the plan of action for
today?"

"Scott's going to take us fishing."

Having heard that, he couldn't think of anything else
to say and caught himself staring intently at Billie's
profile, willing her to look up. He told himself it didn't
matter if she talked, he just wanted one good look at
that face. That beautiful, secretive face. When she
wouldn't budge, he relented and turned his attention to
the other female in the room.

"So, Stephanie, are you into worms on hooks?"

She made a face. "Not in my wildest dreams."

Mike dug into his bowl of cereal with his fingers and
picked up a strand of soggy Shredded Wheat, dangling
it in front of her like a limp, brown worm. Matt
laughed as Stephanie made a face and slapped at her
brother's hand.

For Billie, the sound was like a magnet. Drawn by
the joy in his voice and the vitality around him, she
looked up and found herself caught in a penetrating
stare.

Matt curled his fingers around the framing to keep
himself in place. The urge to go to her was strong . . .
so strong. Her eyes were dark and mysterious. An ache
spiraled within him as he asked something he had no
right to know.

"And you, Billie Walker—what about your dreams?"

At that moment, she almost hated him for the taunt,
and herself for not being able to answer.

Scott's entrance broke the mood as he flipped the checkbook across the room like a Frisbee.

"Here you go, Dad."

Matt caught it in midair. "Thanks. See you guys later. Oh . . . and catch me a big one. I've got a sudden hankering." The pause in his words was hardly noticeable as he let his gaze drift once more over Billie's pale face. "For fish."

In defiance, she stuffed a spoonful of soggy cereal into her mouth and looked away. Moments later, the back door slammed shut. Only then did she relax. *Damn that man*, she thought. For two cents she'd . . .

No, she wouldn't ponder, not even for a moment, what she'd like to do to him, or, for that matter, with him. To hell with two cents. She'd do it for free and count herself blessed in the process.

Scott carried his dirty dishes to the sink. "So, is everyone ready?"

"Yeah, just lead me to those babies," Mike bragged.

Billie dumped her dishes in the sink and followed her friends out the door.

A light, frisky breeze cooled the flush on her face and pushed at the well-washed fabric of the pink T-shirt she was wearing, molding it to her body. The sun was warm on her long bare legs, and when she stopped and bent over to readjust the laces on her tennis shoes, her denim cutoffs cupped her slim, shapely hips like a second skin.

"I can't believe we're actually going to fish," Stephanie remarked.

Billie straightened. "It sort of sounds like fun."

Stephanie rolled her eyes. "Give me a credit card and a mall any day."

Billie grinned. "Now, Steph, that's no way to be. You need to be open to new challenges . . . new experiences."

"To heck with worms and sunburns. My idea of a challenge is to be first in line on sale day at my favorite boutique."

"Stephanie, you are an awesome shopper, and that's a fact. If you apply yourself, you just might catch more fish than anyone else. And wouldn't that just tick those two off something fierce?"

Stephanie paused as the idea took root. "That would be a hoot," she said, smiling broadly, and suddenly broke into a trot, leaving Billie to follow behind. "Hey, you guys, save one of those poles for me!"

Matt drove up to the stock pond just after noon. He hadn't worried when they'd missed lunch, but the kitchen had been too quiet, and Billie's presence so strong, that before he knew it he'd gulped down his sandwich and iced tea without tasting either and headed for his pickup.

He had a real good reason for searching them out, but by the time he topped the hill above Scott's favorite fishing hole, he'd forgotten what it was. All he could do was focus on the tall, dark-haired woman sitting alone on the dam and try to remember that she did not belong to him—had never really belonged to him. Except once—for several long, sweet moments—on a New Year's Eve.

Stephanie looked up from her seat beneath the shade of a nearby tree and sighed with relief as she saw Matt driving toward them. If she was lucky, he might take her back to the house. She liked fresh air and sunshine, maybe more when it was connected with beaches and the brown bare bodies of California sun worshipers, but this fishing trip had turned into a fiasco. She itched and had bumps on her ankles that Scott said were caused by chiggers. Her shoes were wet and caked with mud, and her clothes were still damp from falling in the water. She wanted a bath and dry clothes in the worst way.

"Scott! Your dad's here," she shouted, and was rewarded by a frown from Mike and a loud shush from Scott.

She sighed as she remembered all too late that making noise was also a no-no.

Matt walked up beside her, eyeing her disheveled state and her hangdog manner. "Hey there, what happened to you?"

"They won't let me fish anymore," she muttered. "It wasn't my fault my line kept getting whiplash."

"Backlash," Matt said, and tried not to grin.

"Whatever. And then I fell in." She sighed. "It's been a long day."

He laughed softly and ruffled her hair. "Hang tough, honey. It's only half over."

Stephanie groaned and laid her head on her knees as Matt sauntered over to where Scott and Mike were fishing.

He knelt, pretending great interest in the stringer of

fish he could see at the edge of the water, when all his senses were tuned to the solitary female on the other side of the pond.

"I see you've had a little luck."

Scott grinned. "A little? Take a closer look."

Matt pointed back over his shoulder. "Stephanie looks beat. Don't you think someone should take her to the house?"

"She's fine," Mike said. "Besides, this is building her character."

Matt got to his feet and gazed across the expanse of water, as if just noticing Billie's whereabouts, although she'd been the first one he'd seen.

"How's *she* doing?"

"She who?" Scott asked distractedly, concentrating on the slight tug he had just felt on his line.

Matt thought her name before he said it, savoring the sound in his mind before it became a word.

"Billie. I was talking about Billie."

Scott glanced up. "Fine, I guess. At least *she* hasn't complained." And then his line suddenly jerked. "Got one!" he yelped, and started reeling it in.

Matt stepped out of the way and, instead of stopping, started circling the pond toward the dam. Toward Billie.

Billie watched him coming and started to panic. What would he say? What should she do? She fixed her attention on the float on her line, feigning great interest in the fact that it was not moving.

He sensed her tension from across the pond and wondered what in hell he would say when he got there.

Do you love my son? Did you meet him before me or after me?

Then he was there, staring down at the top of her head and wishing he had the right to take down her braid and feel the weight of her hair on his hands and arms just one more time.

"Having any luck?"

She shook her head.

"Having fun?"

She shrugged.

He squatted down beside her until he was staring intently at her profile.

"Hey, Memphis."

She looked up. Ignoring the plea in his voice was impossible.

Matt sighed. The look on her face was somewhere between distrust and terror.

"Don't do that, honey."

"Don't what?" Billie muttered.

"Don't be afraid . . . not of me. I don't think I could take it if you were."

"I'm not afraid."

Just to prove she wasn't lying, she tilted her chin in a show of defiance, unaware that she'd offered her lips in almost the same manner as she had on the night they'd first met.

Instant longing rocked Matt on his heels. He stood up abruptly. For a moment he'd been tempted to take what she'd unintentionally offered. That was impossible.

He turned away, cursing beneath his breath and trying not to remember what she tasted like.

"I didn't know Scott was your son."

Matt kept staring at the back side of the pond dam, wondering if his world would ever be right again.

"I know."

"I didn't even know your name, or you mine."

"I know that, too," he said gruffly.

For a short space of time neither spoke, then Billie was the one to break the silence.

"Then why has this happened? And why are you ignoring me?"

"Ah damn, Memphis. I don't know why it happened. As for ignoring you . . ." He closed his eyes against the pain of the truth. "You're my son's friend now. I love Scott more than my own life. There's no way I would ever endanger that. Do you understand?"

Billie frowned, unaware that the float on her line was starting to bob.

"What I don't understand is why everyone is making such a big deal of that. He's just a friend, nothing more. I've known him for over a year and we've never gone on one date. Not one!" she said, unaware that she'd raised her voice.

Matt turned, wanting to believe her, and at the same time knowing it didn't matter. She might not want Scott, but from where Matt was standing, it seemed as if Scott damned sure wanted her.

"Then why did you come with him? If you're not sleeping with my son, why would you come to meet his father and spend a week at his home?"

"Because anything is better than going to my own," she mumbled dejectedly.

And then the fish took the hook and almost yanked the pole from her hands. She stood up with a jerk.

"Set the hook! Set the hook!" Matt shouted, pointing toward the submerging float.

Billie was dancing sideways, caught between panic and delight.

"Do what? Do what?"

"Yank the line hard!" He grabbed for her pole. "You've got to set the hook or it'll get away."

She yanked.

To Matt's amazement and her delight, a good-sized fish came flying out of the water, as if the pond had suddenly puckered up and spit it out like a bad seed.

"Oh my gosh!" she shrieked, as it went flying past her head. She turned, eyeing the flopping fish with something akin to shock. "I caught one! I caught one!"

"You sure did, honey."

He ran toward the fish before it came loose and flopped back in the water. Billie knelt at his side, watching with interest as he delicately worked the hook from the inside of the fish's mouth without tearing the skin. It was the first time she'd ever seen a fish outside of an aquarium or already cooked and on a plate. And now that she had, she wasn't so sure she liked what she saw.

The eyes looked glassy, and the gills on the side of its head were heaving in a desperate, choking manner. Tentatively, she reached out and touched it, marveling at the cool, slick feel of the scales.

"It can't breathe . . . can it?"

The hook came loose just as she spoke.

Matt paused, letting the hook drop into the grass as he readjusted his grip on the fish. Her earlier delight was gone. There was nothing on her face but regret. He looked down at the fish he was holding and connected with what she must be thinking in seeing this for the first time.

"No, honey. It can't."

Tears shimmered, giving her dark brown eyes a bottomless appearance. "Can we put it back?"

"We can do any damn thing that you want."

"Then I want you to let it go."

Matt walked to the edge of the pond, then knelt, loosening his grip on the fish only after he'd completely submersed his hands in the water. With a flip of its tail, it darted forward and disappeared into the muddy depths. Even as he stood, he heard Billie's sigh of relief.

"That's good," she said softly. "That's good."

Matt turned. For a long, silent moment they stared into each other's eyes, lost in a memory they couldn't forget.

You are what's good, Billie Walker. I just wish to hell you were mine.

"Hey, you two!" Scott shouted. "We're ready to go."

And the moment was gone.

Embarrassed by what she'd let him see, Billie grabbed at the pole and the line and caught the tip of the hook in her finger.

At her quick gasp of pain, he spun, and when he saw what had happened, he took hold of the line to ease the tension.

"Don't move."

She didn't.

A small drop of blood began seeping out from around the partially embedded tip as he cut the hook from the line.

"Damn, sweetheart, I'm sorry. Does it hurt bad?"

Sweetheart? If only she was.

"Only a little. It stings more than it hurts."

He tilted her finger to the light, judging the injury against what it would take to get it out. "At least it didn't embed the barb. Want me to pull it out or do you want to give it a try?"

"You. I want you."

He looked up. "Damn you, Memphis," he said, and knew that his voice was shaking.

Her stare never wavered, and he was the first to look away. Gripping her finger as tightly as he could and hoping that the sudden pressure would act as a temporary painkiller, he took hold of the hook and yanked.

Billie gasped. First in shock, then in relief. It was out.

"Wow," she said, as tears came to her eyes. "Now I know how the fish felt."

Matt never knew what made him do it. It could have been the tiny droplets of blood seeping out the end of her finger. It could have been the pain in her voice, or even the tears in her eyes. But before he thought, he'd taken her finger into his mouth.

When Matt's tongue curled around her skin, heat surged through her belly. With a slow, sucking motion, he drew the end of the finger past his lips, warming the flesh and taking away one pain in her body while replacing it with another. The new pain was one a kiss could not assuage. Mesmerized by the feel of his tongue on her body and a part of herself inside him, she swayed on her feet.

Aware that once again he'd crossed a line with this girl he had no business crossing, he stopped.

"Is that better?"

When she didn't speak he looked up and hated what he saw: himself reflected in her tears.

Billie looked away, then back again, compelled by memories she couldn't forget. Like the shape of his face and the cut of his mouth, and the fact that he'd groaned exactly twice when they'd kissed—once beneath his breath, and once in her ear just before he'd disappeared.

"Is it better? No, Matt, I don't think I'll ever be better again."

She walked away, leaving him to deal with the line and pole.

He had no choice but to let her go.

"Where's your fish?" Mike asked, as B.J. walked past them on her way to the pickup.

"I let it go."

She would have kept walking had Scott not stopped her by grabbing her arm.

"What were you and Dad doing over there?"

"Fishing."

Scott frowned. They'd been standing so that he saw little else but his father's back, but he knew something had been said between them that had upset Billie. If his father made a pass, he wanted to know.

"Then why did you cut and run? Did Dad say something to upset you?"

Her laugh was rough and painfully abrupt as she realized what Scott was getting at. "No, Scott, your father was a gentleman. I stuck a hook in my finger, see." She thrust it beneath his nose. "He pulled the damn thing out and turned me loose just like that stupid fish I caught, okay?"

Scott flushed. "Well, I just thought you might have . . ."

Billie threw her hands up in the air and wanted to cry from the frustration of it all.

"You thought what? That someone could possibly make a pass at me? God forbid! Why would anyone bother? Better yet, why the hell should you care? You're my friend . . . not my keeper."

Having said that, she stomped toward the truck, leaving them to gather up the remaining equipment. Moments later Matt came across the pond carrying Billie's pole in his hands.

"Here you go." He handed it to Scott. "You'll have to tie on another hook. I had to cut that one off to get it out of Billie's finger."

Guilt began to emerge as Scott looked at the dangling line minus its hook.

"She really got hooked?"

Matt nodded. "It wasn't too bad, but you might remind her to put some antiseptic on it when you get back to the house."

When Matt started to walk away, Scott called out, "Aren't you coming?"

Matt turned, aware that he was looking at his son as if he were a stranger and wondering if he had the guts to watch him with the woman he wanted. Finally, he shook his head.

"No, I don't think I'd better. Remember my motto? Too much work and not enough time." He got into his pickup and drove away.

The ride home was unusually silent. Stephanie was so happy to be heading toward a shower that she didn't even complain about the constant itch around her ankles. Mike was lost in contemplation, seeing the countryside and his friend in a new and intriguing light.

Billie was numb. She couldn't believe that she'd actually found her cowboy again, only to have him hold her at arm's length because of some misbegotten belief that he was doing the right thing.

If she wasn't so disheartened or had grown up with more self-confidence, she would have taken Scott to task. It was his fault that Matt believed as he did. From the moment they'd arrived at the ranch, he had acted like a gold-plated idiot. She didn't know why, but she knew it had nothing to do with love.

Scott stomped the brakes, sliding to a stop in front of the house. "We're here! Mike and I are going to clean our catch, so you girls can have dibs on both showers."

"Thank goodness," Stephanie mumbled, and headed for the house.

"Hey, B.J., there's stuff for sandwiches in the refrigerator," Scott yelled. "If you girls are hungry, help yourselves."

Billie couldn't answer. The thought of food made her nauseous. She didn't want to eat; she wanted Matt's arms around her. Her finger throbbed, and she looked down at the tip, remembering his tongue curling around it, drawing out the pain, warming the flesh. Making her crazy.

She was at the door when Scott yelled again.

"Hey, B.J.!"

She turned.

"Dad says you better put some antiseptic on your finger."

Without answering, she entered the house, slamming the door behind her.

"What's with her?" Mike asked.

Scott lifted the stringer of fish from the back of the Jeep and shrugged. "Who knows? Women! They're all alike."

Mike arched an eyebrow. "Yeah, and what would we do without them?"

Scott grinned as he held up the fish for his friend's perusal. "Maybe catch more fish?"

They laughed and headed toward the backyard to clean their catch while Stephanie and Billie made for the bathrooms, stripping off their clothes as they went.

Supper was over, and still Matt had not made an appearance. Billie felt anxious, but she couldn't bring herself to ask Scott where he might be. His food was warming in the oven. The kitchen was clean. She'd chosen to read a book rather than join the lively game of Trivial Pursuit that the others were playing, and even then was unable to concentrate on the words. Minutes ticked by until they turned into hours. Just as the clock struck 9:00 P.M., the back door opened. Tension in her body escaped like air out of a balloon. He was home!

He came into the living room, a quieter man than when they'd last seen him.

Scott looked up. "Hey, Dad! Where have you been? You missed the best supper, but we saved you some fish."

Matt paused beside Scott's chair and ran his hand across the top of his son's head, as if by touch alone he had assured himself that Scott was just fine. His voice was low, the tone strained.

"Jimmy Lee Newell was killed in a car wreck earlier this evening."

Scott froze. The smile on his face slipped sideways as the news sank in. Jimmy Lee had been a classmate and, at one time, one of his closest friends. Shocked by the news, he swiveled around in his chair.

"Oh no! How did it happen? How did you find out?"

"I was there."

"Are you all right? Were you in the accident? How did you . . . ?"

Matt slid an arm across Scott's shoulder. "Whoa, son. Slow down. I didn't mean to scare you. I just had the misfortune to be three cars behind when it happened." The muscles across his face tightened as he shook his head and looked away.

Mike clapped a hand on Scott's shoulder. "I'm sorry, Scott. Was he a friend of yours?"

He nodded. "He was a classmate, and when we were younger, a really good friend."

From across the room, Billie quietly asked, "Would you two like to be alone?"

Leave it to Billie to be the thoughtful one. Her question touched both Matt and Scott. Matt's smile was slow in coming as he shook his head.

"No, honey, but thanks for asking. I'm sorry to put a damper on everyone's evening, but I wanted to tell Scott first before he heard it on the news."

Scott tossed the dice back on the board. "I think I should go over to the Newell house and express my regrets. Will you guys be okay for a while?"

They nodded.

"Dad, do you want to go?"

Matt shook his head. "I just came from there. Once was enough."

"I won't be long," Scott said.

Mike stood and stretched. "Don't mind us, take as long as you need. In fact, if you don't mind, I think I'll turn in. We've had a big day."

Stephanie groaned as she got up. "Me, too. I'm sore all over."

Moments later, Matt and Billie found themselves alone in the room.

Matt walked toward the window and watched until the taillights of Scott's Jeep disappeared from view. Billie could tell by the set of his shoulders that letting his son out of his sight was the last thing he'd wanted to do.

"He'll be all right."

Startled by her understanding of his mood, Matt turned, looking intently at the woman who sat with such an air of confidence. She seemed years older than the others, yet he knew it wasn't so. *Remember*, he told himself. *Remember Scott.*

And then she stood up and came toward him. When she held out her arms, he went into them without thought, taking the comfort she offered because he didn't have it in him to refuse.

"Damn, Billie, but it was bad."

She wrapped her arms around his waist, and, even though the evening was warm, he felt cold to the touch.

"I'm sorry you had to see it," she said, stroking the breadth of his shoulders and down his back, wanting to give comfort, yet unsure how.

Matt sighed. Disgusted with his own weakness in wanting her in his arms, he rested his chin on the top of her head.

"We shouldn't be doing this."

"We're not *doing* anything," she countered, and knew a swift moment of satisfaction when she felt him harden against her belly.

Matt gripped her by her shoulders, pushing her back until she was forced to look him in the eyes. His voice was low, almost angry.

"But it's not from lack of want, Memphis, and we both know it."

The power in his grip—the anger in his voice—were more than she'd bargained for, but she didn't care. She wanted this man. She wanted to be naked beneath him in the very worst way.

Without shame, she took his hands and moved them from her shoulders to her breasts, letting him feel the pounding of her heart and the hardness of her nipples against his palms. Her head tilted back as her lower body swayed toward him, silently begging for something he just wouldn't give.

Matt cursed low and beneath his breath. The want on her face was driving him mad, and the softness of her breasts against his hands was almost more than he could stand.

"Damn you, Billie Walker, this just isn't right. I can't. We can't. And I already told you why."

Tears burned at the back of her throat and shimmered across her eyes, but she would have burned in hell before she let him know how much his refusal had cost her. Her smile was bittersweet as she pivoted out of his arms and started to walk away.

"Billie!"

Because she heard a pain in his voice that mirrored her own, she turned, then waited for him to say what was on his mind.

"I'm sorry, more than you will know, but I can't do this to my own son."

She laughed, but the sound came up and out of her throat in a sob.

Unable to see his expression through an onslaught of tears, she bitterly suggested, "Don't let it bother you. After all, this is nothing new. I should be used to being in the way. I don't know why I can never get this right."

He wasn't prepared for her pain. It made him feel

guilty and, somehow, wrong. When he started toward her she stopped him with a shake of her head.

"No! Not again. Not until you trust what I've been telling you all along. There's nothing—absolutely nothing—between me and your son." She took a deep breath, choking on unshed tears. "The only thing we have in common is you. When you're ready to believe me, you know where I'll be."

She walked out of the room, leaving Matt to consider what she'd said. At that moment, if Scott had walked into the house, Matt would have set him down and confronted him with his feelings. But he didn't, and by the time he returned a few hours later, Scott was in no mood to talk about relationships of any kind.

And so the opportunity passed, forever altering the events of the days to come.

Chapter 4

By the weekend, Matt's anxiety was out of control. In less than three days, Billie would walk out of his life just as he'd walked out on her at the airport two years ago. In his mind, he knew it would be for the best. In his heart, he knew this time he just might not get over it. *Damn you, Scott*, he thought. *Why didn't you bring home some cute little airhead with an IQ the same size as her waist. If you had, this wouldn't be so difficult.*

But knowing the truth and facing it were two different things. Matt knew he had no business caring for Billie, but he couldn't stop what he felt any more than he could have stopped breathing. And because his guilt was so overwhelming, it affected his behavior, making him seem cold and uncaring when it was actually the opposite.

Billie wasn't experienced enough to see through the wall he'd put between them. She'd always pretended her life was normal, pretended that she mattered to the only parent she had. But now, with Matt shying away from any sort of contact, she assumed that he just didn't care anymore and miserably accepted the fact.

After all, why should he be any different than others she knew?

Even Scott noticed something was wrong, but was too subdued by the death of Jimmy Lee Newell to do more than wonder. Attending his old friend's funeral had been sobering for him on more than one level. Jimmy Lee left behind a wife and child. Scott didn't even have a steady girl. Jimmy Lee was exactly two months younger than Scott, and he was already dead. Scott was forced to face the fact that youth was no guarantee of a long and happy life. And because of his indecision, he started grasping at things he didn't believe in, and looking for love in all the wrong places. Namely, Billie Jean Walker's arms.

"Come on, B.J.," Scott coaxed, sliding his arm across her shoulder and tickling at the back of her ear. "Stephanie won't go because of her sunburn. I've got to have someone to dance with, and Mike's too ugly to two-step with."

Mike wiggled his hips in a poor imitation of a sexpot. "That's all you know. I clean up real good."

Scott grinned. "Yeah, but you're just not built right, buddy, if you know what I mean."

Billie rolled her eyes and batted impatiently at Scott's hand as she slid out of his halfhearted embrace. Shaking a finger beneath his nose, she warned, "I might go if you promise to keep your hands to yourself. For Pete's sake, Scott, ever since we arrived at the ranch, you've been acting like a fool. When you're not winking, you're trying to feel me up, and frankly I'm about sick of it. The only reason I came to Texas with you was because I trusted you, and because I liked you—but only as a friend. I'm not your type and you're definitely not mine and we both know it."

Scott frowned. The truth was a bit hard to take. He knew he was acting like an idiot, but he couldn't seem to find a way to stop himself.

"How do you know what my type is?" he challenged.

Billie snorted beneath her breath and started ticking off names on the ends of her fingers.

"Let's see . . . stop me if I miss one. Since I've known you, there was Bettina, Michelle, Lissa, and God forbid that we forget Paisley." She waved her fingers beneath his nose. "What did they all have in common, Scott?"

Mike laughed. "I know, I know, teacher. Ask me! Ask me!"

She ignored Mike's interruption. "They were all top-heavy blondes . . . am I right?"

Scott's chin jutted mutinously.

"That doesn't mean that I can't . . ."

"Oh, but it does," she said. "My hair is black. I don't giggle. I am not a 34D, and I do not wear bikinis."

He glared. "Does this mean you won't go?"

Billie sighed. "No. It just means that *if* I go, you behave yourself."

Scott grinned. "It's a deal."

When he started to hug her, she doubled her fists and took a step back. He laughed, ignored her puny threat, and picked her up off her feet, spinning her around and around in teasing delight.

"You like me, and you know it," he said.

In spite of herself, Billie grinned. "Put me down, you fool," she said, laughing, and to her relief he did. "And *like* is the operative word. Remember that, and we'll get along just fine."

Her smile died when she turned to find Matt watching them from the doorway. The look on his face hurt her, and because she knew he would infer the wrong thing from what he'd just seen, she threw up her hands and started out of the room.

Scott spun. "Hey, Billie! Where are you going?"

"To wash my hair." When she walked past, the look she gave Matt would have squelched the mood of a pissed-off cat. "Can't go dancing without looking my best now, can I?"

Matt ached. The urge to grab her and run was almost overwhelming, but he'd seen her in Scott's arms, laughing, teasing, sparkling in a way she'd never done for him. He'd also sensed Scott's joy in the moment and figured the rest out for himself.

"Hey, Dad! We're going to the Tumbleweed tonight. Why don't you come with us?"

He was tempted, but it took exactly two seconds for him to make up his mind. He wasted the first one actually considering the option, and the second coming to his senses.

"No way. You don't need a parent tagging along. Have fun. Just be careful, okay?"

Scott grinned. "I'm always careful."

Matt frowned as he walked away. There was something about Scott's behavior that bothered him. He'd been acting strange ever since Jimmy Lee's death. The fatal accident had been a shock to everyone, but he suspected that besides Jimmy Lee's family, it had hit Jimmy Lee's peers the hardest. Accepting death was a difficult lesson to learn, and Matt should know. He'd lost his own wife at an age when their whole lives had been stretched out so far ahead that neither one had been able to see the end.

That was when it had come. Suddenly. Abruptly. Irrevocably over in the space of time it took for the drunk driver to hit her head-on.

A door slammed in another part of the house. It was Billie going into her room. The thought of her dancing and spinning in his son's arms all night just might make him nuts. He considered his options and decided that he was too old to get drunk. The only thing he could do was live with the fact that he'd missed his chance with Billie Jean Walker and get on with his life.

The noise inside the Tumbleweed was just a decibel shy of a roar. Music was playing, but it was hard to distinguish the melody from the raucous laughter, the clink of glasses, the occasional shouts of anger, and the high-pitched giggles from girls in tight jeans dancing with men in big hats.

Billie was tired, and her head hurt. Although the first half of the night had gone better than she'd expected, the last half was working its way toward disaster.

It was obvious by the glare in Scott's eyes as he watched her from across the room that he was still fuming from the brush-off she'd just given him. She didn't care how long she'd known someone, he wasn't putting his hands in her hip pockets and plastering her up against a bulging zipper just to spin her around the room. She'd spent the better part of the last hour trying to get Mike and Scott to take her back to the ranch, but to no avail. And from the growing accumulation of empty beer bottles on their table, if they ever decided to leave, they would be in no shape to drive. She hoped she could remember the way home.

As she watched, a girl paused at Scott's table, leaning over his shoulder and whispering something obviously naughty in his ear. The gleam in Scott's eyes was visible from across the room, as was his intent, when he stood and pulled her into his arms.

Billie held her breath as Scott staggered, obviously too drunk to walk, and when the flirt began swinging and swaying against him to a tune only they could hear, she knew things were bound to get worse. They did. And it didn't take long.

Trouble came in the form of a muscle-bound, fire-breathing cowboy they called Bulldog. Either he'd been named from the rodeo event that he loved, or the dog whose looks he shared. Billie didn't think she'd ever seen an uglier man in her life . . . or a madder one. Bulldog seemed to think that he had first claim to the woman in Scott's arms.

It took less than a minute for the fight to begin. When an empty, brown long-neck flew past her head and shattered on the wall behind her, Billie made a run for the pay phone. From what she could see, Scott and

Mike were in desperate need of help . . . and so was she.

Matt hadn't meant to sleep. In fact, when he'd lain down on the living room couch, he would have sworn that he'd never sleep again. Visions of Billie in some-one else's arms had swirled through his head until he'd closed his eyes in self-defense. Somewhere between dismay and despair he'd drifted off, and when the phone suddenly shrilled next to his ear, he came up-right and off the couch in a single motion, confused as to where he was and what he'd just heard. When it rang again, he cursed softly beneath his breath and swiped a shaking hand across his face as he yanked the re-ceiver from the cradle.

Unaware that fear had coated his voice with a rough, angry tone, he growled. "Hello?"

"Matt?"

He came awake. At once. With no further hesitation. "Billie . . . honey . . . is that you?"

"Uh . . . Matt, I think you better come . . ."

The sound of shattering glass and then Billie's soft squeal of dismay sounded in his ear. He distinctly heard her tell someone to put her down, and then the line went dead.

"Son of a bitch," he exclaimed, and grabbed his boots. He had lived through enough wild years of his own to recognize the sound of a bar fight when he heard one.

He picked up his hat and keys on the way out the door, trying to remember where Scott had said they were going. It wasn't until he took the turn onto the highway and gunned his pickup toward Dallas that he remembered that it was the Tumbleweed, on the outskirts of the city.

He stomped on the gas, hoping they were still there. If Scott and Mike had started to barhop, Matt had no way of telling where they might be. Dallas had a surfeit of places to party, all of which, if one was in the wrong frame of mind, spelled trouble.

The room was in turmoil. Billie couldn't believe that the fight was still going. She'd long since lost sight of Mike and Scott, and assumed the worst. Her call to Matt had been in desperation, and she feared, too late. The cowboy who'd interrupted her call and then slung her over his shoulder was out for the count on the floor a few tables away.

Now she was caught between a wall and a half-drunk trucker who'd decided to claim her for his own. Each time she tried to get away, he'd laugh and grab her by the arm, then slather another slobbery kiss across her face before throwing his next punch at the nearest man.

Just when Billie was about to give up on being rescued, a gunshot sounded, and then another. An odd, eerie silence swept across the room, stilling the combatants in freeze-frame with hands still fisted and punches half-thrown.

Matt Holt stood with legs braced and eyes flashing as he waved the sawed-off shotgun he'd pulled from beneath the bar over the heads of the Tumbleweed patrons.

"I don't give a damn who started this, but I know who's gonna stop it!"

A slight grumble of disgust came from an opposite corner of the room. To make his point, Matt cracked the barrel and ejected the empty shells. Without taking his eyes off the crowd, he slipped two new ones into the chambers and flipped the barrels, locking them back into place.

"I didn't hear that," he said softly. "Anyone want to repeat what was said?"

Silence reigned.

"You are a sorry-ass bunch of Texans," he said as he started walking through the room, nudging limp bodies with the toes of his boots as he searched the crowd. Just thinking about the panic he'd heard in Billie's voice made him mad all over again.

The people watched in uneasy silence, willing to let the man with the gun have the floor, but Matt didn't care how nervous he made them. He had to find Billie . . . and his son. They were bound to be here. Scott's Jeep was still outside.

When the crowd parted, Billie let out a shaky sigh of relief. She'd never been so glad to see anyone in her entire life. Thinking the worst was all over, she shouted his name, pushing aside the trucker who'd cornered her.

"Matt!"

But the trucker wasn't ready to let her go. He hauled her up against his chest in a rude, iron-hard grip. "No, you don't, sugar. You're mine. I won you fair and square."

At the sound of her voice, Matt spun, then took one look at the terror on her face and the bruises on her lips and got mad all over again. His voice was just above a whisper as he gripped the shotgun a little more firmly.

"Turn her loose, you son of a bitch. You don't touch what's mine."

Billie gasped. The anger on his face was unmistakable, as was the claim that he'd made in front of the entire room.

The trucker blanched. He held up his hands and stepped as far away from Billie as he could get. "Now, mister, I didn't mean no harm. We was just havin' ourselves a little fun. See there, I didn't hurt her none."

Relieved to be free, Billie started toward Matt. But he shook his head and pointed with the barrel of the gun toward the door.

"My truck's outside the door. Get in."

"But what about Scott and Mike?"

He raked the room with a cold, angry glare, as if daring anyone to argue with his plan of action. "I'll deal with them . . . and everyone else. You just get yourself safe and wait for me to come out."

Billie did as she was told, and, to her surprise, Matt emerged a few minutes later behind four men who'd obviously volunteered, with a little persuasion from a mad-as-hell cowboy and a loaded shotgun, to carry the unconscious pair to the truck.

Unaware that Decker, the owner of the bar, had followed them all outside, Matt pointed with the shot-gun toward his truck.

"Just dump them in the back."

The men did as they were told, and then disappeared into the bar, grateful to be out of range. As Matt was shutting the tailgate, he noticed Decker standing in the shadows near the door.

"You might need this again," Matt said, and tossed the gun back to its rightful owner.

Decker caught it in midair. "Real sorry this had to happen here tonight, Matt. We don't usually have such a ruckus."

Matt nodded. "I'm not blaming anyone in particular. I came for what's mine."

Decker frowned. He understood ownership. He also understood that Matt Holt wasn't the kind of man to mess with.

As Matt was pulling out of the driveway, the sound of sirens could be heard in the distance.

"Just in time," he said, half to himself, and headed toward the ranch, which lay in the opposite direction.

Billie went limp and, letting her head drop against the back of the seat, she caught herself repeatedly trying to swallow past a lump in her throat. She almost had herself under control when Matt's fingers swept across her leg and grabbed her hand.

"Are you all right?"

It was one ounce of sympathy too much. She started to cry.

Reaching across the seat, he pulled her roughly against his chest with one hand as he steered with the other. "Go ahead and cry, sweetheart. If I wasn't so damned mad, I might join you."

She buried her face in the curve of Matt's neck and sobbed. "He wouldn't let me go."

"Who, Scott?"

"No, that cowboy. Scott was already mad at me."

Matt sighed. He didn't really want to listen, but it might explain this whole mess.

"I'm sorry, honey. Did you two have a fight?"

Billie groaned, and pulled back from Matt's embrace. "Everyone had a fight! Didn't you see?"

He hid a slight grin. "Actually, I believe that I did, but you know what I meant. Did you and Scott have an argument about something personal?"

She hunched herself against the opposite door, trying her best to glare through lingering tears.

"There is *nothing* personal between us. Never has been. Never will be. Therefore, our argument was not *personal*. But he was still mad at me all the same."

Matt's fingers tightened on the steering wheel. He kept his gaze focused on the road ahead when all he really wanted was to pull over and take her in his arms.

"Point taken," he muttered. "Then why *was* my son mad at you?"

Billie turned away, mumbling something beneath her breath as she stared at the shadowy image of her own reflection in the window.

"I'm sorry," Matt said. "I didn't hear you."

She turned and glared. "I said, I don't need to be felt up just to dance. I told him so. He doesn't take rejection well."

Angry flags of red suddenly stained the muscles jerking in Matt's cheeks. Just hearing her say aloud what was going on between them was worse than anything he'd imagined. The idea of anyone touching Billie in an overt and sexual manner made him livid. Even if it was his son. Even if he had the right. He groaned, then cursed. This was a hell of a mess, and there was no mistake.

At that moment, Matt faced the truth of what he was feeling. He was in love with Billie Walker, or so damn close that the semantics of his feelings didn't matter, and . . . he was jealous as hell of his own son. Things couldn't really get much worse.

"Look, Billie, things will work out. Couples have fights all of the time, and couples make up. It's the way the world works."

To his surprise, she punched him on the arm, her voice just shy of a scream. "We are not a couple! We will not make up because we had nothing to break! He was my friend, but he's not any longer! I can tell you now that going home to my father has suddenly become a lot more appealing than it was a week ago. At least there I know where I stand."

Matt frowned. There she went with those odd references to her home and her father again, and witnessing her anger toward Scott's behavior was something of a revelation. If only he could believe her. But he'd seen too much with his own eyes to trust her statement. Women said things in the heat of anger and passion that they didn't always mean. He'd learned that from experience, too.

"Maybe things will look better in the morning."

She refused to respond, and he had to settle for her small snort of disbelief.

Finally, they reached the ranch. Matt parked without killing the engine, and when Billie got out, he gave a quick glance at the pair in the back of his truck, who were still out cold, and then walked her to the porch. When she entered the house, he followed her inside, reminding himself that hands-off was the only way to deal with this situation.

"Are you going to be all right?"

Her shoulders slumped. "Yes, I'm fine, thanks to you. When I called, I never got to tell you what was wrong or where we were. I was so afraid you wouldn't come that I couldn't even think."

The need to hold her was suddenly too strong to ignore. He pulled her close, hugging her gently and smoothing back the hair from her face.

"Ah, Memphis, I'll always come when you call."

A new ache settled inside Billie's chest, replacing the anger that had been there earlier. She nuzzled her face against his shirtfront, relishing the feel of his arms surrounding her.

Matt closed his eyes and groaned beneath his breath. This felt so right. Why was it so damned wrong?

"Billie! What on earth?"

At the sound of Stephanie's sleepy voice, they jerked apart and turned. Matt gave Billie one last hug and pushed her gently toward her friend, who was standing in the doorway.

"Take care of your buddy, Stephanie. She's had a real rough night."

Stephanie managed to pale beneath her sunburn. Her eyes widened and her mouth dropped as she looked at Billie's beer-stained shirt and slightly swollen mouth.

"What happened?"

"You were the smart one to stay home," Billie replied. "Scott and Mike got drunk, then got into a fight. If I hadn't called Matt to come get us, we'd all probably be in jail right now waiting for bail."

She took Billie by the arm. "Good Lord! When will those guys grow up?" And then she looked around. "By the way, where are they?"

Matt paused on his way out the door, yanking his Stetson a little tighter on his head. "They'll be in later," he said shortly. "I'm not through with them yet." Then he slammed the door behind him.

Stephanie shuddered. "Oh my gosh, I wouldn't want to be in their shoes. He looks mad enough to kill."

Billie sighed, and looked down at her clothes, picking lifelessly at a half-torn pocket on the front of her shirt. "If I wasn't so tired, I'd go outside and help him."

Stephanie tugged at her arm. "Come on, honey. You need a shower and a good night's sleep."

"No, actually, I need my head examined."

Stephanie grinned. "Things will look better in the morning."

It was all Billie could do not to cry. "Where have I heard that before," she said under her breath, and followed Stephanie into their room.

Matt reached the truck just as Scott moaned. When

he leaned over the truck bed and looked in, Scott was trying to crawl to his knees.

"What a pair," he muttered in disgust, getting back into the truck, slamming it in drive, and spinning out on the gravel as he headed toward the barns.

By the time he came to a sliding halt by the stock tanks, both Mike and Scott were rolling around like empty bottles.

"Wha' the hell you drivin' like that for?" Scott grumbled, and then winced when his dad slammed the door hard enough to rock the truck on its wheels.

Mike had curled himself into a ball and was leaning against the far corner of the truck bed, holding his hands over his ears. His head hurt so badly that it felt as if it just might fall off. He didn't care where he was or how he'd gotten there, he was extremely grateful to wake up someplace besides the floor of the Tumbleweed.

Matt lowered the tailgate and leaned forward, grabbing Scott by a boot and then dragging him out of the truck. Scott hit the ground on his ear, groaning in dismay at the unjust treatment he was receiving right before he threw up on himself.

Matt began to curse, and it was loud enough that the horses in the far corral heard the tone of his voice and started circling inside the fences in a nervous trot.

"Damn, Dad, wha' made you—"

"Shut up," he yelled, and grabbed a water hose that was coiled on a nearby fence. "Damn you, Scott. I've been mad at you plenty of times in your life, but I've never been ashamed of you until tonight."

As drunk as he was, as miserable as he felt, Scott knew a moment of pure shame. He hated to be less in his father's eyes.

He rolled to his knees, intent on crawling back up to his feet, when Matt turned on the water. The spray hit him head-on and sent him toppling back down on his butt.

"Hey! Don't!" he cried, batting at the water with his hands and trying to keep it out of his eyes.

"You got drunk and left a woman who'd trusted you to take care of her in the hands of a roomful of strangers who were only slightly less drunk than you two. How the hell do you think *she* felt?"

When Scott did nothing but hang his head and let the water pummel him, Matt threw the hose down in disgust, letting it run freely until Scott was, quite literally, sitting in a puddle.

"Besides that, you threw up in my truck. Wash it out, and then get yourself up to the house and into bed. I've said all I'm going to about tonight, but you've got some tall apologizing to do to your girl. If she hadn't thought to call me for help, you would all have wound up in jail."

Too angry to say any more, he pivoted, then walked away, as sorry as he'd ever been in his life that he was a father. He felt like a failure. He'd spent his life trying to make things better for Scott, and tonight it would seem that he'd made them too good . . . maybe too damn easy. He couldn't believe that a son of his would not have had the foresight to take care of his woman before he took care of himself.

"Oh Lord," Mike muttered, as he crawled toward the tailgate on his hands and knees. "Your dad is awesome when he's mad. We're in deep shit, aren't we?"

Scott couldn't answer. He attributed the lump in his throat to his recent bout with nausea, but if he'd been honest with himself, he would have known that it was dismay at his own behavior that was keeping him mute. His dad was right. Billie and Mike were his guests. He'd almost gotten them all arrested, and Lord knows what Billie had endured. The last thing he remembered was the look of disgust on her face when he'd pulled the cute redhead into his arms.

Why did I do that? I only meant to make her jealous. But why? I don't love Billie, not like that.

With an aching heart, he picked up the hose and started the cleanup with himself. The water ran swiftly over him, dousing his shirt and soaking into the denim of his jeans until he was drenched, yet he still felt dirty.

"You go on to the house," he told Mike. "I'll clean up the truck. I'm the one who made the mess."

Mike didn't argue. He was just hoping he had the strength to walk the distance from the barns to the house. If not, he supposed that Scott would find him later.

Matt was shaking when he entered the house. In all the years since Scott had been born he'd never been that mad at him. For a moment, just before he'd turned the water on his son, he'd had an almost-uncontrollable urge to punch him in the face. The knowledge made him sick with guilt. It was as if he'd forgotten that Scott was his son and that he'd looked upon him as a man who'd hurt someone he loved. Namely Billie.

"Oh God." Matt shuddered as he leaned against the door and covered his face with his hands. "Don't let me lose perspective in this unholy mess. And more important, don't let me lose control of myself. Scott—and Billie—mean too much to me."

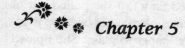 **Chapter 5**

I came for what's mine!

Billie rolled over in bed, awaking with a start and expecting to see Matt standing over her. When she realized she'd been dreaming, she flopped back down onto the pillow in disappointment and pulled the sheet over her head to keep out the sun streaming through the window. Even now, with her eyes closed and her head covered, the memory of last night's episode at the Tumbleweed came flooding back. Matt's vow was the last thing she'd thought of before falling asleep, and now it would seem she'd start the new day the same way.

Stephanie still slept, but for Billie, rest was over. She rolled out of bed and headed for the bathroom down the hall, aware of the deep, uneven snores coming from the room where Scott and Mike were sleeping, and even more aware of the silence behind Matt's door. It was daylight. He would already be gone.

A few minutes later she was back in her room, digging through her suitcase for some clean clothes.

The day after tomorrow she would be in Memphis. Ignoring the ache in her heart, she started to dress.

The well-worn blue jeans she chose were for comfort, not because they exaggerated her long legs and slim hips, and the dark red tank top she pulled out of her suitcase was picked for coolness, not because it adhered to her body like wet paper to glass. She tiptoed out of the room with an elastic band in one hand and her tennis shoes in the other, welcoming the quiet in the near-empty house and the scent of coffee coming from the kitchen.

She ate toast and jelly standing up while reading a day-old paper someone had left on the counter. When she'd finished, she walked out on the porch and sat down on the steps to put on her shoes. The sun was warm on her face and arms as she bent to her task. As she walked across the yard, the heat of the sun and the weight of her hair made her dig in her pocket for the elastic band she'd brought with her.

She paused beneath a shade tree. Using her fingers for a comb, she separated her hair and began making a braid. She was halfway through when she heard the sound of an approaching vehicle and turned to look. It was Matt.

Matt's first order of business had been to retrieve Scott's Jeep from the bar parking lot. He'd taken Nate with him to drive it home, and then had gone into Arlington to pick up some feed. He had to keep busy or go crazy thinking about the mess he'd left behind him.

The fight he'd had with Scott was the worst in their entire lives, and the fight he'd had with himself, even more so. He had spent a night in hell, condemning himself for thoughts he couldn't control.

Exactly thirty-two steps separated him from Billie Walker's bed. He knew because he'd walked it during the night when he couldn't sleep. He'd stood at the foot of her bed, staring down at her in the darkness and remembering the look of relief on her face when he'd entered the bar. Remembering, also, the tears she'd shed on their way home. He wanted to hold her then just as badly as he still did now, and there was no way it was going to happen. In spite of her claims to the opposite, he still believed that Scott had romantic feelings for her. In Matt's eyes, that made her off-limits.

A short while later, with a load of feed in the back of his truck and his mind a thousand miles away from the business at hand, he drove into his front yard, saw Billie standing in the shade, and forgot where he'd been going. He slammed on the brakes, shoved the gears in park, and got out of the truck, leaving the motor running and the door wide open. He needed to see for himself in the bright light of day that she had suffered no lasting effects from last night's brawl.

Bracing his hands on the rail fence that separated them, he leaned forward, watching with absent fascination the way she was twisting a band to the end of her braid. In an abstract sort of way, he imagined he knew just how that band felt.

"Mornin'."

What he said was not what she heard.

I came for what's mine!

The words hung between them. Billie watched the

intent look in his eyes and wanted to scream. *Say it again, Matt. Say it now and make me believe you.*

A muscle jerked at the corner of his jaw, but his gaze never wavered from her face. Finally, it was Billie who gave up the dream and answered him back.

"Good morning. Looks like you've been busy."

Morning light was too bright to hide her small wounds. He frowned, then vaulted the fence in one leap. Before she had time to react, his hand cupped her cheek as he tilted her face up for a better look.

"Your mouth is still bruised. Damn that trucker. I should have punched out his lights just on general principle."

Billie shrugged. "Part of it's my own fault. Maybe if I'd made a bigger fuss he would have—"

"No!" The word exploded from Matt's mouth. "Don't make excuses for someone else's mistakes. The man who had you cornered was old enough to know better, but too drunk to care. If it was anyone's fault, it was Scott's."

Billie hated the anger on his face and felt guilty that it was directed at his own son. Because of her, they were at odds.

"What happened between you two last night?"

"Not nearly enough," Matt answered, and then changed the subject by tugging at the braid hanging over her shoulder and adding a smile. "Want to help me bottle-feed a calf?"

Her eyes widened. "Really?"

Matt smiled. "Really."

She beat him to the pickup.

"Hop in," he said, and stood aside for her to climb into the cab.

She hesitated, then pointed to the bed of the truck. "Could I ride back here instead?"

Matt grinned. "Once a kid, always a kid. Sure, you can ride in the back, but it's full of feed. Wait a minute, and I'll let down the tailgate. You can sit on that."

The moment he let it down, Billie slid into place. He couldn't ignore the delight on her face. He wanted to step between those long dangling legs and wipe that smile off her face with a slow, endless kiss. Instead, he gave her knee a quick pat and urged her to hold on. Billie did as she was told, and when the pickup started moving at a much slower pace than the one at which it had arrived, she tilted her face to the sun, closed her eyes, and just smiled. For now, the day was as close to perfect as it could get.

A short time later Billie stood to one side, watching as Matt prepared the milk that the calf would drink. After measuring the dry formula into a large plastic bottle, he added the correct amount of water to the mix, popped the nippled cap into place, and started to shake.

"An oversize milkshake for an oversize baby," Matt said, and handed her the bottle to hold as he washed his hands beneath a nearby faucet.

"Why doesn't the calf nurse from its mother?"

Matt dried his hands on the seat of his pants and took the bottle out of her hands as he led her across the lot toward a nearby corral.

"This one doesn't have a mama. She died."

Billie leaned over the fence, watching as the little white-faced calf ambled toward Matt.

"He knows you." Billie laughed as the calf nudged Matt's knee with its nose, scenting the milk in the bottle he held.

"Sure he does. All babies know their mothers. I'm not nearly as pretty as his was, but I'm all that he has."

She experienced an odd sort of sympathy in spite of the fact that the baby had four legs and she only two. She knew all about being motherless. And from the gentle manner in which Matt guided the calf's mouth to the bottle it would seem that he knew all about motherless babies, too. That's when she remembered he'd raised Scott by himself.

She rested her forearms on the top rail, watching man and animal communicating in the way they knew best.

The calf made loud, sucking noises as his tongue wrapped around the elongated rubber nipple, then he started to tug. When he bucked his nose against the bottle in an instinctive movement to get more, Matt laughed aloud and looked up at Billie.

"Want to give it a try?"

Billie nodded, then crawled over the fence before she had time to change her mind. A little taken aback at the intense manner in which the calf was feeding, she hesitated.

He laughed. "Take hold of the bottle; he won't hurt you, honey. He's more interested in what's inside than who's holding it."

Billie did as she was told, breathing a sigh of relief

when the calf paid no attention to the transfer. And while she held on, he continued to feed until it was all gone.

Foamy, white milk bubbles now hung on both sides of the little calf's mouth, evidence of how intensely he had fed. Although the bottle was empty, the calf chose to suck air rather than give up the rubber teat.

Matt pulled the bottle out of the calf's mouth. "Hey, buddy, that's it for now. More later."

Billie laughed when the calf butted the back of Matt's knee.

"He wants to play, doesn't he?"

Matt tossed the empty bottle over the fence, then squatted down until he was eye-to-eye with the little whiteface. "Naw, he wants his head scratched. I've sort of spoiled him."

While she watched, Matt obliged by roughly scrubbing his knuckles on the knot between the calf's ears. "You're a good father—in more ways than one, Matt Holt."

Stunned by her unexpected praise, he paused, and when he did, the calf kicked up its heels and made a quick, unannounced dash toward the opposite corner of the corral.

He stood, then turned and looked at her. The breeze was playing havoc with escaping tendrils of the hair around her face. The sun had put color in her cheeks, and the look in her eyes made him weak with longing. His voice was gruff as he acknowledged her praise.

"I can't believe you can still say that after the way you were treated last night."

Billie sighed. "I told you there's nothing personal between Scott and me, so I know I didn't hurt his feelings, but when I turned him down, I hurt his pride. He's young. He reacted badly. It doesn't make him a bad person."

He took a step closer, needing to see past the shadows in her eyes to the truth. "You're not much older yourself, Memphis, and yet you kept your head. God knows what would have happened if you hadn't had the foresight to call me."

"I'm a woman. We mature faster than men, remember?"

Her answer caught him unaware. For a moment, he just stood and stared, trying to think of a smart comeback; but to save his soul, he couldn't come up with anything but the obvious. His fingers twitched with longing as he raked her body in one long, hot sweeping gaze.

"Yes, ma'am. I'd venture to say that you are a woman . . . in every sweet, sinful sense of the word."

Billie's eyebrows arched. "Sinful?"

He took another step forward. "From the beginning of time, girl. Remember Adam?"

She gave him a look that would have wilted a lesser man. "Pooh! I don't even like apples all that much."

Common sense told him not to touch her, but he couldn't help it. The fire in her eyes was too much for a hell-raiser like him to ignore. He threw back his head and laughed, and when she wasn't looking, yanked her off her feet and into his arms, spinning around and around with her until a small dust cloud was hovering just above their feet.

"Don't like apples! Lord, but that's a good one!"

Their lips were too close, their bodies even closer. Matt knew if he stopped spinning and laughing, he'd be in trouble for sure. Finally, he could delay it no longer. He was getting dizzy, and she was holding on far too tightly for his peace of mind.

He put her down and took a single step back, his eyes alight with joy as he shook his head in amazement. He interjected a lighthearted note to hide the fact that he hadn't wanted to let her go.

"You, sweet lady, are dangerous. You need to wear a warning sign so all the poor, unsuspecting males will know ahead of time that you've got a sense of humor to go with that pretty face."

Billie blushed and stammered, then looked away. Praise was unexpected, and coming from Matt, all the more precious. In all of her life, she could never remember a man giving her a compliment that she believed—until now. Trying to regain her footing in their give-and-take, she looked up.

"Don't play pitiful with me, Matt Holt. We both know who's dangerous, and it sure as hell isn't me."

And then she pivoted and ran, climbing up and over the fence before he had time to react. When she heard the thud of his boots as he jumped, she knew that he'd followed. Instinctively she spun, a look of near fright on her face.

The expression on her face stopped him. Whatever he'd been considering went out of his head as he absorbed the fact that she could even believe he would do her harm. He glowered as he bent down and picked up the empty bottle he'd tossed earlier.

"Don't look at me like that. The last thing I'd ever do is hurt you."

Billie sighed. She hadn't meant to hurt his feelings.

"I wasn't running from you. I was running from me," she said softly. "I'm not very good at witty repartee."

"Darlin', the last thing on my mind was talking," he said, and disappeared into the barn with the calf's empty bottle.

His words made her think things she'd be better off to forget, so when he passed by where she stood, she stuffed her hands in her pockets to keep from throwing them around his neck. She'd already shamed herself once in trying to make him believe she was an unattached, free woman. She didn't have it in her to take another rejection from him. With a heavy heart, she started walking back toward the house, unaware that they'd had an audience.

It was just past 11:00 A.M. when Scott woke up to the sounds down the hall of Mike retching. It was enough to make his own aching head and rolling belly give a lurch but, to his relief, he kept it all down.

Shifting to the side of the bed, he sat with his head in his hands, contemplating his toenails and waiting for the room to quit spinning as he announced his intentions:

"I will never get drunk again."

Mike staggered into the room, his face as white as his T-shirt and undershorts. "I've heard you say that before," he said. With a groan, he crawled back onto his side of the bed, careful not to rock anything that could move.

"Yeah, but this time I mean it," Scott said, unable to speak above a whisper.

"You've said that before, too," Mike said, and pulled a pillow over his head. "Oh God. My head's killing me, and I don't think it's happening fast enough to save me from your father's wrath."

The memory of Matt's anger made Scott slump even more. "Don't remind me. I've never seen him so mad, but you don't have to worry—he won't say a thing to you. It's not Dad's way. He minds his own business and assumes that everyone else will mind theirs."

A knock on their door sent Scott scrambling for his pants. His head was swimming, and he staggered while trying to stuff his feet into places they didn't want to go. When he was decent, he dropped back to the bed and held on to the sides to keep the room from spinning.

"Come in," he said, and then winced. Even the tone of his voice seemed to hurt.

Stephanie looked inside. "Are you guys decent?" Then she frowned. "I suppose I should have used another word, like sober, maybe?"

Mike cursed beneath his breath and pulled the pillow a little tighter across the back of his head.

"Get lost, Sis."

"Boy, you two sure stirred up a hornet's nest, didn't you?"

Neither one of them saw fit to answer, which did not deter her a bit from continuing.

"I thought Matt was going to explode. He all but dumped Billie into my arms, then took off out the door like a man on a mission." She grinned, and wiggled her finger beneath Scott's nose, then poked her brother in the back of his leg. "You two, I assume, were his targets and, from the way you're behaving, I'd guess he hit a bull's-eye, right?"

"Have mercy, Sis. Your use of clichés is appalling."

"So is the smell in here," she said, and flounced out of the room, careful to sidestep the sodden clothes that Scott had walked out of last night.

"I'm going to take a shower," Scott said. "And then I'm going to make some coffee. Do what you want. I've got some serious talking to do, and I don't want to be tossing my cookies when I do it."

Just the mention of tossing anything else made Mike groan. Scott grabbed clean clothes on the way out and slipped into his father's room to use the shower.

Once inside, he leaned against the door, absorbing the familiarity of the bedroom and the sights that he'd grown up taking for granted, like the sight of his dad's best Stetson hanging on a hook near the door, the denim blue bedspread and pillows in place on the bed, which his father always made up minutes after he arose each day, the framed picture of his mother that Matt faithfully kept on display—even though he'd admitted to Scott many years ago that if he hadn't gotten her pregnant, they might never have married.

Scott swallowed past a lump, knowing that above all else, his father's honesty was the one thing he could always count on. A pair of dirty jeans were draped across a chair by his bed, ready to dump in the laundry when he next came through the room. As Scott passed them on his way to the shower, he impulsively stopped and picked them up. Tossing his own clean clothes on the bedspread, he held the jeans to his waist and measured the leg length against the length of his own, just as he'd done off and on through the years. He sighed. Even though he was now as tall as his dad, after last night's stunt, he was a long way from being the man that his dad was.

He dropped the jeans back on the chair and walked into the bathroom, closing the door behind him. After he started the shower, the rush of running water and the headache thundering between his ears drowned out the sound of a telephone ringing, as well as the message that was left on the answering machine.

Much later, with the intention of having some dry toast and black coffee to settle a rolling stomach, Scott entered the kitchen. The first thing he noticed was the answering machine's blinking red light, and he absently punched it, unprepared for the message.

Well, Matthew Holt, if you must indulge in such antics, you would be wise to wait for darkness or at least somewhere other than the wide-open spaces where God and everyone can see you. However, it's only an opinion, not an order, which is just as well, because you've never paid a whit of attention to what anyone thought.

If was Daisy Bedford's voice, but for the first time in his life, Scott saw no humor in the message. His stomach lurched as he walked out onto the back porch and saw his father and Billie standing by the corral.

Scott tried to tell himself that it wasn't what it looked like. But the longer he stood there, the dimmer his chances became of finding another reason that fit, other than the fact that they must have been messing around. Coupled with his own neurosis and Daisy's meddling, he forgot that he'd been the one to transgress. He forgot about the apology that he'd worked on during his shower. He forgot everything except the fact that Billie reacted to his father in a way that she did not to him.

A bitter sense of injustice invaded what was left of his sober mind. By the time she started toward the house alone, Scott had worked himself up into a fit of righteous indignation and waited for her by the door.

Lost in thought, Billie was shocked when Scott suddenly appeared before her, grabbing her roughly by the arm.

"Well, good morning to you, too," she said shortly, and shrugged out of his grasp.

Scott flushed with renewed anger. It must be true! All he'd done was touch her, and she was already having a fit. And after the way he'd seen them behaving, it all added up.

"Look, B.J., we need to talk. Let's go around back to the patio, where we won't be disturbed. Okay?"

She followed his lead. She wanted less to hash over the remnants of last night's debacle than she did to clear the air between them once more.

Scott took a deep breath, then combed both hands through his hair, knowing there was nowhere to start but at the beginning.

"I know I more or less made an ass of myself last night, and what's worse, I'm sorry that I left you to fend for yourself. Stephanie told us that you got roughed up. You can't know how sorry I am that this happened to you. Will you please forgive me?"

Billie's heart went out to him. He looked as sick as he obviously felt, and if she was any judge of character, she believed that he was truly sorry. Impulsively, she slid her hand up his arm to let it rest on his shoulder.

"Scott, look at me."

To his credit he did and, in doing so, elevated his status a little bit more in Billie's eyes. She smiled slightly as his pain-filled blue eyes stared at the bruises and slight swelling she knew were still visible on her lips.

"Oh God, B.J., I'm so sorry for what he did to you," he mumbled. Before she knew it, he'd pulled her into a rough hug.

She patted him on the back. "It's okay. I'm fine, and thanks to your dad, you and Mike missed getting arrested."

At this point, the mention of his father's heroics in the face of his mistakes was difficult to accept.

"Yeah, thanks to Dad," he muttered.

His belligerent look was a big change from moments ago, when he'd been so contrite.

"Don't make light of what he did," she said shortly. "You were already facedown on the floor with your nose in the sawdust when he came into the bar. He stopped the fight with the bartender's shotgun and got all of us out before the police arrived." Her voice was cool and to the point as she nailed his conscience with a slow, even, Tennessee drawl. "Personally, I was grateful not to have been arrested."

Scott paled, and then flushed. "You don't have to shove it down my throat. I said I was sorry."

"And I said, apology accepted. Let's leave it at that, okay?"

Later, Scott would look back and remember that if he'd shut up right then, everything might have turned out differently. But he hadn't, and it didn't, and because he was his father's son, he made another mistake.

"I don't want to leave it. And while we're discussing each other's mistakes, I think you ought to know you've been making a fool of yourself with my dad. Even the neighbors have noticed."

Neighbors? For a moment Billie couldn't speak past the shock of having been accused of something she had not done.

"What on earth are you talking about?"

Scott grabbed her by the arm. "You know good and well what I'm talking about. I see the way you sniff after him like a bitch in heat. Why don't you leave him alone?"

He leaned close, whispering against her ear. "If you just want a good screwing, I'd be more than happy to oblige."

Billie gasped, then froze. For several long painful seconds neither she nor Scott moved.

The moment he'd said it, he would have given a year of his life to have been able to take it all back. But it was too late, and from the look in Billie's eyes, dying a year early wouldn't have helped a damn bit.

The slap came without warning, resounding beneath the low-slung rooftop and shocking Scott out of his trance. Billie's breasts were heaving, her eyes blazing with a fury he'd never believed possible. And then, right before his eyes, her anger dissolved into tears.

He felt sick.

"Oh damn, B.J., I didn't mean—"

She spun and walked past him into the house, slamming the door behind her just as Matt walked into the kitchen from the other direction.

He didn't know why they were there, but the tears on her face were impossible to ignore. Within seconds, she was in his arms.

"Honey, please don't cry. Tell me what happened," Matt begged, and pressed a gentle kiss at the edge of her brow just as Scott came into the house.

The look on Scott's face was enough to make Matt quake. He knew what this looked like, but, so help him God, he would have done it again the same way.

"What's wrong between you two now?" Matt asked. "I walk into the kitchen and find Billie in tears, and you come in looking like someone ate your last cookie. If you two are having problems, just say so and I'm dust."

Scott doubled his fists, unsure of where he stood, but certain that it was on the outside looking in.

"The only problem between us is you!" he said, and then couldn't believe that he'd come out and said it.

Billie jerked in disbelief, then spun out of Matt's arms.

"Scott, have you completely lost your mind?"

"I'm sorry I ever brought you home with me," he said, and knew from the look on her face that, once again, he'd devastated her by his rejection. "You're nothing but a tramp. If I'd—"

Before he could finish, Matt had him by the collar and was shoving him toward a wall.

"Shut up!" Matt said softly. "Just shut up now before you say too much! Billie doesn't deserve the way you've treated her, and from the way you've been acting, she damn sure deserves more than you."

Scott couldn't think for the shock of having been slammed up against a wall by his own father like some two-bit stranger. Unfortunately, his disbelief lasted exactly five seconds, after which he reacted by taking a swing at him. Matt promptly ducked.

"I suppose she deserves someone more like you?" Scott shouted, struggling to get free of his father's grasp.

"You're acting crazy!" Matt yelled. "I would never come between you and someone you cared for. You've got to believe—"

Billie's scream tore through the air, dousing their fury and sending them spinning around in shock. She was crouched in the corner of the room with her hands over her ears and tears streaming down her face.

"Stop! Stop! For God's sake, don't fight!" She choked on a sob as her voice dwindled to a mere whisper. "Not over me . . . not over me."

Matt froze, then turned from Scott to her in a panic. "Billie, sweetheart—"

"Don't!"

He stopped at her demand. Scott cursed softly.

She took a deep breath and shuddered. Trembling in every limb, she stood until she was facing them eye-to-eye, determined that they understand what she was trying to say.

"I'm sorry, so sorry. I never meant to ruin the beautiful relationship you two had. I, more than anyone else, would know how special that is because it's something I'll never have with my own father. Now I want you two to get out and leave me alone. Go somewhere and make up. Forget you ever knew me, both of you!"

Scott felt sick inside. From the beginning this had all been his fault. He hadn't wanted B.J. for a girlfriend, and, if he was honest with himself, he knew that he still didn't.

A knot in Matt's gut jerked a little tighter. Still shaking from the confrontation with Scott, his greater fear was for Billie. All color had faded from her cheeks, and she was swaying on her feet. In spite of what she'd just said, he didn't have it in him to walk off and leave her alone.

"Billie, you've got to listen to me. Don't let—"

"No! You listen to me," she said, and hiccuped on another sob. "None of this is worth losing the person you love best." She pointed at Scott. "And you should be ashamed. Not only were you lying to your father when you pretended to care for me that way, but you're lying to yourself if you think there was ever anything between us. Personally, I resent the hell out of you for not being honest."

Her gaze wavered from Scott back to Matt, and then she covered her face as she gained fresh strength to continue. When she lifted her head, her lips were trembling, but there was a firmness in her voice that had not been there before. She fixed her attention solely on Scott, determined that he listen to what she had to say.

"As for being honest, if *I* had been on the day we arrived, maybe none of this would have happened."

Matt knew what was coming and took a deep breath. She wasn't going to tell this alone. Part of the deception had been his.

When he started forward, once again she shook her head, knowing she would be unable to finish if he touched her again.

It was then that Scott knew something more than the argument was involved, but at this point was ready to let it all go. He was already sorry that it had escalated to such a monumental misunderstanding.

"Look, B.J., just forget it, okay? I'm sorry I made a big deal out of you and Dad. Feel free to—"

She swiped at the tears on her cheeks as she met Matt's gaze. Resignation weighed heavy on her shoulders as she slumped, then turned back to Scott.

"No. It's time you listen to me for a change." She leaned against the wall for support. "I met your father over two years ago in the Denver airport."

To say Scott was shocked was putting it mildly, but

when he looked at his father's expression, he realized she was telling the truth.

"Why didn't you ever say anything about knowing him?"

A slight smile moved across her face as she looked at Matt, letting herself absorb his magnetism.

"Because I never knew his name, nor he mine. He called me Memphis. In my mind, he was just a big cowboy, but he was the embodiment of everything I'd ever wanted in a man. I'm sure that I fantasized about what happened between us. I'm also sure that your father probably forgot about me the moment he was gone, but in my heart, that meeting was the most special thing that had ever happened in my life. You have no right to judge me or your father. I shared more with him in the short time we were together than you and I have in the year and a half we've been friends. And damn you, Scott, I have not betrayed our friendship . . . it's you who's betrayed my trust."

Shamed by the truth of what she'd said, Scott turned and started to walk away when Matt grabbed him by the arm.

"Scott . . . son, is this true? You really don't have romantic feelings for her?"

He shrugged out of his father's grasp and kept walking out the door.

Scott's silence was answer enough. Matt looked up at Billie, and then walked across the room and took her into his arms.

"Oh God, Billie, I'm so sorry."

She went limp, too drained to deny herself or him the much-needed closeness of an embrace.

"Matt, Matt, what have I done? What have I done?"

"Nothing," he muttered. "You're not at fault, and everything's going to work out fine. Once Scott gets over being ashamed of himself, he'll apologize to you. You'll see."

She didn't believe him, and even if she had, it wouldn't have mattered. Everything that had been said was too ugly to forget.

Matt sensed her distrust, and there was nothing he knew to say to change the past. And then he remembered something she'd said earlier and held her a little closer as he whispered against her ear.

"Memphis . . . darlin'."

Billie sighed. If she lived to be a hundred, she would never forget the way his voice wrapped around a syllable.

"What?"

"I didn't forget you. In fact, I paid a cab driver one hell of a lot of money to get me out of that terminal before I did something we'd both regret. To this day, I have yet to walk through an airport without looking for your face, and every time it snows, I remember what it felt like to kiss you."

All movement ceased within her except the heartbeat that was suddenly racing out of control. She lifted her head and looked up. Truth was staring her right in the face.

"Cowboy, you take my breath away."

He lowered his head with a groan, and when their

lips grazed, then centered, he felt an empty space inside of him closing. His hands shook as he tunneled them through her hair, picking at the braid that she'd made hours earlier, much as he'd picked the pins from her hair those years ago. And when it fell free and lay heavily across his arms and hands, he pulled her that much closer.

Billie soared. The touch of his hands, the strength of his body, the tenderness of his kiss all served to prove that she was treading deep water with no chance of survival unless one of them made a quick move.

With a gasp, then a soft, wounded cry, she broke their kiss and buried her face against his chest. Knowing it would have to last her a lifetime, the urge to take what she could get of this man was overwhelming.

"Ah, Memphis, you are the best thing I—"

"Don't say it, Matt. Just hold me."

He did.

❆❆❆ Chapter 6

Matt stood on the front porch, gauging the sky for weather and wondering where Scott had gone. After the fight they'd just had, he felt a strong need to set things right, but he had to find him before that could happen. He raked his property with a discerning eye, gauging what he knew against what was out of place. Except for a turkey buzzard circling overhead and cattle grazing in a distant pasture, nothing seemed to be moving or missing.

Scott's Jeep was right where the hired hand had parked it this morning and didn't look as if it had been moved. Mike and Stephanie had disappeared about the same time as Scott, and Matt suspected that they'd been unwilling witnesses to the fight in the kitchen. Long after Scott had disappeared and right after Matt had gotten Billie calmed down and asleep in her room, he'd discovered the latest message from Daisy Bedford. As he listened he'd wondered how much of that had contributed to Scott's misplaced anger.

Anger tightened his features as he glared in the direction of the old woman's house, then jammed his hat firmly on his head. With a day's work yet to be done, he stepped off the porch and glanced back at the house. Surely, he thought, nothing else could possibly happen until he got back. He hadn't counted on the fact that Billie considered herself a thorn in the Holt family that must be removed.

"What the hell do you mean, she's gone?"

Matt's eyes widened in shock as Scott repeated his news. When Matt's expression turned to one of pain, Scott looked away. Sick at heart, he stared down at his plate, unable to see his father's devastation and know that it was all his fault. He tried instead to focus on Mike and Stephanie's subdued conversation as they put supper on the table—and failed miserably.

A big dark hole had been ripped in Matt's peace of mind and was widening with every breath he took. Finally, he got enough sense back to ask, "Didn't she leave a note?"

Scott shrugged. "When we returned from horseback riding, the Jeep was gone. The only note was one she'd left on the table telling us that we could pick it up at airport parking."

The dust of the day was still on Matt's clothes as he stared at the empty chair beside his place. For the last six days Billie Walker had been in it at every meal. Even when he knew he could do nothing about it, her presence had still given him comfort. And now she was gone? Just like that? Without even a good-bye?

Pain splintered his reasoning as he gritted his teeth and stalked out of the room.

"Gee, that's too bad," Mike said. "I think he's really upset."

Stephanie sniffled. She was still locked into the fact that Billie and Matt had shared a romantic interlude that, in her eyes, was right out of a novel. And now, just as in the proverbial book, the lovers had been torn apart by dissension within the family.

Scott groaned. "Yeah, and it's all my fault. How was I supposed to know there was any history between them?"

"There was no history between you and Billie, but that didn't stop you," Stephanie said sharply, and plunked a bowl of mashed potatoes in front of his plate.

He winced, yet didn't have it in him to be angry. She was right. He shoved his chair back from the table and got up with a sigh.

"I'd better go talk to Dad. I'll be right back."

Mike dropped into the vacated chair, hungrily eyeing the bowls of steaming food.

"Oh fine," he muttered. "No telling what time we'll be eating now."

Stephanie slid a bowl of green beans near his plate. "I can't believe you'd even care. Mere hours ago you were barfing up your toenails."

He glared. "You're a real pain in the ass, did you know that?"

Her right eyebrow arched. "I love you, too."

Scott paused outside his father's door, debating whether to open it, when he heard something break. It gave him the impetus to rush inside.

"Dad, are you all right? I heard—"

The mirror over the dresser had been shattered into dozens of pie-shaped slices and was still hanging within the frame by little more than luck. One of Matt's boots lay on top of the dresser where he'd thrown it, the other he still held in his hand. He glanced down at it as if debating the wisdom of sending it after the first. At the sound of Scott's voice, he turned.

There was so much pain in his father's eyes, Scott wanted to cry.

"Dad . . . Daddy, I'm sorry."

Matt blinked. Scott hadn't called him that in more than ten years. With a sigh, he dropped the other boot and took his son in his arms. "I know, Son, I know," he said gruffly. "So the hell am I." He thumped Scott's back in a rough, manly fashion, and then turned toward the dresser, looking at the mess he'd just made as if he couldn't remember how it had happened.

Scott slumped, trying to look at his father when he asked it, yet still ashamed of what he'd done.

"Why didn't you say something about knowing B.J. earlier?"

Matt paused in the act of shaking glass from his boot and turned. "Because I thought she was your girl. I thought fate was playing a real dirty trick on me when she turned up with you." His mouth twisted as he dropped both boots to the floor. "Which, in fact, it still was. It's a hell of a jolt to lose someone like her twice." He unsnapped his shirt and dropped it on a chair, then walked into the bathroom and shut the door between them.

Scott sat down on the bed, then buried his face in his hands. Never in his wildest imaginings would he have believed that his own father and one of his friends could have ever shared something this serious, and yet it would seem it was so.

"Oh God," Scott mumbled. "Please let this be all right."

When Billie Jean Walker got out of the cab in front of her home hours later, her eyes were red and swollen and her throat ached from the tears she'd shed.

The flight home had been hell. Everyone on the plane had assumed she must have suffered a terrible tragedy, which, in fact, she had. Billie hadn't the heart to tell them that the only thing she had lost was hope. She'd simply accepted the condolences given and closed her eyes against the pain that had come from leaving Matt behind. And now, here she was in the only place she called home, and she'd never felt more alone, or lonely.

As the cab driver sped away from the curb, she hefted her bags to a more comfortable position and started toward the front door. Halfway up the walk, she froze. There was no mistaking the implication of the realtor's sign in the middle of the lawn.

"Damn you, Jarrod, what have you been up to now?"

When she got to the door, she thrust her key in the lock and went inside without announcing herself. At this point, she didn't care what she might walk in on. She wanted some answers, and she wanted them now.

The air inside the house was almost rancid. The lingering scent of cigarette smoke and liquor mixed with the stale smell of old food and dust was overpowering. She shuddered. It was the first time in her life she'd ever come home to something like this. Fury governed her actions as she slammed the door and dropped her bags on the floor. If the rest of the house was this way, she was going to wring his sorry neck.

"Who's 'ere?"

Her stomach turned as she recognized her father's voice.

"It's me, Jarrod. It's Billie."

A low string of unintelligible curses filtered out into the hall. Billie gritted her teeth as she followed the sound of his voice.

"Yes, thanks, I *am* glad to be home. It's so nice to be missed," she muttered, well aware that it was the last thing Jarrod Walker was probably thinking.

She entered the den, readying herself for what she might see, and still was not prepared for the destruction. The room was in a shambles. If she didn't know better, she would have believed they'd been robbed.

"Jarrod! What on earth have you done?"

"She lef' me," he groaned, as he staggered to his feet, waving a half-empty bottle of Scotch at the room in general.

Billie rolled her eyes. "Which she?"

His face twisted angrily as he spun and flung the bottle he'd been holding, uncaring that she had to duck as it hit the wall and shattered just to the left of her ear.

"You don' understand," he said, and then swayed on his feet. "A man needs love and companionship."

A fresh wave of anger swept through her, leaving her shaking with fury that had nowhere to go.

"Oh, I understand better than you think. Everyone needs love, Jarrod, even someone like me."

He lifted his head, staring at her through a drunken haze. His once-handsome features had dissipated over the years and were slack now from the liquor and the extra weight that he carried.

Billie shuddered at the hate on his face and knew that it was directed at her. How odd, she thought, that he disliked so intensely something that he had helped create.

And then he flung out the one thing he knew that would hurt.

"I nev'r wanted you to be born."

Billie smiled, but it was not from pleasure. "Now, Jarrod, that's old news. Let's concentrate on what's new . . . say, for instance, that FOR SALE sign in the front yard."

His concentration wavered as he realized the ramifications of what was about to come.

"I jus' need a fresh start," he said, trying to formulate words around a tongue far too thick for his mouth.

Billie doubled her fists, resisting the urge to punch him one in the mouth.

"Then by all means, make one," she offered. "However, you won't do it with my house and my money. Not any longer. I'm way past the age of consent, *father, dear.* You can't sell what doesn't belong to you."

Jarrod staggered from the unexpected venom in her attack. As drunk as he was, he realized that something, or someone, had given Billie a confidence she'd never before had.

"You don't know wha' you're talkin'—"

Billie started toward him from across the room, her voice rising with each word that she spoke. By the time she was in his face, she was screaming.

"I *do* know what I'm talking about. Mother might have taken the easy way out of life, but she did one thing right before she swallowed a cupful of pills and left me shackled to you—she changed her will and left everything that you married her for to me, didn't she?"

When he refused to answer, Billie screamed it again, only this time mere inches from his nose.

"Didn't she?"

"Damn you," Jarrod said, and thought about hitting her square in her face, but the fire in her eyes was just enough to deter him from doing the actual deed.

"No, damn you, Jarrod Walker, for walking the earth. You're the sorriest excuse for a human being that I've ever known, and I'm embarrassed that you're my father."

His already-ruddy face suffused with color as rage swept over him like a fire across dry grass. How dare this *weed* of misspent seed taunt him for something he wouldn't even admit to himself?

Tossing away what was left of his restraint, his fist shot out and connected with the side of Billie's jaw. The crack it made when knuckles hit bone was as jarring as the carpet onto which Billie fell. Tears sprang to her eyes, but not from the pain of the blow. For Billie, it was nothing more than the final straw to a week in hell. Without missing a breath, she crawled to her feet and got right back up in his face.

"Do that again, and I'll call the police. And if you're still here by the time I get my clothes unpacked, I'm calling Mel Deal."

This time the threat she made was viable. Jarrod blanched. The last thing he wanted was to be on the bad side of the man who controlled their purse strings.

"So call the sorry-ass lawyer, see if I care. You're a weak little bitch who'll wind up jus' like your mother—damn her worthless soul to everlastin' hell."

The threat was nothing new. Billie had heard it all of her life. Every time Jarrod got mad at her, he predicted that she would one day take her own life just as her mother had done. It shouldn't have hurt anymore. But it did.

Determined not to let him know how deeply the words had wounded her, she turned her back on him and walked to the phone. Jarrod frowned.

"You callin' the police?"

Billie turned and stared him straight in the eyes. "Are you still here?"

Her defiance was unexpected, and, in that moment, Jarrod knew he had somehow lost his control over her. His shoulders drooped as he walked out of the room, a weak and beaten man.

As soon as the door closed behind him, all the fight went out of her, and she slumped to the floor. When someone answered the phone on the other end of the line, it was all she could do to remember whom she'd called. Only after they'd identified themselves did she remember what she'd been about to do.

"Century 21 Realtors. How may I help you?"

She bit her lip to keep from crying. "This is Billie Walker at 7343 July Road. I've just returned home and found out that my house was put on the market without my permission. I have no intention of selling it and would appreciate it if someone from your office could come out and remove the sign and take the house off your listing."

The woman was still talking when Billie hung up. Discussing the whys and hows of her miserable life were, at the moment, impossible. Overcome with despair, she hugged her knees and buried her face in her arms, wincing as she accidentally brushed across the place on her cheek where she'd been struck.

"Dear Lord, help me get through this with my sanity intact."

One day at the ranch turned into two, and then into a week. Mike and Stephanie Hodge were long gone, after having said their apologies and good-byes at the same time.

Matt said all the right things and made all the right noises, but when Scott left to take them to the airport, he felt liberated, yet not in the way one would suspect. Now that he was alone, he was free to grieve for the hole Billie's absence had made in his life, and grieve he did. One day stretched into another as his grief took different turns.

At first, he worked every day until he fell into bed too tired to eat, and took chances with his life that he hadn't taken since he'd become a father. His behavior caused Daisy Bedford to go on a rampage. She left more warning phone calls in a month than she had in the years they'd known each other.

When Scott began to agree with her, Matt knew his days were numbered, and still he couldn't find it in him to stop the downward spiral of self-destruction. When he finally turned to a whiskey bottle, the pain, along with his memory, disappeared.

Matt started drinking. Scott went from disbelief at what his father was doing to fear at the underlying rage with which it was done. When Scott realized he couldn't stop it or him, he began to watch Matt like a hawk, afraid to turn his back on him and only to find him later facedown in some ditch, dead.

Yet as worried as he was, he didn't have it in him to try to stop him, because his own guilt was bigger than his righteousness. All he could do was keep an eye on his father and hope that he would be there when it mattered. But, oddly enough, it was the getting drunk that broke Matt's streak of self-pity.

Matt's head hurt. From the outside in and inside out. In places too small to measure and everywhere else at once. His stomach burned, and when he rolled over in bed, he groaned, unable to remember eating ashes the night before, although the taste was in his mouth all the same.

"God have mercy," he mumbled, crawling out of bed

and staggering toward the shower. "Now I remember why I quit drinking. The booze is one thing, but walking on ceilings plays hell with my hair."

The humor was wasted as he stepped into the shower and turned it on full force. It came out cold before it came out hot. When he could breathe without wanting to die, he ended the shower as abruptly as it had begun and wondered how long he'd been like this. He had no memory of when it had started, or how long he'd been at it. His only thought as he dried and dressed was for Scott. Had he said or done anything that might ruin what was left of their relationship?

A short time later, as he was heading toward the kitchen, he heard the unmistakable sounds of a lawn mower's engine and made a detour toward the window.

The midmorning sun beamed relentlessly upon Scott's bare brown shoulders, while perspiration tunneled between the ridges on his flat, muscled belly. Matt leaned his forehead against the window and watched the concentration on his son's face, remembering him as a child and marveling at what a strong young man he'd grown up to be. Pride in the child had grown to pride in the man. Matt took a deep breath and walked out onto the porch, knowing he had to face him sometime, and in Matt Holt's world, sooner was always better.

Scott saw movement from the corner of his eye. He paused just as he was about to turn a corner in the yard and looked up. When he saw his dad standing at the edge of the porch, he felt an overwhelming sense of relief. He didn't have to talk to him to know he was back to his old self. He could tell by the way he was standing that it was over!

With shaking hands, he killed the engine, then started across the yard. When he was standing at the foot of the steps, he looked up, gauging the extent of lucidity in his father's eyes, and then smiled, satisfied by what he saw.

Thank God, Matt thought. *If he can smile at me after all of this, maybe it will be okay.*

"Well, well," Scott said, and grinned again.

Matt frowned. "What?"

"So you decided to come up for air."

"Look, Scott, I don't know what I—"

Scott shook his head and interrupted, "If you are about to apologize to me, then save it. If anyone should be saying I'm sorry, then I think it's me. I screwed up royally, and if I could take it all back, I would. However, I can't, so talking about what happened isn't going to change a thing."

A surge of relief sent a small smile to Matt's face. At least one thing was accomplished. He and his son were back on level ground. The phone began ringing inside the house, but both men ignored it.

"Thanks, Son."

"You're welcome," Scott said, as he continued to grin.

"What's so funny?"

Scott's eyebrows arched. "I was just thinking."

"About what?" Matt asked, and then wished he hadn't.

"You know, during the last couple of days, I think I

just got my first glimpse of the hell-raiser people always said you used to be."

Matt's eyes narrowed. He had been afraid of this.

"And they were right. I wouldn't have had the guts to do what you did," Scott said, well aware that he had Matt's full attention.

"To do what?" Matt asked.

"Ride the dirt bike into Billy Bob's and circle the dance floor before riding back out the front door. You scattered patrons in all directions and scared the hell out of some greenhorn on the mechanical bull."

Matt dropped onto the front steps and put his head in his hands.

"I didn't."

"Well, actually, Dad, you did."

"I went into Fort Worth on that bike?"

"Yeah."

"Why would I do that?"

Scott grinned. "Because I'd already taken away the keys to your truck."

"Hell."

Scott laughed aloud.

"It's not funny," Matt said. "I don't . . . I wouldn't . . . I haven't—"

"Look, Dad, it's okay. I mean, you more or less had one coming, don't you think? After all, I screwed up your love life in a pretty big way, and then, before you and Billie had a chance to straighten it out, she up and disappears. After all of that, I'm just glad you're still talking to me."

"Disappointments are no excuse for making an ass

of oneself," he said. "I'm sorry for any embarrassment my actions have caused you, and I can promise that it won't happen again."

Scott grinned. "Thank you for the words of wisdom. I'll try and remember them the next time I mess up. As for embarrassing me, I don't think so. Actually, my worth on the streets of Fort Worth went up big time. If I want to impress some pretty thing now, all I'll have to do is tell her that I take after my father's side of the family."

Matt stood up and glared. "Weren't you mowing the yard?"

Scott grinned. "Yep, I believe that I was."

"Then I suppose you'd better finish it up," Matt said shortly. "When you're through, we need to check the cattle. After that, there's a section of fence that needs replacing. Our bull and Turner's bull have been squaring off at each other on the back side of the east range. At least they were, last time I remember."

"Yes sir," Scott said, and then gave his father a half-assed salute.

Matt's eyes narrowed in a challenging manner. "You're acting pretty sure of yourself these days. Does that mean you're feeling cocky enough to try me again?"

Scott laughed, remembering last summer, when he'd had the wild notion of being able to beat his father in a wrestling match. "No way," he said as he headed back to the mower. "You are still *the man*."

Matt tried to smile at the exaggerated swagger in Scott's walk, but the hole Billie had left in his heart was still too painful for him to appreciate anything other than being able to breathe.

"Hey, Scott!"

Scott turned.

"Yeah, Dad?"

"Thanks."

He grinned. "You're welcome."

Man to man, they stared at each other from across the yard, and then Matt was the first to break the look when he walked back into the house and shut the door firmly behind him.

Scott nodded. Enough said.

Moments later, as Matt was pouring himself a cup of coffee, he heard the engine on the mower revving and sighed in relief. One hurdle over and only God knew how many to go.

Just as he was about to take his first swig, he noticed the blinking light on the answering machine and remembered hearing the phone ring while he and Scott were talking. He punched the button and stood savoring the first jolt of caffeine to his system as he waited for the message.

I see you've come back to the land of the living and it's about damned time, Matthew Holt. That was a sorry example to set for your son. At his age, men hover between being an ass or an adult. If he follows in his father's footsteps, there's every indication he'll be braying, won't he?

Daisy! He sighed, unable to find it in him to be mad. Not this time. Not when her message was too close to home.

"I hear you, old lady, loud and clear," he announced to an empty room. Then he set down his empty cup and walked out of the kitchen with slow, measured strides.

The way he looked at it, there was only one way to get through this heartache, and that was one day at a time. And because he was so locked into his own misery, he didn't realize until a month later how deeply Scott felt the guilt for what had transpired.

The phone bill was staggering. Matt stared, dumbfounded by the total. Without taking time to look at the listings, he spun on his heel and headed for the door, his son's name already hanging on the edge of his tongue in anger.

"Samuel Scott!"

The roar in his father's voice was reminiscent of the days of Scott's youth, as was the linking of both of his names. In the past, it had always spelled dire consequences for his backside.

It so startled him that he jerked and bumped his head on the upraised hood of his Jeep. Pain raked his scalp as he cursed beneath his breath. When he thrust an oily hand in his hair to check for a wound, it only made matters worse. Now he didn't know whether the moisture he felt was from blood or oil.

"Dang, Dad, you nearly caused me to decapitate myself."

Matt came off the porch waving the bill in his hand, then shoved it beneath Scott's nose.

"It might have saved me the trouble! Four hundred

and twenty-two dollars, dammit! What the hell were you thinking?"

Scott didn't have to look to know what it was. "Oh man," he muttered. "I didn't think it would be that much."

Matt couldn't think of what to say next. Infuriated, he began thumbing through the pages, intent on discovering the whereabouts of the long-distance girlfriend who had warranted all the calls. As he read, anger broke and spilled, running out of his body in one long, agonized breath as he read line after line of calls made to number after number in the city of Memphis, state of Tennessee.

Scott held his breath, afraid to talk, but afraid not to explain. Moments later, he could tell that explanations were unnecessary. That was what gave him the courage to speak.

"I tried to find her, Dad. I lay awake at nights remembering what a shit I had been to her—and to you. I wanted to tell her it was all right. I wanted her to come back, to give us another chance."

Emotion clouded Matt's vision. The numbers all ran together as he gripped the pages tightly between his fingers. Finally he gained enough control to speak, and even then his words came out in fits and starts, as if admitting what he knew was too painful to say.

"We both messed up," Matt said harshly. "When I met her, I knew then . . ." He took a deep, shuddering breath. "I knew in my heart that I had a chance at heaven. Instead of following my instincts, I ran. I didn't trust my own feelings. To make matters worse, I got a second chance and still blew it. I should have said something the day you arrived instead of leaving it all on her shoulders." It hurt to remember the pain on her face. "She kept telling me there was nothing between you two, but I didn't believe her. Maybe part of me didn't want to believe her because then I would have had to confront what I really felt for her."

Scott took the pages from his father's hand, lightly scanning the evidence of his ill-fated search.

"I called every Walker in Memphis and got every kind of response except the one I wanted. I got cussed at, and answering machines, and hang ups. And then there were the times when I thought I was on to something. The funny thing was, several of the people I called had once known either Billie or her father, sometimes both."

In spite of hearing something he didn't want to face, Matt had to ask.

"So, what did you find out?"

Scott shrugged and looked away, pretending great interest in the new oil stain on his old T-shirt.

"Not much."

Matt frowned. "Boy, you're gonna have to do better than that. I know when you're lying to me."

Scott lifted his head. For a brief moment their gazes locked. He was the first to look away.

"One of them had kids who'd gone to school with her. Another said the last time she'd driven by the house where they used to live, she'd seen a FOR SALE sign in the yard. No one seems to know anything about her or her father."

A small light flickered and died in the back of Matt's soul. It was the last of a hope that he'd harbored, and when it snuffed, he winced in reflex.

It was the kind of pain that comes too quickly to register. The kind that has to get past the shock of it all to start hurting. His shoulders slumped as he turned and started back toward the house.

"Dad . . . ?"

He turned.

"I'm sorry about the bill. I intended to pay it all along."

"Forget it," he said harshly. "Just forget everything. Do me a great big favor and don't mention Billie Jean Walker—or Memphis—to me ever again, okay?"

Scott nodded, then shuddered when the front door slammed behind Matt.

Scott left for L.A. the first week in August, and Matt stood on the porch and waved until he could no longer see the dust behind him.

For all intents and purposes, the incident with Billie Walker was over. It was only at night, when the house was silent and Matt's memories were filled with the ghosts of a lifetime of mistakes, that he let himself feel the pain. It had dug in with the persistence of a tick and was holding on, sucking the joy from his life for all it was worth. In a way he welcomed it. It was, for Matt, proof that he still lived and breathed beyond the numbness that had invaded him.

And so it continued until one rainy October weekend when the darkness of the night outside was only shades lighter than the shadows inside his soul.

✿ ✿ ✿ Chapter 7

A chill gust of October wind caught the edge of Billie's winter coat, tunneling beneath the hem of her skirt and adding to the general numbing of her body that had already taken place during the past few weeks. However, her initial misery had little to do with the weather.

It had started on the day she'd called her lawyer, Melvin Deal, and told him what Jarrod had tried to do.

Today it was over.

After a long, drawn-out court battle, her father no longer had access to anything that belonged to her, including her home, her money, or the bulk of her estate should she die.

Billie's face was gaunt, her eyes red-rimmed and haunted as she stood on the top steps of the Shelby County Courthouse, waiting for Mel to bring his car around. Out of deference to the weather, she pulled the collar of her navy blue coat a little tighter around her neck. Her chin quivered, both from the cold and from despair. There was no joy in having to fight a parent before the courts, not even if you came out the winner, not even if you were right.

Just as she saw Mel's car, a sparse scattering of snowflakes began drifting down from the skies. With a heartfelt sigh of relief, she started down the steps just as someone grabbed her arm, impeding her progress.

Swaying unsteadily on the narrow concrete steps, she turned, then gasped. Jarrod held her in an unsteady grip that seemed to tighten with every breath that he took. His eyes were wild and glazed with anger. His nostrils flared, his upper lip curled back in a disdainful sneer as he glared down at the woman who bore his name.

For some reason Billie thought of the expression Matt Holt had been wearing when he'd rescued them in the bar, of his low, angry voice announcing, "I came for what's mine."

With a bittersweet pain, she knew that life had played her for a fool. The man she belonged to didn't want her, and the one who wanted her wouldn't claim her.

Jarrod shook her fiercely. "You're going to be sorry for what you did today."

Billie struggled to get free, but letting him know she was frightened was the last thing she would do. With what was left of her nerve, she tilted her head and straightened her shoulders, answering him with a voice that was as cold as the wind that swirled around them.

"Don't threaten me, Jarrod. You brought this all on yourself."

He leaned close until she felt his hot breath on her cheeks.

"I don't know how, and I don't know when, but there

will come a day when you'll get yours, girl, and when that day comes, I'm going to be there . . . waiting."

Billie refused to respond to the threat, trying to imagine what her mother had ever seen in this man. Her voice was almost noncommittal when she thrust her parting question into the silence.

"Why do you hate me so?"

Jarrod sneered. "Because you look like *her*, and she was weak and useless. She couldn't do anything right. She couldn't even give me the son I wanted. The only thing she ever did right was die."

Billie's eyes narrowed, letting his awful statement roll off her psyche. "It really meant that much? If I'd only been a boy, things would have been different between us?"

But it was obvious that Jarrod Walker felt no remorse for his beliefs.

"A man should have a son to carry on his name."

Billie shuddered. "Then thank God I was born a girl, because your name and your hate will die with you, father dear."

Shock suffused his features.

She took advantage of the opportunity by jerking her arm free and taking the steps as fast as she possibly could, imagining that at any moment she'd feel the imprint of his hand in the middle of her back and it would be all over. But it didn't happen. When she reached the street, she all but fell into the front seat of Mel's car.

Melvin Deal took one look at the panic on her face and growled, "What the hell was that all about?"

She leaned her head against the seat and closed her eyes, willing herself not to cry. Not anymore.

"Just a final parting of the ways. Nothing less. Nothing more."

"Are you sure, honey? If he was threatening you, I can get a protection order."

Billie shook her head. "Drive, just drive. I want to be as far away from this place as I can possibly get."

For a man who was the contemporary version of Ichabod Crane, Melvin Deal had a lot on the ball. He hunched over the steering wheel, folding his long, lanky length into a pose of concentration, wrapped his bony fingers around the stick shift of his sports car, and yanked the gears into drive. Their exit left several feet of rubber on the pavement in front of the courthouse. When they were blocks away, he glanced at Billie and frowned. She looked like death warmed over.

"How about coming home with me? Adelene is fixing pot roast, and you know how she loves to fuss over you."

After the tension she'd endured in the courtroom, the thought of having to make polite conversation with anyone was more than Billie could bear.

She smiled, hoping to soften her rejection. "No, thank you, Mel. I just want to go home."

He worried his lower lip as he waited for the light to change, then blurted out what he was thinking.

"Are you afraid to stay there alone?"

Billie rolled her eyes. "After surviving all of this, there's nothing left to be afraid of." *Except loneliness.*

But she didn't bother to add the last aloud. She had accepted that much on her own.

"It's too bad you had to lose a semester of school because of this mess," he said.

She shrugged. In her mind, the biggest loss that she'd suffered came from finding and then leaving Matt Holt all over again. Between that and the knowledge that her father wished she might disappear off the face of the earth, school had been the last thing on her mind. But Mel was concerned, and she felt obligated to explain what she'd done.

"Earlier, when all this started, I talked to the dean. He seemed very understanding about the situation and promised to help work me back into the system when I was ready to return."

Mel nodded. For a girl who'd more or less raised herself, Billie Jean Walker had a good head on her shoulders and a lot more ambition than the bastard who called himself her father.

"What are your plans for the immediate future? Will you be going back to L.A. soon, or do you plan to wait until after the holidays?"

Her heart tugged, remembering a blue-eyed cowboy who'd once held her and made her feel safe. Dear God, she needed to feel safe. She took a deep shaky breath.

"I don't know what I'm going to do," she said softly. "But if I leave town, I'll let you know."

Mel nodded. He had no other options. After all, she was a woman grown, and today she'd faced a tiger. She was due some downtime.

He braked, then made a sharp turn up her driveway, coming to a skidding halt in much the same manner they'd peeled out in front of the courthouse.

"Okay, girl, you're home, but if you need me, call. Night or day, Billie, and I mean it. Your mother was one of our best friends, and the last thing she asked of me was to make sure I looked after you."

Billie managed a smile. *It's a shame Mother couldn't have stayed around to do the job herself. Today I could use a shoulder to cry on.*

"I know, and I appreciate having you and Aunt Addie in my corner."

He sighed, remembering a phone call on a night long ago.

"If I'd only known what your mother was up to, maybe I could have stopped what happened."

Billie shook her head. "She just didn't have the staying power to deal with Jarrod, and quite frankly, after today, I almost understand."

Mel froze as fear suddenly centered within his mind. "Uh . . . Billie, you wouldn't ever go and do anything . . ."

"No way," she answered sharply. "That's not what I meant. I was implying that I understood her wanting to get away. Frankly, I would have much rather she'd just taken a bus instead of her life."

He grinned. "That's what I thought you meant."

Billie smiled as she opened the car door. He was lying, and they both knew it.

"Thanks for the ride, Mel."

"You call me, you hear?"

All he got for an answer was a halfhearted wave and a view of her back as she made a dash for her door. When she was safely inside, he made a mental note to call the police and have them swing by this address from time to time, at least for another week or so. What Billie didn't know wouldn't hurt her. The idea of that girl alone in that house made him antsy, especially after what he'd witnessed in the courtroom. If Jarrod Walker had had a gun with him today, Mel was convinced that he would have killed them all.

The house was cold and empty, just like Billie's soul. She walked through the clean, orderly rooms without really seeing them, trying to find solace in the familiar. But it wasn't to be. Her nerves were ragged, her spirit all but broken.

When she opened a closet to hang up her coat, the shadows in the corners only emphasized the empty hangers on the rod. She closed the door, unwilling to dwell upon how vacant her life really was. She existed, but she did not live. Breath came and went, but there was no joy, no substance to her day, only the knowledge that whatever happened, she would face it alone.

As she started toward her bedroom to change, the sounds of her footsteps became an eerie echo throughout the house. Shuddering, she stepped out of her shoes and carried them the rest of the way to her room.

She shivered again as she opened the door. Even though the central heat was humming softly in the background, she felt cold clear through. Stripping off her clothes as she went, she was naked by the time she got to the shower. When the water was running swift and warm, she stepped beneath the spray, welcoming the pummeling fingers of wet heat jetting from the showerhead.

She stood without moving until the water began to run cool. Her skin was tingling as she turned off the faucets, and when she exited the shower, the soft, thick folds of the bath towel enveloped her body, warming her even more.

Without dressing, Billie turned on her electric blanket and crawled between the covers. Just before she fell asleep, she thought to take the phone off the hook. For now, the only reality she wanted were the dreams that she knew would come. The dreams of a tall, dark-haired cowboy with suntanned skin and clear, blue eyes, who kept her safe within the boundary of his heart.

For Matt, darkness came early but not unexpectedly. Daylight and good weather were at a premium in late fall, especially this year. There hadn't been two sunny days in a row this week, and from the sounds of the rain dripping off the roof and the weatherman's predictions, there wouldn't be another, at least not for a while. Thanksgiving was over a month away, and for Matt, it would have to be just another day. Scott couldn't come home, and Matt had no desire to fly out for just a four-day weekend.

He tried to find comfort in the warmth of the fire burning in the fireplace, of knowing he had food and shelter at his fingertips. There'd been many years in his life when he'd had one of the above, but not necessarily all at the same time. He was a man who had the good sense to appreciate what he had without wishing for the impossible. He shifted restlessly in his chair, trying to remember the positive.

School was going great for Scott. Cattle prices were up. He had hay in the barns and beef on the hoof. Hell, it had even been weeks since Daisy had felt the need to interfere. He should have been satisfied. He was not.

A log popped behind the fire screen, and instinctively he turned to look, assuring himself that the sparks stayed where they belonged. For several long moments he gazed into the flames without seeing the color or feeling the heat, lost instead in memories that wouldn't go away.

There were memories of Billie's smiles and laughter as she'd helped him bottle-feed the motherless calf, of the joy she'd experienced at catching a fish, and then the immediate need to throw it back. But remembering the good meant remembering the bad. Forgetting the pain in her eyes and the tears on her face as she'd begged him and Scott not to fight was impossible. He sighed, wondering as he had so many other times before what there was about Billie Walker that he couldn't let go.

He sat staring into the fire for so long that he lost all track of time. It wasn't until he heard the sound of an approaching vehicle that he roused and dragged himself from the chair, wondering who would come out on a night like this and hoping that it wasn't some neighbor in need of help. He was in no mood to get wet again today.

Without giving his caller time to knock, Matt opened the door, peering through the darkness and the rain to the figure he saw emerging from a mud-splattered car.

"Who's there?" he called, and stepped farther onto

the porch, trying to discern who it was who'd come calling in the storm. And then she tilted her face just enough for him to see, and the knowledge of who it was hit him like a blow to the stomach.

"Billie?"

At the sound of his voice, she paused to look up, and the expression on her face sent him bolting off the porch into the storm. Rain slapped him in the face and instantly plastered his clothing to his body. His voice was rough with shock, but his hands were gentle as he grasped her by the shoulders. When she sighed, and then swayed, he caught her to him, shouting out his anger only to have it torn from his lips and drowned in the rain pelting down upon them.

"What the hell's wrong with you? Are you sick or just crazy?"

He didn't wait for an answer as he dragged her up the porch and into the house. When the door shut behind them, the warmth of the room was a vivid reminder of how cold and wet they'd become.

Her eyes were filled with pain. The trembling of her lips had nothing to do with the cold. But it was the lassitude with which she drew each breath that frightened him most. Concern for her well-being overcame his earlier anger and shock.

"Billie, honey, talk to me, tell me what's wrong. Scott tried to find you but couldn't. Where have you been?"

She shuddered, and her voice was so weak it was almost nonexistent. "I think in hell . . . and I'm still trying to find my way back." And then her chin quivered, and she started to cry, blending tears with the raindrops still clinging to her face. "Oh Matt, I need help. I can't do it by myself. Not anymore."

He didn't ask what it was she couldn't do or why she had even come. He was just too everlasting glad that she had.

"And you don't have to." He lifted her off her feet and into his arms, then started toward his bedroom.

When her head rolled, then dropped against his shoulder, he hastened his steps. Something bad had happened to her, and from the condition she was in, he was afraid to ask what.

Billie was vaguely aware of her surroundings as Matt carried her into his room. The blue bedspread was familiar, as was the rest of the furniture. But when he set her down, she was forced to hold on to his arms to keep herself upright.

"Sorry," she mumbled as her teeth began to chatter. "I didn't realize I was so cold."

His hands were gentle as he began to strip the sodden clothing from her chilled body. "It's okay, baby, it's okay. I'll have you warm in nothing flat."

The room went in and out of focus as her resistance started to ebb. It was only after air struck bare flesh that she realized he was taking off her clothes. In momentary panic, she started pushing at his hands.

"Matt . . . what are you doing?"

"I'm going to get you warm, and then you're going to rest. After that, we'll talk . . . okay?"

Having said it, he paused long enough to look up, and when she did likewise, she forgot to be embarrassed. The expression on his face was so full of compassion that she knew her instincts to get to him had been right all along. Modesty went begging as the need to trust someone other than herself overcame her.

"Okay," she relented, and dropped her head, letting him get on with what he was doing.

When the last of her clothing fell to the floor, Matt couldn't think straight for trying to ignore the cold, pale beauty that was revealed. But when she shivered beneath his hands, panic made him forget everything but the need to get her warm.

Guiding her into the shower, he stood her beneath the flow of warm water and breathed a quiet sigh of relief when she relaxed and leaned into the spray. But his relief turned to a new wave of anxiety as she staggered and, once again, almost fell.

"Well damn, this won't work," he muttered, and started stripping off his own wet clothes.

Moments later, he slipped into the shower, shutting out everything but the warmth, the water, and the woman.

Billie was vaguely aware that he'd stepped in behind her. Before she had time to object, his arms slid around her torso, and she no longer had a fear of falling. The strength of his hold, the warmth of his skin next to hers, the rough texture of the hair upon his chest were sensations that she'd experienced before, but only in her dreams. A shudder swept through her as she exhaled slowly and relaxed. It felt so right to be standing within the safety of a good man's arms.

Matt used his own strength to brace them both as she went limp. The weight of her breasts against the backs of his hands was difficult to ignore, but when her head slid into the niche beneath his chin, the surge of love he felt for her was so strong that he, too, felt weak.

"Stand easy, darlin'," he said quietly, willing his body not to betray him. Not now.

"I knew you'd help, I just knew it," she mumbled, and then, before he could prepare himself for the shock, she turned within his embrace, slid her arms around his neck, and held on.

Matt groaned beneath his breath. He was as close to a woman as a man could get without being inside her. Every soft, delicate curve of her body was there beneath his hands. Her breath was faint against his neck as the shower spray plastered her long, dark hair to her shoulders and his chest. He gritted his teeth and closed his eyes, willing himself to maintain control. By the time her skin was warm to the touch, and she'd stopped shivering against him, he was in desperate need of another shower, but one that was stone cold.

He turned off the water and helped her out onto the rug as he might have a child, wrapping her hair in one towel and her body in another. When he had her safely seated on the closed toilet seat, he grabbed a towel for himself and wrapped it around his waist, tucking in the ends to keep it from falling at his feet. It didn't help his condition, but psychologically it put a distance between them that he sorely needed.

When he was halfway through the act of towel-drying her hair she began to cry. Softly at first, and then in big, aching gulps that tore the heart right out of his chest.

"Ah darlin', don't," he begged, and once more lifted her into his arms and carried her back into the bedroom before placing her in the middle of his turned-down bed.

She turned toward him like a flower to light as he straightened and moved away. "Don't leave me, Matt. Don't leave me alone."

"I won't. Not ever again."

With a flick of his wrist, he tossed their wet towels onto the bathroom floor, then turned out the light. When he slid into the bed beside her, she rolled into his arms like a magnet, and when her tears ran wet across his hands and onto his chest, he held her fast, silently cursing whoever or whatever had caused her such grief.

"It's okay, it's okay," he promised, as he pulled the covers up around them both. "Let it all out, then let me hold you."

A sob hiccuped around her last words. "Oh God, Matt, don't you know? That's why I came."

Morning was less than a thought away when Billie woke up to find herself face-to-face with a hot blue gaze. It was then that she remembered what she'd done. Naked as the day they were both born, they lay in each other's arms, too close for comfort, and still too far away.

Her pulse rocketed as his mouth curved gently upward, and when he lifted a finger and moved a stray curl from the bridge of her nose, she caught herself holding her breath, wondering what else he might touch . . . might move.

"How long have you been watching me sleep?"

"Long enough."

She swallowed nervously.

"Are you all right?"

She thought of what she'd left behind. "No."

His smile slipped. "Want to talk about it?"

"No."

He frowned, judging the wariness on her face against the longing in her eyes, and went straight to the point.

"You shouldn't have disappeared like that."

Billie sighed, and when she would have looked away, Matt caught her chin and tilted her face back up to his.

"Don't turn away from me, Memphis. You came back. I suppose for a reason. You've got to trust someone sometime—it may as well be me."

Tears welled in her eyes. "Thank you for taking care of me last night."

He sighed, then rolled until she was lying atop him. Pulling her head beneath his chin, he wrapped his arms around her, stroking the soft curve of her back beneath the covers in a constant, soothing motion.

"You're welcome."

A lump formed at the back of Billie's throat. This man was a contrast in textures she couldn't ignore. Big to the point of imposing, she should have felt threatened, but it was his gentleness that was her undoing.

"Matt?"

"What, darlin'?"

"Will you make love to me?"

His hand stilled in the middle of her back as his nerves went on alert. Suddenly he was doubly aware of her breasts flattened against his chest, of the warmth of her body pressed so intimately against his own. He closed his eyes and swallowed before rolling once more, until she was flat on her back and he was braced above her. Levering himself up on one elbow, he stared into the longing he saw etched on her face.

"It would be my everlastin' pleasure."

The breath she'd been holding escaped on a sigh, and when he shifted across her, she stiffened slightly.

"I'm not too good at this," she warned.

Matt's eyes were alight with joy and with love. He dug his fingers through her hair, then cupped the back of her head as he tilted her lips for a kiss. Just before their mouths met, he bent down and whispered, real close to her ear, "That's okay, darlin', I am."

Then he took her lips by storm, sweeping across their tender surface and laying claim to them, and everything else he touched. In the space of mere minutes, Billie caught and lost her breath so many times that she gave up trying to regain a rhythm. When the work-roughened palms of his hands moved across the fragile texture of her skin, she gasped, and when the callused tips of his fingers dipped between her legs and began to stroke, she arched off the bed, following the shaft of pleasure that swept through her body. All she could do was gasp.

"What, darlin'? Do you like that? Do you want me to stop?"

"Oh, Matt . . . oh yes . . . oh no!"

He smiled as his head dipped toward her breasts. She did have a way with words.

His mouth was like a streak of fire across her skin, burning everything in its path and leaving behind an invisible mark of his possession. He traced the shape of her nipples with the edge of his tongue, and when one hardened against his lips, he drew it into his mouth and then nipped. Not too hard, just enough to shatter what was left of her mind.

And, with every caress of her body, his own resistance weakened. A dull roar was growing louder and louder inside his head, blocking out all but the sounds that she made. Attuned to the smallest gasp, the tiniest shiver, Matt knew she bordered on coming undone, and he wasn't going to let her go it alone.

With a desperate yank, he opened the drawer at his bedside table, reaching for protection.

"I'm protected," she whispered.

"So am I," he said, and with shaking hands, he sheathed himself, then moved up and over her and was again sheathed, but this time in sweet Billie's warmth.

Matt gritted his teeth as he slid inside.

"Sweet Jesus," he whispered, as her arms snaked around his neck.

She was hot and tight, and he'd never felt so welcome in his life. When she suddenly wrapped her legs around him and pulled him deeper, closer, he found himself the one in danger of coming undone.

Everything changed. They were no longer two people on the verge of ecstasy: they had become one. Every movement of body to body stoked a fever, raced a pulse, built a fire. Each whisper of love soothed a soul, healed a heart, forged a bond.

The dance they had started was moving to a frenzy neither one could deny. When the pleasure had changed to the point of pure pain, it happened.

Spiraling waves of joy suddenly shattered upon them, then began to ebb and flow, moving from the point of origin to each part of their bodies and ending only when there was nowhere left to go. Bone weak and too spent to talk, Billie still would not let him go, but clutched at him instead in near desperation, as if she'd lose herself if she lost touch with him.

When Matt could breathe and think at the same time, he rolled, taking her with him, until she was lying on top of him.

"Matt . . ."

He sighed as he smoothed the hair from her eyes.

"What, sweetheart?"

"You were right."

Blue devils began dancing in his eyes as a grin broke the planes of his face. He wrapped his fists in the fall of her hair, tugging until she was forced to raise up and look at him and the smug look of satisfaction that he wore.

"What?" she asked, trying to hide a bashful smile.

"Just wanted you to know that I most usually am."

Billie laughed, and when she did, the knot of misery that she'd brought with her began to loosen.

She cupped his face with both hands, reveling in the freedom to do so, and then murmured, "You're an impossible man."

He smiled as joy settled next to his heart.

"But you love me," he said, and then caught himself staring into her eyes and holding his breath for an answer.

The words wrapped around her soul, breaking barriers and sealing off wounds. She shifted within his embrace as she absorbed the truth of what he'd just said. "Yes, I suppose that I do."

He exhaled slowly, his eyes alight with love for the woman he held.

"And for that, I thank God."

Chapter 8

All that same day, the house seemed alive with the energy ignited from their loving. When Billie wasn't in Matt's arms, her eyes followed his every movement. It was as if he was her lifeline to sanity.

Later that afternoon, she stood at the window, watching as he left to go feed the livestock. With one last wink in her direction, he stepped out onto the porch and blew a big kiss in the direction of Daisy Bedford's telescope. While Billie was laughing, he jammed his hat tight on his head and bolted off the porch, jumping puddles as he ran. She caught herself grinning. It had been a long time since she'd felt like smiling, and it felt good. So good.

When he drove toward the barns, she turned away from the window with a reluctant sigh. The warmth and comfort within his home was infusing her with a solace she'd sorely needed, and the deadweight of despair with which she'd left Memphis kept easing by the moment. She didn't want to lose the feeling.

Certain that occupying her hands would also occupy her mind, she headed for the kitchen. She had a sudden urge to bake.

Excitement sparked as she dug through cabinets and started assembling ingredients for pies. It wasn't much, but cooking for him was an easier way to show her love than saying it aloud. For now, what they'd shared was too new and precious to toss about lightly, and she was still too afraid of being rebuffed to say it on her own. It wasn't because she didn't trust Matt Holt's declaration of love. She believed that he spoke the truth of what was in his heart, but it was going to take more than a single night in one man's arms to undo Jarrod Walker's years of damage.

From inside the cab, Matt tilted the spike mounted on the front of his John Deere tractor, dropping the last round bale of hay into the feeder. When he started to back up, the dual wheels slipped, then spun, slinging old hay and mud into the air. The cattle, vying for a place at the feeders, didn't seem to notice or care that he had just dotted their hides with chocolate brown drops of wet Texas earth.

As the animals began gathering around the hay to eat, steam rose like smoke from their warm, shaggy bodies, fogging the air between Matt and the herd. When a loud bawl came from somewhere behind him, he instinctively stomped on the brakes and craned his neck, looking to make sure he wasn't backing into some obstinate old cow. When he could see that all was clear, he continued to move away from the scene, the tires alternately catching and spinning until he finally moved onto firmer ground.

He had plenty of time to think as he started the half-mile journey toward the machine sheds, and Billie was the only thought occupying his mind. She had yet to admit why she'd come back. While he'd like to believe it was solely because she cared for him, he wasn't that much of a fool. Something bad had obviously happened to her. What hurt him most was knowing that she didn't trust him enough to talk about it.

Anxiety kicked in as the roof of the barn came into view. He shoved the tractor into a higher gear. Soon he traded tractor for truck, and a few minutes later pulled up at the side of the house and made a run for the back porch. His boots were too muddy for any front door, even his own.

He walked inside and paused. Warmth and the scent of apples and cinnamon hit him in the face like a lover's kiss, and when he saw Billie busying herself about his kitchen as if it were her own, a wave of emotion swept over him. Absorbing her presence, he let himself feel the love.

The cold gust of wind that came with Matt's entrance into the house lifted the tendrils of hair around Billie's neck, signaling his return. With a smile on her lips, she dropped what she was doing, then turned and flew into his arms.

"You're home! I didn't think you'd ever get back!"

Home. In his mind he'd always thought of the ranch house as home, but he realized that before it had just been a house. Love and companionship had been missing. He caught her on the run and, in sudden and inexplicable anxiety, tightened his grip, hugging her even closer. When she laughed and snuggled up against him, his vision suddenly blurred, and he blinked, telling himself it was because of the cold and not unexpected tears. He held her close and kicked the door shut behind him.

"Well, I am home, honey, and you do smell good. What's that you're wearing?"

She grinned. "A little allspice, a dash of nutmeg, and a dollop of cinnamon."

Matt laughed, then lifted her up into his arms and swung her around, forgetting the mud on his boots.

"My compliments to the chef," he growled, nuzzling her neck, then set her back down as he looked past her shoulder to the room behind her. Two steaming pies, crusty brown and oozing sweet juices, were cooling on racks, waiting to be eaten.

Billie clasped her hands together, unaware how much she looked like a child yearning desperately to please.

"I baked."

He smiled. "I know. It smells wonderful in here."

"You do like apple pie . . . don't you?"

There was a smudge of flour on her cheek and what looked like an apple seed sticking to the front of her shirt near the tip of one breast. His eyes followed the path of his finger as he reached out and lightly flicked it off.

At the touch, her eyes widened and her breath caught, but her nerves quickly settled as he calmly moved away.

"It's my second favorite thing," he said softly, and bent down to pull off a boot.

Darn, Billie thought. She should have made cherry. There were four cans of cherries in the pantry. She'd bet he liked cherry best. But when he pulled off the other boot and straightened, she had a sudden notion that food was not on his mind. When he reached behind him and turned the lock on the door, she knew that she'd been right.

It clicked loudly in the silence between them. Suddenly embarrassed, Billie started backing toward the sink. With slow, single-minded intent, Matt followed, shedding his gloves and his coat, dropping them on the floor as he went.

"Um, Matt, why don't we . . ." The handle of the refrigerator poked her in the back. With a nervous grin, she warded him off with one hand while feeling the way behind her with her other. "Now look, you. Your hands are bound to be cold and, if memory serves, your nose will be colder. Why don't you warm up before we . . ."

It was too late. He circled her waist with his hands, then pulled her shirt from the waistband of her jeans. When his fingers moved across bare flesh, she gasped. Before she had time to object, he began to unbutton her shirt, one tiny button at a time. The wide-brimmed black Stetson was still on his head when he started the unveiling, but when he got to the valley between her breasts, he yanked it from his head and sent it sailing across the room behind him. With a gleam in his eyes, his head dipped, and his wind-chilled mouth found its target as he savored the warmth of her skin.

Billie swayed, clutching the back of his head with

her hands, holding him close, and then even closer still. She'd been right. His mouth *was* cold, but there was a fire burning between them that would have melted the devil's own heart.

"Cowboy, you make me crazy."

He paused, then lifted his head, losing himself in the passion he saw on her face. Without speaking, he fingered the collar of her shirt as if testing the fabric. Before she knew it he was holding her shirt in his hands. She stood shivering beneath his unwavering stare, pinned beneath a bird of prey, waiting to see what came next.

She didn't have long to wait.

He dropped the shirt and encircled her with his arms.

Billie shuddered with sudden longing as she felt his breath upon her bare shoulder.

"Matt."

He shook his head. "Sssh."

She forgot whatever she'd been about to say when she heard a slight click behind her and then felt a slight release of pressure as he unhooked her bra. When he slid the straps from her shoulders and let the bra fall to the floor by her shirt, she took a deep breath. And when he palmed the weight of her breasts, testing the hard jut of nipples with the balls of his thumbs, she moaned and leaned into his touch, offering herself to his desires. By the time he began unfastening his jeans, hers were already undone. He had their emotions and their clothing in a state of disarray.

"Matt . . ."

Once again, he silenced her with a look, so she slid her arms around his neck instead, relishing the feel of bare skin against fabric as his arms pulled her close, then closer. When he backed her into the corner and stepped between her legs, his arousal pressed intimately against her, and she resented the remaining clothing that still kept them apart.

Matt gritted his teeth as her breasts pushed against his chest. So soft, so yielding. With a near-vicious yank, he popped the snaps on his shirt, needing body-to-body contact in more ways than one.

The erotic feel of his hard muscles against her soft curves decimated what was left of Billie's control. With a groan, she hid her face against his neck, but he moved her aside and lowered his head.

His mouth circled, then centered upon a nipple, drawing it into his mouth and teasing the tip with his tongue until it hardened into a rough, extended peak of protest. Billie arched against him, pulling his head closer, fisting her hands in his hair to the point of pain. Still he persisted. In a gut-wrenching gasp for breath, he lifted his head. Air moved across the taut, wet peak, making her shudder.

His eyes narrowed as her control continued to slip. That was good, he thought. He wanted her that way—coming apart in his arms as he came inside her.

With slow, single-minded intent, he slid his hand across her bare, flat belly and lower, moving nylon and denim aside in his search for something sweet . . . something hot.

Billie tensed as he paused. When his fingers slid

through the thatch of soft curls between her legs, searching, continually searching, she moaned. And when he found the object of his search, she dug her fingers into his shoulders and closed her eyes.

With a smile she did not see, he started to stroke, up and down, around and around. When the room started to spin, her legs went weak. With a pulse point slamming from nerve point to nerve point, hammering within her just as Matt had done last night, she started to beg.

"Oh, Matt, please . . . please . . ."

Her skin felt as hot as the honey that flowed upon his fingers. His voice was low and guttural as he concentrated on maintaining control.

"Please what? Tell me what it is that you want."

Billie arched against his hand. "You! Dear God, I want you."

With a yank, he moved clothes aside and himself into place.

"Hurry," she begged, as tiny shock waves of need ricocheted from border to border inside her belly.

He thrust up and then in, and when she closed all around him, he gritted his teeth in fierce concentration to keep from spilling himself then and there. Her fingers were digging into his shoulders, her eyes closed in ecstasy. In that moment, Matt knew there might be sweeter things in heaven, but not on this earth.

"I love you, Billie Walker," he said harshly, and he began to move.

It didn't take long for the world to fall off its axis.

Less than a minute of unguarded passion and Billie was no longer able to stand alone. With a low, achy moan, she closed her eyes, locked her fingers around his neck, and held on as he rocked against her in near-desperate thrusts.

In spite of the chill of the day, a fine beading of perspiration broke out across Matt's skin as he tried to focus on the act itself, wanting to draw out the pleasure. It was impossible. There was too much need between them, and too much heat.

With a groan, he cupped her hips and moved even closer and deeper inside. Thrust after aching thrust, he took her standing, until the muscles in his legs were beginning to tremble. Just when he thought it would never end, it came upon him. From every corner of his being, the madness drove and enveloped him. With a final thrust, the essence of all that he was burst and spilled into her. There was nothing left to do but ride out the shock wave in each other's arms.

Billie stood at the living room window, peering out into the night, absorbing the differences between his world and hers. Outside, the distinguishable sounds she could hear were the low, plaintive bawl of a lost calf, intermittent yips from a pack of coyotes on the hunt, and the occasional and distant rumble of trucks on the highway far off in the distance.

A far cry from Memphis, as well as L.A. Here, no sirens blared, no tires screeched. Except for the pale-blue glow of his security light, the absence of artificial light was noticeable and welcome. Down the hall she could hear the sound of running water. Matt was taking a shower. This time, alone.

A small smile moved in place as she leaned her forehead against the chilled windowpane and thought about this afternoon. About their loss of control. It had happened so fast. One minute Matt was standing in the doorway staring at her from across the room, and the next she'd been in his arms. She shivered with longing, remembering the blaze of passion on his face as he'd undressed her. The man made love with as much reckless abandon as he went through life.

"Hey, Memphis, you aren't thinking about running out on me again, are you?"

Billie turned. He stood in the doorway, hair still a little damp from his shower, wearing old jeans, a faded sweatshirt, and clean white socks. Without that trademark Stetson shading his face, and his old black boots that added unnecessary inches to his tall, muscular frame, he seemed less formidable and intense.

She smiled. "It took me too long to get the guts to come back. I don't plan on leaving all this soon."

Her odd choice of words struck him, and once again he wished he knew more about her life before they'd met . . . and what had happened to her this past summer after she'd left the ranch. There were too many secrets between them for him to rest easy. When the smile she was wearing shifted, he decided it might be wise to change the subject and said the first thing that came to his mind.

"How about some popcorn?"

Relieved by the innocuous question, she followed

him into the kitchen, watching from the doorway as he dug a packet out of the cabinet and tossed it into the microwave.

"It's not quite as romantic as popping it over the fireplace, but it's a hell of a lot neater."

She laughed, then proceeded to take out a bowl for the finished product. When he tore open the top, the rich, salty aroma of hot popcorn drifted beneath their noses.

"Umm," she said, and leaned over the bowl.

Impulsively, Matt took a popped kernel from the top of the bowl and held it suspended above her mouth.

"What do you say?" he teased, expecting her to say "pretty please."

The smile on his face seemed lit from the inside out. Billie ached from the love she felt for this man.

"That you have the most incredible eyes and the sexiest mouth I've ever seen on a man."

Matt's grin slid sideways into a cocky smirk. "I suppose that will do," he said, and popped the corn into her mouth, then picked up the bowl, took her by the hand, and led her back to the living room.

He dropped to the couch and, stretching his long legs out on the cushions, patted the spot in between. "Sit here."

Billie slid into place, cradled by his bent knees, her back resting against his chest, her head just below his chin. His arms encircled her as he kissed a spot just below her right ear, then set the bowl of popcorn in her lap.

For long, precious minutes they shared the snack

and the closeness, savoring both as if they might be their last. When they were down to the last few bites, they started to play.

"Open your mouth," Matt ordered, waving a popped kernel of corn in front of her lips.

"You eat it," she argued, batting at his hand. "I'm too—"

He slipped it between her teeth, then yanked back his fingers before she could bite. When she laughed, he smiled to himself and impulsively hugged her.

The caress was not unexpected, but it was so comforting that she wanted to cry.

Oh Matt, and to think I almost didn't come back.

Suddenly, she wanted to explain—about everything.

She set the empty bowl on the floor beside them, then took his arms and wrapped them around her like a blanket, savoring the strength of him, the gentleness, and the rock-steady rhythm of his heartbeat.

"Matt?"

He shifted slightly to give her more room between his legs and nibbled at one of her ears.

"Umhmm?"

"I had to take my father to court."

He stilled. Instinctively, his arms tightened around her, holding her closer, safer.

"What the hell for?" he asked, then cleared his throat, afraid that she'd think his anger was directed at her and not at the man who'd fathered her.

She sighed. "It's a long, ugly story."

"So . . . it's a long, cold night," he said, and began combing at the tendrils of loose curls around her face, stroking his fingers through her hair in a soothing motion, gentling her as he did all things under his care.

She closed her eyes against the ugliness of the story.

"As best as I can tell, Jarrod Walker married my mother for two reasons. Her money . . . and the means by which he could acquire a son."

Matt frowned. The calm, almost-matter-of-fact tone of her voice seemed ominous by its lack of emotion.

"And?"

"He got me and blamed her."

Matt cursed softly and beneath his breath, but Billie heard it all the same.

"Oh, it's no big deal. I got over blaming myself for that matter years ago."

"Then what is the deal?" he asked. "Surely your mother was there for you." Billie was much too quiet for his peace of mind. "Billie . . . honey . . . she was, wasn't she?"

"I suppose so, up until the day she swallowed a bottle of pills. Then she left her money and the man she had married to me." A bitter laugh accompanied her words. "Actually, I think I would have been happier without either."

"My God! How old were you?"

She shrugged. "Eight . . . nine . . . I forget. Those years all sort of run together."

"Where did you live after she died?" he asked, and felt her grow tense.

"With him."

Dear God, how many years of mental abuse has she suffered? And Matt had no doubt that it was abuse. It was the only explanation for her lack of trust, for the way she seemed to close in upon herself when things got bad, and probably the reason she'd come undone when he and Scott had fought about her.

Her whole body was trembling, and the notion that she'd suffered so many years alone made him sick.

"Ah, Billie, I'm sorry, so sorry," he whispered, and held her that much closer, that much tighter.

Quiet enveloped them.

A short time later, he remembered that she'd only told half the story. "Sweetheart, you never said why you had to take him to court."

She sighed. In spite of it all, it had to be said. "When I left here last summer I went straight home. When I arrived, I found a FOR SALE sign on the front yard and the house in shambles."

"My God, why?"

"Because wife number six had dumped him . . . or was it seven?" She shrugged. "I forget, and it really doesn't matter. He said he needed a fresh start."

Matt tried to imagine a child growing up in such a hellish situation. All these years he'd believed that Scott had been deprived because of losing his mother, but compared to Billie, it was obvious that he'd been the luckier of the pair.

"I'm sorry, honey, but I still don't understand. Why court?"

She laughed bitterly, and he could almost feel the pain and anger in her.

"Because he tried to sell something that didn't belong to him, and when I called him on it, he went crazy. Remember, all that money he married my mother for is now mine."

Matt was unable to understand a man who could father a child and then not want to nurture it. "If he resented you that much, I'm surprised he stayed with you."

"Oh, Jarrod had no intentions of leaving until he got everything he wanted."

"But how did he expect to do that? Was he the executor of the estate?"

"No, a lawyer who was a friend of my mother's was in charge of all that. In fact, if it weren't for Melvin Deal, Jarrod would have spent it all years ago."

Matt straightened, then turned Billie in his arms, needing to look at her when he asked.

"Talk to me, Billie. You're not telling me what's between the lines."

"After we argued, I changed my will, then took him to court and got him out of my life . . . only he doesn't seem to want to go. I left Memphis because I couldn't stand the harassing phone calls and the threats. I'm tired of his stupid predictions. He doesn't know me and doesn't want to. All he sees is my mother in me." She shuddered on her last words. "I'm not like her. I'm not."

"Why does that matter, honey? What does that mean to you?"

"He says I look and act just like her. He says I'm weak, and one day I'll hit a wall I can't climb over. When I do, he predicts that I'll take the easy way out . . . just like she did." She grimaced and looked away. "Don't you see? If I had died before I changed my will, the damned money would have been his."

Shock spread across Matt's face. His complexion went from pasty white to a dull, angry flush as rage all but overwhelmed him. He took Billie by the shoulders and shook her slightly until she was forced to look up.

"God damn him, are you telling me your father dared you to kill yourself?"

"At least once a week since I was ten years old."

The despondency in her voice and the slump in her shoulders frightened him. His hands shook as he pulled her close. When she fell against him in a disheartened slump, he started to rock. Back and forth she swayed within his arms, and when she started to cry, his rage grew. He muttered a litany of curses, which mingled with the choked sobs of her hot tears until it was all one endless, gut-wrenching sound.

Long after they'd gone to bed, Matt lay wide-eyed and staring up at the ceiling, holding Billie as she slept. With each passing hour, the rage within him grew. Once, when he heard her breath catch in her sleep, he looked down to see tears slipping from beneath closed eyelids and onto her cheeks.

"Don't cry, darlin', don't cry." He pulled her closer against him, careful that the warm covers didn't slip from her shoulders in the chill of the room. "I don't know how or when, but one day I'll get the chance, and when I do, I will make that man pay for what he's done to you."

His voice was little more than a whisper, and Billie was still quite sound asleep, yet at his vow, she seemed to settle. It was all the satisfaction that Matt was going to glean, and like the man he was, he settled for what he could get. Sometime later he dozed. When he awoke, it was morning.

Chapter 9

"Scott called."

Matt paused in the act of hanging up his coat to gauge the weather of Billie's mood. It was almost too still.

"So, what did he have to say?"

"I didn't answer. It's on your machine."

Matt frowned. "Why did you do that?"

She shrugged and looked away. "I don't know. It's your house, your son, your call. I didn't want to interfere."

Matt grasped her by the shoulders. "Damn it, Billie, don't do this. I would hate to live the rest of my life playing referee between you two. Besides, he cost me nearly five hundred dollars in phone calls when he was trying to find you and apologize. Give him a break, okay?"

Billie's eyes rounded. "You're kidding!"

Matt sighed, and cupped her face with his hand. "No, darlin', I'm not."

She was quiet, almost thoughtful, as she considered the news. All this time she'd believed Scott still harbored some imaginary grudge against her for loving Matt and not him. Finally she sighed.

"So, I might look him up when I go back to school."

Matt frowned as he realized the implications of what she'd just said, and it shamed him to realize that he hadn't even wondered why she wasn't in school at this time.

"You sat out this whole semester, didn't you?"

"The court stuff was such a mess . . . and I was afraid to leave home until I was certain everything was clearly in my name."

Angry color slashed Matt's cheeks. "Damn your father to hell. Doesn't he know . . . doesn't he care what he's cost you? And I'm not talking dollars and cents."

"He's already damned himself," Billie replied. "As for caring about costs or me . . . no, actually he doesn't."

"Well I do," he growled, and dug his hands through her hair, tilting her lips to his mouth.

The union was swift and urgent, and when they broke apart, both were breathing intensely harder than they had been moments before.

"You know what I want to do, don't you?" Matt said.

Billie smiled, letting go of the nervousness that had held her in check. "Take off my clothes and drive me out of my mind?"

He groaned, then laughed. It was a rough, jerky bark of emotion that had little to do with mirth.

"God, woman, but you do know how to get right to the point, don't you?"

"Call Scott," she said, and started out of the room.

"Where are you going?"

"I thought I'd give you some privacy."

He muttered beneath his breath about the obstinacy of the female race, then picked up the phone and began to dial. When Scott answered the phone, he didn't even give him time to talk. The first words out of his mouth came without thought.

"She came back."

Scott Holt dropped onto his bed with a deep, relieved sigh. He didn't have to ask to whom his father was referring. The woman had been on both of their minds for months, although for entirely different reasons.

"Is she still there now?"

"Yes."

It was only one word, but it was all he needed to hear. "Thank God," Scott said, and wiped a shaky hand across his face. "Is she all right?"

"No, but we're working on that."

"Am I still a problem between you two, because I could talk to her and explain that I'm over my asinine spell," Scott offered.

Matt's eyes narrowed as he thought of the man who was at the root of all of Billie's troubles.

"No, it's not me that's causing her problems. It's not even you. And, unfortunately, it's a long, ugly story which we won't go into right now. So, what's up?"

Scott knew when he'd been rerouted and accepted the change of subject with equanimity.

"Christmas. Are you coming out, or am I coming home?"

Matt smiled. "We haven't had Thanksgiving yet. What's wrong, boy? Don't tell me you're homesick?"

Scott grinned. "Okay, I won't tell you."

Matt chuckled.

In another part of the house, Billie sat on the side of Matt's bed, hearing the joy in his voice and the laughter that he and his son were sharing and wondered if there was a place for her in between them.

"Good Lord," Matt muttered, swiping at the sweat running down the sides of his cheeks. "I wish this weather would make up its mind. Last week I thought it might snow. Today, it's nearly eighty degrees and climbing."

Billie let him ramble, content just to be at his side.

"Hand me the wire stretchers, will you, honey?"

She slid down from the tailgate of the truck with the tool in hand, sidestepping a loose coil of old barbed wire that he'd just replaced.

He watched her progress with a nervous eye, well aware of what barbed wire might do to her tender skin. "Careful, don't damage the goods."

"So, I'm goods now," she asked, and handed him the stretcher.

His eyes darkened as a tense smile swept across his face.

"It was just a figure of speech, Billie. You know I don't think of you that way."

She tried to smile, but it didn't quite come. "I know, I was only teasing." But they both knew she didn't mean it.

With a frown, Matt fastened the stretcher on to both ends of the new wires, careful not to let himself be caught in the barbs. With single-minded focus, he finished what he'd come to do.

Fascinated by the intense way in which he worked, and how the muscles in his arms corded as the wire tightened, Billie stood nearby without moving. By the time he was finished, her nerves were as taut as the wires. It was only when he began gathering up his tools that she spoke again.

"Matt?"

His eyes were on the area in which he'd been working, making certain that he was leaving nothing behind, and so his answer was only halfhearted.

"Hmmm?"

"Would you still love me if I was ugly?"

He froze, with his gaze to the ground. When he was able to talk without yelling, he looked up at her. Even then the anger was still in his voice.

"Damn you, woman, you still don't get it, do you?"

Suddenly she shivered in spite of the heat of the day.

"Get what?" she whispered.

"What it means to love."

"Yes, I do," she said. "I know lots of things. I know that you like it when I—"

"No! Hell no!" he shouted, and then winced at his lack of control. "That's not love, that's making love, and that's not what I meant."

She looked away as tears sprang to her eyes, aware that she never seemed able to measure up to what a man expected.

Contrite, Matt pulled off his gloves and tossed them in the back of the truck. He placed a hand on either side of her face and gently turned it, until she was forced to face him.

"Hey, Memphis, I'm sorry I yelled, but sometimes you make me crazy. I love you so damned much, and I feel like I'm spinning my wheels. Truth be known, you're my first love, even my only love, and that's a sad fact for a man my age."

Billie frowned. "But what about your wife? Didn't you—"

"That was a case of raging hormones and a teenage crush. You know our marriage wasn't by choice, it was of necessity, and if I don't do another thing in my life, I will never again put another woman . . . or myself . . . in that same fix. If I hadn't gotten Susan pregnant, it would have been over in months, maybe less. She knew it. I knew it. But we truly believed that we'd done the right thing by getting married. Even though the magic wasn't there, we were doing a damned good job of raising Scott when she was killed."

"I didn't mean to . . ."

Matt wouldn't let her go this easily. "Love is blind, Billie. One hundred percent, dark as hell, blind. If it's there, and it's true, then size, shape, and color don't matter. Only what's inside here." He touched her head. "And what's inside here." He touched her heart. "So, the answer to your real stupid question is yes, I would love you even if you were ugly. And I will love when you when you're sick, and when you're angry at me, and when we're both too old to remember what caused us to fuss. Okay?"

Although she nodded, Matt heard the deep sigh that accompanied it. He sensed her confusion and, at that moment, felt more hatred for a man he didn't know than he'd ever thought possible. Her father had done a number on her in more ways than one.

"Come here."

She did as he asked.

He leaned down, slanting his lips across hers, tasting the heat of the day, the salty remnants of perspiration, and, he imagined, even a bit of her sadness. Just as he was considering the notion of making love on the side of this hill, he remembered Daisy Bedford and her telescope, and stepped back with a groan.

"Thanks to a nosy old neighbor, I don't dare let this go any farther."

Billie blushed, then grinned, imagining what the old woman would think if she caught them in the act.

"It might do her some good."

Matt's eye's lit up as a wide smile broke the seriousness of his expression.

"Oh, I don't know about that. Remember, darlin', I'm real good at what I do. When she realizes what she missed, she just might have herself a stroke."

The audacity of his remark sent her into giggles, which was exactly what he had intended it to do. By the time they started back to the ranch, Billie had completely forgotten about their conversation. Matt, however, had not. Without understanding why, he felt the need to gird himself for a battle that was yet to come.

Just before Thanksgiving he realized his instincts had been right all along.

"Can we get a turkey? And do you like mincemeat? I make good pies. Even if you don't like mincemeat, I promise you'll like mine."

Matt grinned as he sat astraddle one of the kitchen chairs, listening to Billie's chatter. The intensity on her face surprised him. He'd never seen anyone as focused on a holiday meal as she seemed to be, but he couldn't resist teasing her anyway.

"Oh, I'll like whatever you cook, darlin'. I liked your apple pies a lot, remember?"

A swift flush swept up her neck and onto her face as her hand paused on a page in the cookbook she was looking through. Remember? Lord, she would never forget how he'd walked in from the cold and taken her by storm. They'd been so lost in making love that it had been hours before either of them even remembered the pies that she'd baked. She took a deep breath and turned, gauging his mood by the twinkle in his eyes. When she realized he was teasing, she retorted, "You are impossible."

"Now, Memphis, I thought I'd already proven to you that anything's possible."

She blushed even harder, but refused to look away. "Darn you, Matt Holt, I'm serious."

He folded his arms across the back of the chair and leaned forward, resting his chin on his hands.

"So am I, honey. So am I." When she started to sputter, he laughed. "Yes, we'll get a turkey, and I love mincemeat."

In spite of his torment, there was a warm, homey feel to their play. Billie lifted her chin.

"Thank you very much," she said, and turned back to the cookbook.

He grinned. "You're very welcome." Matt groaned as the phone rang, ending the moment. "I'll get it," he said, and pushed himself up from the chair.

"Holt Ranch."

There was a slight catch in the breathing on the other end of the line, as if the caller had not expected to hear his voice. Matt started to hang up, thinking he was about to get an obscene phone call, when the caller seemed to get a second wind.

"Is Billie Walker there?"

Caught off guard, he answered without thinking. "Yes, she is. Just a moment, please." He handed Billie the phone.

"It's for you."

She frowned, then lifted the receiver to her ear, and took a deep breath.

"Hello?"

"So now it's all clear."

The cookbook she was holding fell from her hands and onto the floor.

"How did you get this number?"

Jarrod laughed. "Mel's desk is a mess, isn't it? He leaves things scattered for days, sometimes even weeks, before he files them away. I've always wondered how he knows where he's supposed to be on any given day."

Billie closed her eyes and knotted her fist, telling herself that this didn't matter. Everything she had was safely out of his clutches. And she didn't love him, or for that matter, even want him to love her. Not anymore. So why was she so frightened? He couldn't hurt her now . . . could he?

"Billie, honey, what's wrong?" Matt asked, then realized that she'd completely tuned him out.

"Why are you telling me this?" Billie asked. "The fact that you're underhanded is not news."

Jarrod cursed.

"And I've heard all of that before, too," she said, gaining strength in the fact that, although she could hear him as clearly as if he were standing before her, he was actually hundreds of miles away. "Get to the point. I'm busy."

His laughter wrapped around her like a tight, grimy fist.

"I'll just bet that you are, you little whore. I should have known when you came home with your tail in a fluff that you'd been straddling something besides a damned fence. Don't fool yourself. He doesn't want you; he wants your money."

Her eyes blazed, and she gripped the phone so tightly her knuckles turned white. As hard as she tried to stay calm, her response came out in a shriek.

"You're wrong! You're wrong! All men aren't like you, Jarrod."

At the sound of the name, Matt froze. He didn't

know what was being said, and he didn't have to. Billie had gone from pale to shaking, and if she hadn't been leaning against the cabinet, she would have been on the floor.

He took the phone from Billie's trembling fingers at the same time that he took her in his arms. When she buried her face against his chest and swallowed a sob, he knew that he'd done the right thing. He lifted the receiver.

"Jarrod Walker?"

Jarrod choked in midcurse. "I don't know who the hell you are, but if you think you've found yourself a gold mine, you're wrong. I'm not letting some tomcat with a hard dick take what's mine."

"You may not know me, and if you're real smart, you'll keep it that way. However, I know your kind, and I can't believe you'd be so stupid as to think you can take something back that you already gave away. I know what makes you tick. You like hearing her cry, don't you?"

"You don't know a thing about—"

"But I do know this," Matt said. "You leave her the hell alone or you'll answer to me."

Jarrod gasped. The challenge was unexpected. "You'll be sorry. You'll be sorry. I'll get you, all of you!" Although it was an impotent threat, it was all he could think of to say.

Billie couldn't hear what was being said on the other end, but she could tell by the rage spreading across Matt's face that it wasn't good. And then he smiled, and she knew if Jarrod Walker had been able to see

Matt Holt's face at that moment, he would have turned tail and run. Matt spit words in cold, concise increments.

"Better men than you have tried and lost, buddy, but hell, I'm all for freedom of choice. Feel free to give it your best shot. You do need to remember something if you get a hankering to visit. This is a real big ranch. It's easy to get lost out here, so you be careful now, you hear?"

Something about the tone of his voice told Jarrod that this was a man he didn't want to face. Not now, not ever.

"Just tell her this isn't over!"

With that, Jarrod slammed down the phone, breaking the connection and what was left of Billie's spirit.

"Oh my God, I'm sorry! I'm so sorry!" she whispered, and tried to pull away from Matt's embrace.

Matt grabbed her fiercely. "Don't you dare turn away from me. That wasn't your fault. Don't apologize for that son of a bitch. Not when I'm within earshot you don't!"

Billie struggled, refusing to look up. "You don't understand," she objected. "He makes me feel dirty and guilty. It's my fault you were exposed to such ugliness. If I hadn't been here, none of this would have happened. I hate it!" she said, and in spite of her determination not to, she started to cry. "I hate it, and I hate him!"

Matt pulled her closer, then panicked when he caught a glimpse of the look on her face. Her gaze was empty and unfocused, her lips trembling from unshed tears. Only then did he realize how fragile her hold on sanity truly was.

Stay calm, he warned himself. *She's had about all she can handle.* His hands stroked across her back in a slow, easy motion, soothing . . . gentling . . . loving.

"I know you do, sweetheart, I know, and I don't give a damn what you think about him. Just please, please, don't make me pay for what he's done. Don't shut me out, or you'll kill us both."

It was a harsh but true accusation, and one she could not ignore. With an abject sigh, she swallowed her tears and relaxed within his embrace.

"I love you, Matt."

He groaned, wishing he could absorb her pain and make it his own.

"I love you, too, Billie Jean. Just don't quit on me, okay?"

"Okay."

It was only one word, but for now, it was enough. And more important, it was time to change the subject.

"Come on, sweetheart, let's get back to that grocery list. And don't forget to buy apples. I think apple pie just might be my favorite after all, Thanksgiving or not."

Billie poked through the frozen-food case, reading label after label on the mountain of frozen turkeys ready for sale. Decisions needed to be made, and Matt was nowhere in sight. The last time she'd seen him he'd been standing in the cereal aisle talking to an old friend.

With a troubled sigh she leaned even farther into the freezer case, struggling with a half-buried bird that looked to be just the right size. If she could only get the weight tag out from under these other two, she might know.

"Unless you're plannin' on company, that bird's too big."

Surprised by the unexpected advice, Billie lost her grip on the tag and yanked her fingers back just in time to keep them from getting smashed between an avalanche of rock-hard meat.

"Here, this one's just about the right size."

Billie stepped aside and tried not to gawk as a tall, gray-haired woman of indeterminate age dumped a twelve-pound turkey into her shopping cart. The old woman's clothes were nearly as worn as she looked. Her faded jeans were loose and baggy, and an old, blue flannel shirt hung on slumped shoulders, dangling halfway to her knees. The boots on her feet were cracked and turned up at the toes, and she'd wadded her long unkempt hair into a bun at the back of her neck. Her skin was as creased as her clothing, but it was her eyes that gave her away. They were dark, and glittering from the life that still burned within.

For a long, silent moment they stood, staring into each other's eyes, taking each other's measure. Finally, it was the old woman who broke the uneasy silence.

"You're younger than I expected," she said gruffly, as if reassessing herself.

Billie blinked. "Have we met?"

"Nope." Then the old woman seemed to make a decision and suddenly extended her hand. "But I reckon we ought. My name's Daisy Bedford, I live . . ."

Billie's eyes lit up, and she accepted the handshake.

"I know where you live," she said, and smiled. "And I suppose I should have recognized your voice."

Daisy's eyes crinkled, but she pursed her lips and frowned.

"I don't know why that might be," Daisy muttered, and then poked at the frozen turkey in the cart. "However, that bird should be just about the right size for two."

Billie didn't know why, but the words, "or three" came out of her mouth before she had time to reconsider what had popped in her mind.

The subtle invitation caught the old woman off guard. "What are you gettin' at, girl?"

"I'm inviting you to Thanksgiving dinner with Matt and me."

The skin on Daisy's face folded like a fan as she threw back her head and laughed.

When she could talk without breaking into chuckles all over again, she slapped her leg and shook her head in wonderment. "That's real nice of you, girl, but Matt Holt would have hisself a fit if you—"

Just then, Matt came around the corner of the grocery aisle with his finger against his lips as a plea for Billie not to give him away.

She tried hard not to grin, but it was hopeless as she watched him step up behind Daisy, slide an arm around her shoulders, and give her a loud, juicy kiss on the cheek.

"Now, darlin', why would I have myself a fit? You know I'm just waiting for the day when you say you'll be mine."

If blood could have boiled in Daisy's veins, steam would be coming out her ears. The look on her face was somewhere between shock and disbelief as she swiped the kiss from her cheek and batted his arm from her person.

"Get away from me, you fool," she exclaimed, and quickly shoved her own shopping cart between them. "Go mess with someone who cares."

Billie grinned. She could tell that, in spite of their bickering, they did care for each other.

Matt slipped an arm around Billie's shoulder. "Then that would be this one," he said, and planted a kiss on her cheek, watching in delight as a soft pink flush quickly stained Billie's face.

Daisy snorted. "It's your life, girl. I wasn't never one to meddle in other people's affairs."

Matt cocked an eyebrow and grinned. "That's what I hear."

To her credit, Daisy Bedford had the grace to blush.

Matt turned his attention to Billie. "So, why would I have myself a fit?"

"I invited Daisy for Thanksgiving dinner."

This time, it was Daisy who cackled, as a look of pure shock swept over Matt's face.

"You did what?"

"I invited her to eat with us."

"What on earth for?" he sputtered, eyeing the look of glee on Daisy's face.

"See, girl! I told you!" Daisy crowed.

But Billie refused to budge. Instead, she faced Matt with an unwavering stare that he couldn't break.

"She's your neighbor. She's going to be all alone. I thought that she might—"

Daisy suddenly took umbrage at being a charity case. "I didn't say a piddlin' thing about my eatin' arrangements. Why for all you two lovebirds know, I might be goin' out on the town. I don't need anyone feelin' sorry for me! No, I don't!"

If she hadn't looked away, Matt might have believed her. In spite of the years of antagonism between them, he saw and heard a loneliness in her manner that he wouldn't have believed. And then he looked back at Billie and realized she was still waiting for his reply. He threw up his hands.

"Well hell, don't mind me," he said, and glared at Daisy. "As for charity, you'd be last on my list. Does that make you happy?"

Billie gasped. She wouldn't have believed that Matt could be so cruel. But when Daisy suddenly broke into a wide, engaging grin, Billie found herself lost in the byplay between the two neighbors.

"Since you put it like that, then I'd be happy to come," Daisy said. "What do you want me to bring?"

Billie gawked. She'd expected anything from Daisy Bedford except instant capitulation. When Matt suddenly turned away and pretended interest in the stock on a shelf, she realized what he'd just done. He'd found a way for the old woman to accept the invitation without losing face.

"Whatever you like," Billie said.

"How about sweet potatoes? My man always liked the way I fixed sweet potatoes."

Billie smiled. "That would be just fine. Then we'll see you for dinner Thursday, okay?"

Daisy nodded and started to walk off when she stopped and turned to fling one more defiant remark into the shocked silence.

"Were you meanin' city dinner or country dinner?"

The question confused Billie, but Matt knew what she meant. He dropped a can of green beans into the cart and answered for her. "Country dinner, Daisy, and don't be late. I like to eat while the food is hot."

She glared. "I'll get there when I get there," she mumbled, and wheeled her cart out of sight before either of them had time to change their minds.

Billie was lost. "What's country dinner?"

He grinned. "In the country, we eat dinner at noon and supper at night. In the city, people have lunch and then dinner at night. Daisy just wanted to be sure she didn't miss all the fun."

"Are you mad at me for asking her without consulting you first?"

In spite of the fact that they were directly in the aisles between frozen and canned foods, Matt took her in his arms.

"No, Memphis, in fact, I'm real proud of you."

"Why?"

"Because you did something from the goodness of your heart that I should have thought to do years ago."

"What's that?"

"Make peace with someone before it's too late."

A strange little ache jolted Billie as she thought of her own life and the mess it was in. Jarrod would never want peace. All he wanted was money.

Chapter 10

Billie stood at the living room window with her gaze fixed on the empty road stretching toward the horizon, watching for Daisy Bedford's arrival. A chill wind whistled around the corner of the house and, in spite of the warmth of the room, she shivered. It was a mournful, empty sound that echoed deep inside her heart.

Lost in thought, she didn't know Matt had walked up behind her until he slid his arms around her waist, then pulled her back against his chest.

"Hey, Memphis . . . what are you looking at?"

Love for this man swept over her so quickly that it frightened her, and in a fit of panic she let her fear boil over onto something less drastic, such as the arrival of their one and only Thanksgiving guest.

"It's spitting snow. Do you think she'll come?"

Matt hugged her closer as he buried his nose in the nest of curls at the crown of her hair, breathing in the sweet scent of his lady.

"Don't worry, she'll be here. Daisy wouldn't miss this even if it was blowing up a blizzard."

Billie turned in his arms until they were standing

face-to-face. With an absent but gentle gesture, she traced the curve of his lower lip with the tip of her finger.

"Thank you for letting me do this."

His eyes sparkled wickedly as he nestled her within the cradle of his hips. "Do what? Make love to me with your eyes, or eat dinner with Daisy?"

"Matt . . ."

"I was only teasing. I told you before, I'm looking forward to this, except I don't dare let her know. I'd never hear the end of it if I did."

"How did this cold war even start between you two? Weren't you once friends?"

He shrugged. "From where I'm standing, we still are. As for why it started, it beats me. All I can figure is as long as I was a grieving widower, I was high on her list of saints. A couple of years later I started trying to get back into real life, and when I did, she flew off the handle."

"Maybe this dinner will reestablish your friendship."

"And maybe it won't. Don't count on that old woman to be predictable, okay?"

Billie stood on her tiptoes until their mouths were only inches apart. "The only one I count on is you," she whispered, and leaned forward, testing the surface of his mouth with her own.

Matt inhaled slowly as her lips centered, then parted. He groaned and pulled her closer, resisting the urge to grind against her until he was hard and hurting, and she was begging for more. Just when he was considering taking this another step beyond kissing, a horn honked. They broke apart in confusion to look out the window. It was Daisy.

Billie blushed, and Matt cursed. "Oh well, that's just great," he muttered. "I wonder how long she's been sitting out there watching the show?"

To Billie's everlasting relief, a timer went off in the kitchen, giving her a reason to leave Matt to greet the guest.

"That's the dressing!" She bolted from the room before Matt could grab her.

"Coward," he called out after her, then winced as Daisy rapped sharply on the door.

Gritting his teeth, he stalked to the door and opened it wide. The old woman stood on the doorstep bearing a covered dish and a disparaging frown. He refused to let her know that her arrival had rattled him.

"Hey there, Daisy, come on in." And like the gentleman he was, took her by the arm and helped her over the threshold.

She stepped inside with her chin held high, her boots clomping sharply on the hardwood floor. If there was going to be a first blow struck, she was determined to be the one to do it.

"From the way the window was steamed, I figured you'd burned the food." Then she set down her bowl and shrugged out of her coat, without giving Matt time to play host. "Here. Hang it up for me, will you? I'd better get these spuds to a warmin' oven. It's cold enough outside to freeze the tits off a boar hog."

He took her coat and grinned.

Her chin tilted higher. Although it had been years

since she'd set foot in his house, she took direct aim for the kitchen, holding her sweet potatoes before her as if they were the crown jewels.

"And a happy Thanksgiving to you, too," he said, hanging up her coat.

Daisy leaned back in her chair and loosened her belt two full notches. "Lord have mercy. You're a good cook, girl."

Billie beamed. Praise in her life had been rare, and she soaked it up now like parched earth would a soft rain.

"Thank you. I like to cook, but I rarely have the chance. It's not so much fun to cook for one, you know."

Old pain came and went so swiftly in Daisy's dark eyes that Matt almost didn't see it, but he'd been watching these two all during the meal and was beginning to read them quite well.

In spite of their age differences, they had one thing in common that he could tell. They kept more of what they thought within, rather than sharing it with the world around them. So when Daisy suddenly became interested in the silverware pattern, he knew Billie's innocent remark had hit home in a very personal way. Daisy had been cooking for one for more years than he could remember. Compassion prompted him quickly to change the subject.

"Got any more apple pie left?" he asked with a grin.

Billie looked up, her face suddenly flushed.

"I don't know where I'll put it," he went on, "but

you know how it is . . . sometimes you just can't get enough of a good thing."

Billie couldn't believe it. He was making sexual innuendos he knew she couldn't ignore. Her mouth dropped.

It was all he could do not to laugh aloud. God, but he liked to get her riled, and love her back into a good frame of mind.

Daisy's eyes narrowed. Something was going on between these two besides conversation and eating. And she didn't know when she'd seen Matt Holt so dumbstruck on a woman. She almost smiled. It was about damned time.

"You know, Matthew, you'd do well not to let this one go. Not only is she pretty, but she's a real good cook. That's a rare combination with modern women these days." Then she winked at Billie. "No offense, girl. Just statin' a fact."

This was getting too deep, even for Billie. "I'll just get that pie," she said, and jumped up from her seat.

Matt glared at Daisy. "Well! Coming to dinner served more than one purpose for you after all."

"And how's that?"

"You didn't have to waste a phone call to give me the latest piece of your mind."

This time it was Daisy who flushed. She slapped a hand on either side of her plate, rattling the cutlery and the glasses as she leaned forward.

"I don't know what you're talkin' about."

Matt lost his train of thought just as Billie shoved the pie beneath his nose.

"A la mode?"

When he looked up, the warning was vivid on her face. With a sigh, he looked at Daisy over the pie and grinned. It was a go-to-hell smile that had won him plenty of hearts in his youth. On the face of a man, it was deadly. Even Daisy was not totally immune.

"Truce?" he asked, and offered her his pie.

When Daisy realized that their bickering was upsetting the girl, she sighed. Just when it was getting good.

"Truce," she muttered, and shoved the pie out of her face. "You wanted it. You eat it."

Matt set it down before him with a sharp plop and picked up his fork.

"Thanks, darlin', I do believe I will."

"Darlin', my foot," Daisy grumbled, and hoped the pleasure his words gave her didn't show.

Billie sat back down with a slow sigh of relief, putting her chin in her hands as she surveyed the remnants of their meal. All in all, she didn't know when she'd had a better day. Not once in her entire life had she ever felt this safe or this secure. Even Matt and Daisy's squabbles had seemed more akin to family disagreements than actual anger.

"Matt . . . Daisy?"

He paused, a bite of pie halfway to his mouth, while Daisy broke her glare.

"Hmm?"

"This was my best Thanksgiving ever."

Shame overwhelmed him as he gazed across the table at Daisy. She looked as surprised as he felt. They'd done nothing but bicker all through the meal.

Even if it had been harmless, it should have been distracting. Instead, Billie was actually claiming this day as something to treasure.

He set down his fork and then scooted back his chair. Ignoring Daisy's presence, he pulled Billie into his lap. She blushed and sputtered, feeling a little embarrassed, yet too pleased to deny him the right.

"I swear, Matt, we have company."

"Hush." He settled her firmly upon his knee. "She's seen a man hug a woman before. And if she hasn't, it's way past time."

Daisy tried to look pissed, but damned if she didn't like this fellow's go-to-hell attitude. He reminded her of her Manley, the way he was before the cancer started eating away at his body and then his mind.

"Don't mind me," Daisy said. "You've pulled your stunts in plain sight of God and everybody for years. Why stop now?"

Matt ignored her.

"What *are* you doing?" Billie asked, still nervous as to what he might do at any given moment.

"I'm about to apologize for acting like an ass. Then I'm going to thank you for the best meal I've had in more years than I can remember. Then I'm probably going to have to kiss you just to see if you taste as good as you feel."

Delight came swiftly, following on the heels of a little more embarrassment. Matt's kisses were devastating on any level. Having an up close and personal witness to any brand of lovemaking was something she would have to consider. But there was a glitter in those blue eyes she couldn't ignore, and with a soft, helpless laugh, she glanced up at Daisy and shrugged.

"You'll have to excuse me a moment. I'm about to be had."

Daisy grimaced, although she was secretly pleased that a woman had brought Matt Holt to his knees. "Like I said before, don't mind me. I'm too old to bother and too tired to care."

Matt took this as his cue to begin.

"Billie, darlin', thank you for the meal, and I'm sorry I picked on your special invited guest. The food was spectacular but not nearly as much as the company. This day was wonderful only because you and Daisy were here to share it with me."

Tears came to her eyes as she sat within his embrace.

"As for the taste . . ." He tilted her chin downward, slanting his mouth across her lips. The connection was sweet but brief, and as he leaned back, he ran his tongue lightly over his lower lip. "I was right," he said. "Sweet clear through."

A soft snort interrupted the moment. Matt grinned at the high flush on Daisy's cheeks.

"Hey, Daisy darlin', I've got an empty knee."

"In your dreams, boy. In your dreams."

Matt tilted his head back and laughed. She should have known he'd try to have the last word. Men like him always did, even when they knew it was wrong.

"Are you gonna eat that pie or what?" Daisy chided.

Matt's laughter had dwindled to a chuckle. "You don't need to worry about what I'm going to do," he said. "And that includes eating my pie." He gave Billie one last hug and scooted her off of his knee. "Billie, honey, why don't you and Daisy go into the living room and relax. You worked hard fixing this meal. It's only fair that I clean up."

"Oh, I don't mind," she said, a little unsure of being left alone with such an opinionated woman.

"Well I do," Daisy said, and took Billie by the arm. "Come on, girl. That's one offer a man makes that you should never turn down."

Billie led the way out of the kitchen.

"Have a seat, Daisy. I'll just put another log on the fire."

Daisy dropped into the chair nearest the fire and put her feet up on the footstool, aiming the soles of her boots toward the heat.

"My, but there's nothin' warmer than a good wood fire, don't you think?"

Billie nodded as she took a chair opposite the old woman's perch. When she didn't seem ready to begin a conversation, Daisy took it upon herself to continue.

Eyeing the rich dark color of Billie's burgundy slacks and sweater, she waved her hand toward where Billie was sitting. "You fixed yourself up real pretty today. That color goes nice with your hair."

"Thank you."

A little embarrassed by the compliment, Billie smiled and picked at a piece of lint, uncertain of what to say next.

Daisy frowned, wondering how on earth someone

like her had ever connected with someone like Matt Holt. On the surface, she'd never seen two more diametrically opposed personalities.

"You're a sight younger than Matthew. You know that, don't you?"

Billie couldn't help but grin. Matt was right. This woman didn't waste time or words.

"Yes, I know."

Daisy sighed. This wasn't getting her anywhere. She aimed her toes toward the fire, wiggling them comfortably within the well-worn boots.

"Look, girl, I know he's a charmer. As old as I am, I'm not immune to a sweet smile. But you need to take your time gettin' to know a man, and you haven't known Matt Holt long. He's got lots of history."

This time, Billie felt on firmer ground. "I know all about that. He's been up front with me about everything, including his marriage. Besides, I met Matt more than two years ago, and I've known Scott for nearly that long. We aren't exactly strangers."

This was definitely news! Daisy sat up straighter. The frown on her face deepened perceptibly as she realized she'd been one-upped.

"Well, then! I don't suppose you need any more of my advice," she conceded.

Impulsively, Billie leaned forward, gently touching the old woman's jeans-clad leg in an easy pat.

"On the contrary, advice just tells me you care. And you do, don't you, Daisy?"

Daisy frowned. "Do what?"

"Care for Matt."

The semipermanent glare that she seemed to wear softened as she met Billie's gaze.

"I might. But you don't need to go tellin' that mister anything of the kind. He's already got a head too big for his hat."

Billie smiled. "Your secret is safe with me."

Matt walked into the room. "What secret?"

"Now isn't that just like a man. If we was to tell you, then it wouldn't be a secret," Daisy said.

Matt eyed the pair with wonder, trying to imagine what on earth they could have possibly been discussing that would lead to sharing a secret of any kind.

"So, are you saying you want me to walk out and come in again?" he asked.

"Didn't say a darned thing about comin' back, now did I?"

Matt grinned as Billie made a place for him beside her. He slid an arm around her shoulder and nestled her closer as he stretched his long legs out before him.

"Today I am a happy man," he said, and winked at Billie. "My stomach's full, my house is warm, and I'm surrounded by two of the most intriguing women I've ever met in my life."

Billie smiled, and Daisy snorted in playful disgust. "Like I told you, girl. You can't trust a good-lookin' man."

Matt threw back his head and laughed while Billie settled into the spot he'd made for her. She listened with an absent air as the two old friends continued to nitpick while she chose to absorb the love that seemed to fill the room.

Long after Daisy had gone home, she could still feel her presence and took comfort from the fact that today had been a milestone for everyone concerned.

During the meal, Matt and Daisy had actually shared more than words, while Billie had shared a part of herself. Granted it was a small part, but it was more than she'd ever done before. Loving Matt Holt was easy. The big step in Billie Walker's life would be trusting him enough to believe that he would keep his word to love her back.

That night while Matt was shaving, Billie entered his bedroom and stood in the doorway, looking at the picture of his wife on the dresser. The smile on Susan Holt's face never quite reached her eyes, and there was a wistful expression around her mouth that hinted at dreams never realized. She'd been so young and left so much of herself behind when she'd died.

"Does that bother you?" Matt asked.

Startled by the sound of his voice, her focus shifted from the picture to him, and then swiftly looked away, embarrassed to be caught looking so intently at a part of his past.

"No, not really."

He knotted the towel a little more firmly around his waist and stared at the picture of the woman who'd borne his child. "It's not there for the reasons you think."

The rough, almost-angry tone of his voice surprised her. "It doesn't matter what I think. It's none of my business what you—"

"That's not true," he growled, then pulled her farther

into the room and into his arms. "You are my business, Billie. I love you, remember?"

He smelled good and clean—of soap and water and a spicy after-shave. His bare body was still damp, but warm, so warm.

She rested her cheek against his chest. "I remember."

His heartbeat was strong and steady against her ear, and she caught herself trying to match the rhythm of her breathing to his. It was a silly thing to do, and she knew it, but in her mind it made them even more inseparable, as if one could not exist without the other. Then, the moment she thought it, she stiffened. *I can't do this. I can't let myself be so dependent on a man that I will cease to exist without him.*

Matt felt her withdrawal and sighed. Damn! What would it take to make her believe? He had said it over and over. He had shown her in every way he knew, and the trust still wasn't there.

He led her to the bed, then sat down. "Sit here." He patted a spot beside him.

When she dropped into place, he gave her a quick, friendly hug. For several seconds there was nothing between them but silence as Matt searched for the right words to explain what he'd meant. Finally, he knew there was only one way, and that was to start at the beginning and tell the whole truth.

"The picture's not there because I still grieve for her. In fact when she died, I lived with guilt more than grief because I didn't love her the way I should have."

Billie stared at a spot on the floor, letting his words sweep over her. "You don't have to say this."

"That's where you're wrong. To make what's happening between us work, there has to be total honesty. I want . . . no, I need for you to understand."

She waited.

"I told you before that I got her pregnant. But you've got to look past the simple fact that we'd made a baby together to see the whole picture. Susan was smart. Really smart. She'd spent eleven years of her life succeeding in school for the chance of a full college scholarship. Her father was dead. Her mother was on welfare. She wanted something better out of life than the constant struggle of trying to make ends meet.

"But instead, one night of carelessness ended both of our dreams. Scott was born two months before we graduated. I was already working two part-time jobs while trying to finish high school just to keep us afloat. She was sick a lot. Her grades fell during her pregnancy, and she lost out on the chance for a scholarship. I couldn't send her to school. I didn't even have the money to send myself."

"Oh, Matt, I'm sorry."

"Don't be. It was no one's fault but our own." Then he looked away. "What hurt was, from the first year, we knew we'd married for all the wrong reasons. Whatever it was she'd felt for me was gone, and whatever feelings I had left for her were so wrapped up in the fact that she was the mother of my child that I didn't really know how I felt. But we'd made a bargain with each other, and we kept it."

He combed his hands through his hair. Lost in the

past, he stared at a spot on the floor. "Years passed, and our life became routine. Oh, we laughed and talked and shared the joy of watching our child growing up before our eyes, but the love wasn't there." Reluctantly, he looked at Billie. "Not for her . . . or for me."

"I don't know what to say."

Matt's eyes were bright with intent. "You don't need to say anything. Just understand. I keep that picture to remind me of the mother of my son, as well as to remind me of my mistakes. I don't ever want to be responsible for breaking any more hearts . . . or destroying any more dreams."

For a long, silent moment Billie absorbed the powerful emotions of his words. And while she thought, she suddenly remembered something that had puzzled her to this day.

"That was why you walked away from me in the airport, wasn't it?"

He smiled ruefully. "That, and the fact that you were too close to being jailbait. My God, Billie. Your life was just starting. I'd been where you were . . . for that matter, where you are now. I won't take away your dreams. No matter what I feel for you, I will not steal your chance to succeed."

His words frightened her. They sounded too much like a good-bye. She smiled bitterly as she wrapped her arms around herself to keep from shaking.

"Succeed? Succeed at what, Matt? A college degree does not guarantee happiness."

"Neither does a marriage license, unless it's for the right reasons."

"By that, I suppose you mean if it's a shotgun wedding, it's doomed to fail."

He glared. "No, that's not what I meant, and you know it. I'm telling you that sacrificing dreams is no way to rectify a mistake." Then he relented. "Don't misunderstand what I've said. If I had the chance to do it again, I wouldn't change a thing, because that would mean I wouldn't have Scott, and I can't imagine my life without him. But if there hadn't been a child involved, Susan and I would never have married. That's something I've had to live with for a long, long time. Marriage without commitment is hell. Marriage without love is impossible."

"Then you're safe from me," Billie said as she jumped up from where she sat and started to undress for bed. "I have no designs on trapping you or any man into a marriage of necessity."

Matt sighed, wishing he'd never started this conversation. "You still don't get it, do you, honey?"

"Get what?"

"That I love you. That what I was talking about does not refer to us. It refers to the past."

She smiled and tried not to let herself care too deeply for the near-naked man on the bed.

"Did you ever tell Susan you loved her?"

His face darkened as a deep red flush suddenly stained his cheeks.

"Well, yes, but I . . ."

"But what? You didn't mean it. Or you changed your mind?"

"Damn it, Billie. I was sixteen years old! When you

were that age, how many boyfriends did you have in the space of six months? Two . . . three? Teenagers change their minds as often as they change channels."

"I didn't have any," she said quietly.

"Why not?"

"I couldn't find one to trust."

She walked into the bathroom, quietly shutting the door between them.

Anger slid out of him, leaving him weak and helpless as he buried his face in his hands.

Chapter 11

The confrontation between Billie and Matt had been inevitable. The first bloom of passion was giving way to reality, and it hurt. The hardest lesson she'd learned was that she couldn't hide behind Matt Holt's strengths or use him to fight her battles. But dear God, she wanted to.

It would be so much easier just to stay on the ranch and let him make her decisions, to keep him as a bulwark between her and her nemesis. If she left, she would no longer have backup should her father cause problems again, and knowing Jarrod as she did, it was bound to happen.

Added to that, her conscience had pricked until she'd accepted the fact that Matt had been right all along in telling her the truth about the past. She owed it to him and to herself to apologize.

Comparing his past and their future had been wrong.

The two were not comparable. And why should she believe that?

Because he'd said they were not. For Billie, it would have to be enough.

But Billie wasn't the only one dealing with devils.

Matt awakened each morning with a sense of impending doom. Only after he saw for himself that she was still in bed beside him was he able to relax and focus on the day ahead.

Even then, the never-ending chores were not enough to ease the tension that stayed within him. He couldn't forget the panic he'd felt when he came home last summer to find her gone. Since she'd left once with no explanation, it only stood to reason that she might do it again. With all the finesse he could muster, he tried to pretend there was nothing wrong.

Yet both of them seemed to know that it was only a matter of time before something would be said, or some decision would be made, that would break the tenuous bond of passion that had kept them together thus far. On the first day of December, it was Billie who proved them right.

She dawdled over breakfast, stirring a puddle of sweet, hot syrup with the tines of her fork without touching the stack of pancakes that Matt had put on her plate. The knot in her belly was too painful, and the tears at the back of her throat too thick for food to slide past. If she opened her mouth for a bite, she'd wind up crying instead. So she played with her food and pretended to be unaware of the slow, studied looks that Matt was giving her.

She'd find a way to tell him, she thought. Later, when it wasn't so fresh in her mind.

She should have known Matt wasn't the waiting kind.

"Don't like my cooking?"

The fork slid from her hand and clattered against the plate as she forced a smile.

"Oh no, that's not it! Everything looks and smells wonderful!" In spite of her resolve, tears flooded into her eyes, and his face went out of focus.

At the sight of her tears, the pit of his stomach bottomed out.

"Good enough to make you cry?"

She pushed back from the table and ran out of the room.

Matt thrust his fingers through his hair in panic and frustration. *Oh damn, don't let this be happening.* He got up from the table and followed her. She was standing before the fireplace, her head down, her hands fisted against her belly.

He took a slow, deep breath as he stared at her from across the room, mentally warning himself not to make things worse. Nervousness automatically lowered the timbre of his voice.

"Has this got anything to do with the phone call you made to the Dallas airport this morning?"

Billie spun. Fresh tears fell down her cheeks. Her mouth trembled. She didn't know he'd overheard.

The look on her face told him more than he wanted to know. Rage blended with pain, coloring his words with an anger he couldn't control.

"What? Were you just going to walk out without saying good-bye, like you did last summer, or were you planning to leave another note?" He walked toward her, trying desperately not to shout. "I particularly liked the last one you left. Nothing but directions as to where to pick up the goddamned Jeep."

"Stop it," she moaned, then closed her eyes and put her hands over her ears.

"No, you stop it," he growled, and yanked her hands from her ears. "Damn you, Memphis! Open your eyes! You can't keep hiding from life. If you've got something to say, then say it. If you've changed your mind about us, then say that, too. But you can't leave a man hanging in the wind with one foot on a bucket and the other dangling over hell."

"I've decided to go back to school."

He took a slow step back, gauging her revelation against her body language. That wasn't such bad news. Why had she felt the need to keep it a secret?

"So? That's good, isn't it? You know how I feel about education. I would be the last person to stop you from finishing yours, especially when you're so close to being done."

Billie choked back a sob. "You don't understand. I'm afraid that if I leave, things will change between us, and yet I'm also afraid that if I stay, they will never be the same."

A crooked little smile broke the agony of his features as he traced a tear with the tip of his finger.

"Spoken like a true woman. All full of riddles and secrets, aren't you, love?"

"Oh, Matt, what should I do? I don't know." With a sob, she fell into his arms.

He caught her, then held her close until he feared she could not breathe, and still he didn't have the guts to turn her loose. Not just yet, not when he feared she might run.

But when she wrapped her own arms around his waist and he felt her trembling, he knew he wasn't the only one in pain. It made what he had to say just a little bit easier. Tunneling his hands through her hair, he tilted her face.

"Billie, darlin', you don't need to ask me. You already know what to do. You made the decision when you called the airport, didn't you?" When she would have looked away, his voice sharpened as he held her fast. "Didn't you?"

She took a deep breath and nodded.

Anger died as he accepted his fate. "Okay, I can face the truth when I know it. But know this, Billie Walker!" He tugged at her hair until she was forced once again to look up. "I'm not giving you up, I'm just letting you go. You finish what you set out to do, then come back to me. Do you hear me, girl? You come back to me!" His mouth crumpled in pain as he lowered his head. "Or I swear to God, I'll be coming to get you."

Thick sobs tore up her throat as she hid her face against his neck and began to cry.

"Oh, Matt. Why does love have to hurt?"

"That's just it, darlin', it doesn't have to. I swear on my life, it doesn't have to."

She clung to him. "Since I have a car in L.A., I want to leave my other car here for the semester. Will you take me to the airport?"

He grinned wryly. "Darlin', I'd take you to hell

blindfolded if you'd come back to me when you'd seen the sights."

Billie managed a smile. "I don't think I need to go quite that far. But just in case I do, it's good to know you'd be waiting."

The Dallas/Fort Worth airport was, as usual, a hubbub of activity. Early holiday travelers pushed and shoved their way through the crowded corridors in a rush to get from one place to another.

Billie clutched Matt's hand with shaky persistence, refusing to let their connection be broken by the crush of travelers. The weather outside the terminal was typical for December. The wind was bitterly cold with a windchill of below freezing. In deference to the day, the heavens spit tiny flakes of snow that melted against the windows of the warm concourse as quickly as they hit.

Matt glanced down at Billie's wan expression, gauging her state of mind against the weather in which she would have to fly, and then suspected that weather conditions were the least of her worries.

He shifted the strap of her carryall to a firmer position on his shoulder and tugged at her hand until she paused beside him and looked up.

"What?"

"It's going to be all right."

She sighed. "I know. I just don't want to leave before Christmas, but if I wait, I might not be able to get the courses I need to graduate on time. If the dean weren't already aware of the circumstances that had pulled me out this near to graduation, it would be nearly impossible to get back in for spring semester."

Matt slid his hand beneath her hair and cupped the back of her neck. The expression on his face was serious. His words were sharp and to the point.

"Billie Jean, there comes a time in everyone's life when there are choices to be made. Years ago you chose to get an education and have been acting upon that choice. We didn't plan on falling in love, but it damned sure happened. We chose to deepen our relationship by making love . . . and commitments. But one should not have an impact upon the other. I'm a firm believer in finishing what I start, so why would I expect you to be any different?"

For the first time that day, Billie found a reason to smile.

"What's so funny?" Matt growled.

"Nothing," she said softly. "I was smiling because you give me such joy."

Matt groaned. Ignoring the strangers passing by, he wrapped his arms around her and pulled her close into an embrace.

"Have mercy, Memphis. You pick the damnedest times to rewind my clock. Right now I'd give a whole hell of a lot for an empty room with a lock."

Billie buried her nose against the warmth of his fleece-lined coat and shivered as their bodies aligned. She knew exactly how he felt.

Attention please. American Airlines is now boarding all passengers to Los Angeles at Gate 21. Please . . .

Billie gasped and clutched Matt even tighter.

"God give me strength," she murmured.

Matt's heart gave a jerk. "No, darlin'," he said softly, and tilted her chin, "God give *me* strength. I'm the one who has to let go."

Just as their lips met, she sobbed, and the pain traveled from her to him with love, shattering what resolve he had mustered and leaving him little more than walking wounded. When they lifted their heads, neither could clearly see the other's face for the tears.

Matt cupped her cheeks with both hands, imprinting each separate feature of Billie Jean into his memory for all time.

"We've got to stop meeting and parting like this," he said wryly. "I'm starting to get a serious dislike of airports."

Billie clutched at the lapels of his jacket with shaking hands.

"I love you, Matt Holt."

"Ah God, Memphis, I love you, too."

Without another word, he slipped her bag from his hands to hers and watched her turn and walk away. Twice before she passed through the doorway to board, she stopped and turned. Each time, he watched her indecision come and go. When she finally disappeared, his knees went weak. He took a deep breath and swiped a shaky hand across his eyes.

Dear Lord, you're gonna have to help me bear this.

Somehow he made it to the window and stood without moving until the plane backed away from the terminal and moved onto the runway. Long after it had vanished from sight, he kept staring into the gray, overcast sky, trying not to think of the loneliness that waited for him back home.

It wasn't until a child jostled the back side of his legs that he came to himself enough to move. He remembered nothing of the trip home except the empty seat beside him and the sound of windshield wipers swiping against cold, hard glass.

A few days later, he walked into the house just as the phone began to ring. He ran, ignoring the mud on his boots and the door that he'd left ajar, unaware that his voice sounded breathless and a little bit desperate for news of a woman who'd gone out of his life.

"Hello?"

"Hi, Dad, what's up? You sound out of breath."

Disappointment swept over him. It took a moment until he was able to focus.

"Oh, Scott, it's you."

Scott grinned and kicked back in his chair, using his bed for a footstool. "And I miss you, too," he drawled.

Matt slumped against the wall, willing himself to another level of emotion. "Sorry, that came out wrong."

"I don't think so. I think it came out exactly how you felt. What's wrong?"

He frowned and stared at a spot on the ceiling. "Nothing out of the ordinary," he replied, and then changed the subject in midstream. "Hey, Scott?"

"Yeah, Dad?"

"I need you to do something for me."

"You name it, and it's yours."

"I need you to look out for Billie. You know, sort of

stop in and say hello from time to time. Don't make it look like you're checking up on her; just make sure she's all right."

All the breath slid out of Scott's lungs in one swoosh. It took him several seconds before he could think.

"She's gone? Billie's gone?"

"She flew back to L.A. a few days ago. She's got one more semester to finish." *And wounds in her soul that I don't know if I can fix.*

Scott sighed with relief. "Oh wow! For a minute I thought that she'd walked out like she did before. You scared me."

And she scares me because she hasn't called. "I didn't mean to; I guess I was just preoccupied. I've been stringing wire all morning. Somebody ran through the west side of the fence that borders the highway. It was pure luck that the herd was at the opposite end of the place when it happened, or I'd still be out chasing cows. Is everything going okay with you?"

Scott grinned. "Considering finals are looming, I suppose so. Anyway, I wanted to call and let you know that I was able to get my flight. I almost waited too long to make reservations."

Matt grinned. He could hear the excitement in Scott's voice.

"I sure hope the weather holds," Scott continued. "You know what a mess flying during the holidays can be. I'd hate to be stranded in an airport and miss Christmas dinner with you."

Matt closed his eyes as pain rolled around him.

Once he'd been stranded in one, and magic had happened. He gripped the phone a little tighter and cleared his throat.

"You won't miss a thing. Whenever you get here is when Christmas will be."

Scott grinned. "That's great! I can hardly wait."

"Me neither," Matt said, and then remembered. "I guess you should know that we just might have company for Christmas Day."

"Oh? Someone I know?"

A small smile tilted the corner of Matt's mouth. "Daisy Bedford. I don't know if she'll accept, but I'm going to invite her just the same."

"Old lady Bedford? Whatever for?"

"Daisy," Matt said, correcting Scott's impolite epithet, although to be fair, he'd called her worse more than once. "And because she likes to make sweet potatoes."

"Hunh?"

"I'll explain when you get here. Fly safe and remember what I asked."

"About Billie? I swear, Dad. I'll look her up this week. Besides, my apology is long overdue. Don't worry, I'm sure everything will be fine. She'll probably burn up the phone lines and be back before you know it."

Matt sighed and tried to absorb some of Scott's positive attitude. "You're probably right. Good luck on your finals and call me ahead of time if you want me to pick you up at the airport."

"Will do. Talk to you later."

When the line went dead, Matt hung up the phone. The kitchen door thumped against the wall as a cold gust of wind blew it open the rest of the way. For a moment he stood alone in the middle of the room, looking around at the uncluttered cabinets and the weak winter sunlight coming through the curtains to his right.

His hands curled into fists as the utter solitude of his life overwhelmed him. With a curse, he jammed his Stetson a little tighter on his head and stalked back out the door, slamming it shut behind him as he walked headfirst into a bitter blast of wind.

December in L.A. was mild compared to the cold north winds that swept through Texas, but today it came close to being bleak. Rain fell in slow but steady sheets, running swiftly through the gutters and into the sewers, washing the streets clean. People on foot huddled beneath awnings and crowded into shops, waiting for the deluge to pass while the ever-present traffic made swift passage through water-filled streets, showering cars and people alike with the chill, muddy flow.

Billie plodded from one store to another in a mindless routine as she went about the task of putting her apartment back in order. Even if she had left her heart in Texas with Matt Holt, life still must go on.

Billie was determined to finish what she'd started. Years ago, her first foray into the world of computers had convinced her that she'd found something at which she could excel, and it was something that didn't fight back. If one had the skill, computers could and would do anything that one asked of them. They had been her salvation. She'd found work that satisfied a long-empty part of her.

Falling in love should not have interfered with that fulfillment, but it had. Billie knew that with little effort she would have quit on herself and on life and let Matt carry the burden of her fears and mistakes.

He loved her enough to try.

She loved him too much to let him.

For her sake as well as his, she needed to reach the goals she'd set for herself. That was why she'd walked out just when she'd needed him most.

When the last errand on her list was finished, Billie made a mad dash for her car with bags and packages bumping against her breasts and beneath her chin. In spite of her raincoat, she was soaked by the time she got inside. Her hands were shaking as she jammed the key into the ignition and turned the key. Slipping the car in reverse, she shivered and longed for a good warm bath.

A short time later she reached home. Dripping with every step, she entered the apartment elevator, cursing her luck and timing as a man entered just ahead of her. His name was Wayne. He lived two floors above her, and she'd been dodging his attentions for more than a year.

"Nasty day, isn't it?" he asked.

She nodded. "Would you please press four for me?"

He obliged, and then looked her up and down in a slow, studied gaze. "I've missed seeing you around," he said, and took a step closer. "Thought maybe you'd moved."

"No."

"Looks like you're just setting up shop again," he said, and would have poked through the tops of her packages had she not moved back. "Why don't you let me take you out to dinner tonight? Just a friendly welcome back. No strings."

"No, thank you." Not for the first time, she wished for the guts to tell him his cologne made her think of fish bait.

To her relief, the elevator soon came to a jerky stop. When the doors parted, he was forced to step aside to let her off. He leaned out to watch her departure. "I'd be happy to help carry that."

She lengthened her stride toward her doorway, breathing a small sigh of relief as she heard the elevator grinding its way up the shaft. "Some things never change," she muttered, and dropped her stuff by the door to search for her key.

Just as she stuck it in the lock, the phone inside her apartment began to ring. By the time she got the door open, it was on the third ring. Shoving her packages inside with the toe of her shoe, she slammed the door shut and ran. Breathless from anticipation and the unexpected dash, she answered without taking time to inhale.

"Hello?"

"Billie, is that you?"

The voice was familiar, but not the one that she'd wanted to hear.

"Oh, Scott, it's you."

Her response was so like the one that he'd gotten from his father that he laughed in spite of himself.

"My God," he drawled. "If I wasn't so sure I was gorgeous, I would be getting myself an inferiority complex."

Water dripped from the hood of her raincoat and into her eyes, while a puddle began forming where she stood. In spite of her disappointment, she laughed. Scott had a way of making that happen.

"Sorry. I was out shopping. The weather stinks. I guess the mood rubbed off on me."

"Don't apologize," he said, and then cleared his throat. "I'm the one who owes an apology, remember? Besides, the reason I said that was because I called Dad yesterday, and he answered the phone the same way. You know . . . Oh, Scott . . . it's you. What's wrong with you two? Why haven't you called each other?" His voice lowered. "Please don't tell me you're still mad?"

The mention of Matt's name was enough to send her spirits into a nosedive. She missed him so much that it physically hurt.

"No. No one's mad. It was just hard to leave him, that's all. And I was afraid if I called too soon, I'd be on the next plane to Texas. I made a promise to myself to get settled back in before I made contact."

"Okay, I can accept that. Now, are you going to go out to dinner with me, or what? Mike and Stephanie called. They've found this new restaurant near campus and are dying to try it. However, they say that brother and sister cannot be seen in public together unless they are in the company of others. Something about ruining their reputations or some such bull."

Billie smiled. She didn't realize how much she'd missed her friends. Then she remembered.

"Shouldn't you be studying? Finals are just around the corner."

Scott snorted softly into the receiver. "You're not my mother yet. Are you coming with us, or not?"

She grinned. "I suppose. Where do I meet you and when?"

"Oh no," Scott said. "I promised I would . . . uh . . . I mean I don't think you should. . . ."

In spite of her soaked condition and the chill in the room, a sweet warmth circled her heart. "Matt told you to take care of me, didn't he?"

Scott fidgeted. He wasn't about to tell her the truth for fear she would take it the wrong way. He'd already done enough to create trouble for them and had no intention of causing more. "I'll be there at seven. Stephanie said to tell you the restaurant is semichic, whatever the hell that means."

Her smile widened. "It means that whatever you wear better be clean and pressed."

He groaned.

"See you at seven," Billie said, and then added, "Oh, Scott?"

"What?"

"Thank you for calling."

"You're welcome . . . I think."

The line went dead in her ear. Without hesitation, she broke her connection and released the button, waiting for a clear dial tone to sound. When it did, she began punching in numbers with slow deliberation. She had an overdue call of her own to make. Only after it began ringing did she remember the two-hour time difference. She looked up at her clock and was shrugging out of her raincoat when he answered.

"Matt, it's me."

Matt sank into the nearest chair and closed his eyes in a fervent but silent prayer of thanksgiving.

"Hello, darlin'. I was beginning to think you'd never call."

Billie absorbed the voice in her ear, savoring the deep, resonant texture of the words because they were all that she had.

"So you sicced Scott on me instead."

He winced. If Scott had messed this up, he was going to wring his neck.

"I wasn't trying to spy on you, I just wanted to make sure you were—"

"No . . . don't apologize. I'm not angry, I'm touched, more than you will ever know."

A slow grin spread across his face as he began to relax. "Damn, Memphis, if I was just a little bit closer, I'd show you some touching you'd never forget."

She laughed, and the sound wrapped around his senses, making him ache for more than her voice.

"I miss you, darlin'."

Her smile went awry. "I miss you more."

The knot in his belly pulled tighter. "I sincerely doubt that. However, it does my ego good to hear it just the same.

The line crackled in their ears and Billie heard a soft but distinct curse as Matt's voice faded in and out of hearing.

"What's wrong?" she asked.

"The weather. It's blowing a blue norther out here. You better be glad you're in sunny California."

"I'd be happier if I was there with you freezing my toes off," she replied wistfully, and heard his swift intake of breath.

"And I'd be a lot happier, too," he said quietly.

The line crackled, then popped in Matt's ear.

"Billie?"

She had to strain to hear his words.

"I love you."

"I love you, too," she said, but he was already gone.

The doorbell rang just as Billie was stepping into her shoes. She glanced at the clock. Ten minutes to seven. Either Scott was early, or someone else was at the door, and it had better not be Wayne, the jerk from upstairs.

When she glanced through the peephole, she started to grin. It was a jerk all right, but his name wasn't Wayne. She unlocked the door and opened it wide, wishing she had a camera to capture the moment. It was Scott. And the three-foot-high dunce cap on his head said it all.

Even though Billie was smiling, Scott's stomach was still churning. They'd parted on angry words a long time ago, and amends still had to be made.

"It's just to make my apology official."

"Come in before someone sees you," she said, and grabbed him by the arm.

The door thumped loudly as she shut it behind him. For a moment they stared at each other, remembering the ugly words that had passed between them, remembering the pain Scott had caused. He was so like the man she loved that it wasn't in her to stay mad . . . at least not for long.

"Hey, Scott?"

"What?"

"Turn around, will you?"

"What for?" he asked, but did as she asked.

"Hmmm, it's not there."

"What's not there?"

"The long gray tail."

Now he was really confused. "What long gray tail?"

"The one that asses always wear."

Scott grinned. "Does this mean I am forgiven?"

She pretended to consider the question, although she'd forgiven him long ago. When she saw him starting to sweat, she relented.

"I suppose."

Scott tossed the dunce cap, then swung her off her feet and kissed her soundly on the cheek. "Thank God. My conscience is finally clear."

Billie swatted him on the arm. "Put me down, and don't lie. Unless you've drastically changed, one apology to me will not assuage your poor conscience. You've been the wrack and ruin of too many women as it is."

He grinned, and at that moment, Billie saw more of his father in him than she'd ever seen before.

"Now, B.J., don't be heartless. You know I love women more than anything else."

"Yes, but that's just the problem. You haven't figured out how to love just one at a time."

The grin on Scott's face slipped. Not too much. Just enough for her to know that what he said next came from the heart.

"Maybe I just haven't found the right one yet. When I do, like Dad, I'll know it. I just hope she's as good as you, Billie Walker, because the Holt men don't settle for less than the best."

Billie's throat tightened as tears shimmered across her eyes, blurring Scott's image as well as the room around her. Embarrassed by the unexpected emotion, she turned away, pretending to search for her coat.

"Here it is," Scott said, and lifted it from the back of a chair right beside her.

When he held it up, she slipped her arms into the sleeves, then hugged it close around her. As they started toward the door, she paused, her hand on his arm.

"Scott?"

He stopped.

"Thank you."

He breathed a sigh of relief and grinned. "You're welcome. Now let's hurry. I'm starving."

Billie led the way, with Scott right behind her. When they started toward the elevator, his hand cupped her elbow. It was a small gesture, but one of which his father would have been proud. Holts protected their women, no matter how they ranked in the family. For Billie, it was final proof that Scott had accepted his father's relationship with her. And from the smile on his face, it would seem that he even approved.

Chapter 12

Christmas was everywhere. Store windows abounded in holiday decorations, while shoppers browsed to the traditional songs being broadcast throughout the area. Both upper and lower levels of megamalls vibrated from the thunder of hundreds of feet as people surged in and out of doorways like ants at a picnic. To the casual observer, it looked like chaos, but there was an order to it that even the smallest of children could see. It was no secret why they were here. Presents had to be chosen and bought and then wrapped. Santa was on his way.

Billie stood just outside the doorway of a small but elite boutique, watching the children standing in line to greet the mall Santa, while, inside, Stephanie tore through the shop with list in hand and a gleam in her eye.

As far as Billie was concerned, it was a case of "been there—done that." She had no desire to try on another item of clothing. Her head ached and her feet hurt worse. The din outside the boutique was only a decibel lower than the one inside, but the way Billie felt, any improvement was better than none at all.

She turned to check on Stephanie's progress. From the intense manner in which her friend was going through the racks of clothing, she wasn't close to being done.

Out in the mall, a little boy shrieked as his mother dropped him into Santa's lap for a holiday picture. Billie turned, her heart full of sympathy for the tears running down the toddler's face, as well as for the mother who so desperately wanted her annual memento of the occasion.

"Poor baby," she said, half to herself, and wished for a place to sit down.

The air was filled with dozens of recognizable scents: cinnamon oils, hot buttered popcorn, faux pine from a cart nearby. Bayberry candles adorned the boutique window, emitting a clean, fresh smell that mingled with that of perfumes, hair sprays, and fabrics. Apart they were nothing remarkable. Together, they were overpowering, almost sickening.

Her stomach grumbled, reminding her that she and Stephanie had yet to eat lunch, and making her wish that she had not skipped breakfast as well. The longer she waited, the less enticing the thought of food became. Sounds and voices echoed inside her head. As Billie swayed in place, her hands began to sweat, and saliva surged at the back of her throat. In a panic, she looked back through the boutique window and was relieved to see Stephanie coming out of the store.

"I didn't think you'd ever get here," Billie said, and promptly fainted at Stephanie's feet.

*   *   *

"She's coming around. Step back," someone said.

Billie blinked and opened her eyes. It took her a moment to orient herself with the world, and when she did, mortification took over. She was flat on her back, and the person looming over her was wearing a red suit and hat and had a long white beard.

"What happened?"

Santa Claus smiled. "Welcome back, little lady. How do you feel?"

"Okay, I guess," Billie said. "I got dizzy."

Stephanie sighed with relief. "You scared me half to death." She patted Billie's arm and cheek in helpless panic. "I didn't know you felt bad. You should have said something sooner. I feel just awful making you stand out here so long."

"Help me up," Billie said.

Santa Claus grinned and extended his hand. "Easy does it," he cautioned, as he and Stephanie pulled Billie upright.

"I can't believe I did that," she said. "I never faint."

Santa handed Billie her purse and coat. "That's what my wife said just before the rabbit died."

Billie turned a whiter shade of pale as Stephanie giggled. "We didn't have lunch," she said. "It's my fault. I wanted to get here before the good stuff was gone."

"And I skipped breakfast, too," Billie added.

"Are you sure you're all right?" Santa asked. "I could still call mall security and have an ambulance dispatched."

"No, please don't. I'm just a little queasy is all."

"Then I recommend you two young ladies get some food in your stomachs before you spend another dime."

"Yes sir," Stephanie said, and grabbed her shopping bag. "Billie, honey, do you feel like walking? That yummy Mexican restaurant is just a couple of doors down."

Billie's stomach lurched at the thought of meat, grease, and spices while Santa ambled his way through the crowd to resume his seat. She managed a smile to soften her refusal.

"Anything but Mexican, okay?"

Stephanie frowned. "But that's your favorite thing."

"Not today. I don't even want to smell it."

"Okay. When something looks good, say so, and we'll eat there."

Stephanie took her by the arm and started down the mall, plowing a path through the shoppers for them with her bulging shopping bags.

Thankful for someone to lean on, Billie took long, deep breaths to still her rolling stomach and followed where she was led.

A few stores down she pointed to a small deli. "How about here? I think soup and a sandwich just might do the trick."

There was a line at the door but with a few well-chosen words, Stephanie quickly had them seated at a table. While Billie was still staring blankly at the menu, Stephanie ordered vegetable soup and grilled cheese sandwiches for both.

"Thank you," Billie said. "I couldn't seem to make up my mind."

A concerned expression replaced Stephanie's usually sunny smile. "Are you sure you're all right? You went out like a light."

Billie shrugged as she ran shaky hands through her hair. "I guess so. I still don't know why it happened."

"Do you want me to call—"

"No! Lord no," Billie said, cutting Stephanie's offer off in midstream. "Don't call anyone, especially Scott. He hovers enough as it is."

"Okay, fine, but as soon as I get you home, I expect you to crawl into bed. If you're coming down with something, the sooner you get off your feet, the better."

"I'll be fine," Billie said. "Just as soon as I eat, this hollow feeling will go away."

"You're the boss." And then Stephanie smiled. "Who would have thought that old Saint Nick knew CPR. When you went down, he was out of that seat and down at your side before I could turn loose of my purse." She giggled. "I wonder if he's cute?"

Billie rolled her eyes and grinned. "It doesn't matter what he looks like. He's married, remember? Mrs. Claus . . . the rabbit that died?"

"Oh yeah!" Stephanie made a face. "Pooh. The good ones are always taken."

In spite of what had just happened, Billie managed a laugh. "How can you say that? You don't know if he's good. You don't even know the man."

Stephanie grinned. "Sure I do. I've been writing to him ever since I was two."

"You are incorrigible," Billie said, then leaned back with a grateful sigh as the waitress set down two steaming bowls of soup along with hot, crusty sandwiches oozing thick, melting cheese. She picked up her spoon. "This looks great."

Within moments, the early mood of their shopping trip returned as Stephanie began reeling off her latest finds between mouthfuls of food.

Later, Stephanie dropped Billie off at her apartment with a promise to call, waving as she drove away.

Billie entered her apartment and, with a definite mission in mind, went to pick up a calendar. Something the Santa said had started a worry. *The rabbit had died . . . the rabbit had died.*

She couldn't get the words out of her mind. For a long, silent moment she held the calendar in her lap, as if waiting for it to give her an answer she didn't want to hear. Finally, she took a deep breath and started to count.

Twice she counted, and still the days stayed the same. Dropping the calendar back to the desk with a thump, she pulled herself up from the chair.

"It doesn't mean a thing," she mumbled, and began taking off her clothes one by one.

By the time she reached her bedroom, she was nude. Without searching for her gown, she turned back the bed and crawled in, pulling the covers clear up to her chin before turning on her side and rolling herself into a ball.

"It doesn't mean a thing," she repeated, and quietly closed her eyes.

Finally she slept, and when she did, dreamed she was on the witness stand before a jury of twelve men who all looked like Matt.

I didn't mean to do it! I didn't mean to do it! she'd cried.

But as hard as she pleaded, no one believed in her innocence.

The phone kept ringing. It had been ringing off and on for three days. Billie didn't have to answer it to know who it was. Matt been calling and leaving messages with deadly regularity. Unable to bear the sound of his voice without answering him, she had finally turned off the machine. Now all she had to do was endure the strident demands of Ma Bell until he gave up and disconnected.

Her eyes were hollow from lack of sleep, her movements lethargic. She sat at her desk without moving, staring at a small cardboard box she'd purchased over a week ago and had yet to open.

And then, as suddenly as the ringing had begun, it ceased. She covered her face with her hands and drew a slow, shuddering breath. This craziness had to stop, and there was one thing that would do it. The truth.

"God help me," she whispered, and looked at the box. With trembling fingers, she picked it up and walked out of the room.

A short time later she was back, a fixed expression on her face and a thin strip of paper in her hand. She stood before the clock, counting down the minutes to the rest of her life. When the allotted time had elapsed, she looked down for a long, disbelieving moment at the dot of color that had appeared. She blinked, then wadded it up in the palm of her hand.

"Oh!"

It was a small, insignificant gasp, but the devastation of it all swept through her just the same.

In a daze, she took her purse and walked out. She walked for hours until darkness was upon her. When she finally stopped to look around, nothing was familiar. Not the shops. Not the streets. Not the faces of the people that she saw. A swift surge of panic arose as she clutched her purse against her belly and spun in place, looking for a cab, or a phone, or someone who'd help.

To her undying relief, she saw the familiar colors of an LAPD cruiser as it came around the corner at a slow, steady pace. Without thinking, Billie dashed into the street, waving her hand in a panicked motion.

The car slid to a halt as the window came down. Before the officer could ask, Billie grabbed the door and leaned in.

"Where am I?"

Both the driver and his partner exchanged looks, then the officer on the passenger side emerged. He took Billie by the arm, turning her until he could see in her eyes. Expecting to see signs of drug or alcohol abuse, he frowned. There was nothing but panic.

"What are you on, lady?"

Billie's voice was shaking as she clutched at his sleeve. "Nothing, Officer, I swear. I was walking and didn't realize I'd gone so far. It's getting dark, and all the shops around here are closed, so I can't use their phones. I got scared. That's all."

"You mean you're just lost?"

She nodded and swallowed past a knot in her throat. It wouldn't do to start crying. Not now. She might never stop.

"Yes, I'm just lost." *In more ways than one*, she added silently.

"Where do you live?"

She dug in her purse and showed him her identification. "Near the UCLA campus."

He whistled softly between his teeth. "Wow! You didn't get lost; you went on vacation."

Then he leaned back down and looked at his partner. Again, the look that passed between them needed no words.

He opened the back door and motioned Billie toward an empty seat. "Here, miss, get in. We'll get you to an area where you can get a cab. Do you have the fare?"

Her legs were shaking from an adrenaline rush as she slid into the cruiser. "Yes," she said, and leaned her head against the backseat. "Yes, I have the fare."

The short intermittent bursts of traffic on their radio, as well as their muted conversation, went over her head as she let them take her away. Her mind was blank, her emotions on hold.

Just let me get home. Just let me get home.

The mantra stayed with her through an awkward but appreciative parting from the officers, as well as the cab ride home. When the cab driver suddenly came to a stop, Billie looked up only to realize she was at her apartment complex.

When she opened her purse to take out the fare, a

small strip of paper slipped from her hand and fell unnoticed to the floor of the cab. It didn't matter. The loss wouldn't change a thing.

Billie Walker had done the unthinkable. She'd just become the second unwed woman in Matt Holt's life who was going to bear his child. How it had happened in spite of the protection they'd used was immaterial. That it had happened was more than she could bear. If she told him, he would marry her, of that she was sure. But in her mind she kept seeing him standing before his dresser, staring down at Susan's picture.

I didn't love her like I should have. If I hadn't gotten her pregnant, we would never have married.

"Keep the change," she said, and crawled out of the cab.

When her feet hit the pavement, the thick growth of shrubs around the building suddenly took on ominous airs. In a fresh spurt of panic, she bolted toward the door and inside the complex as if the devil was at her heels. Only after she had reached the safety of her apartment and turned all the locks did she breathe a small sigh of relief.

Now she was home. The moment she'd seen the dot turn color, her decision to have the child had been made. It was the how of it all that she'd had to face. It wouldn't be easy, but she'd be damned before she confessed her condition to another living soul. Not now. Not before she had time to regroup.

And yet leaving Matt totally out of her decision was unthinkable. She couldn't do what she had to do without talking to him at least one more time. If she simply up and disappeared without a word, he'd have every cop in California on her trail and then some.

"Lord, help me find the words," she muttered as she dropped into a chair and stared at the phone near her elbow. Then she sighed. Waiting wasn't going to make anything change . . . or go away. She picked up the receiver and dialed.

It rang forever. Either he was on the other line and just wasn't answering his call-waiting, or the answering machine wasn't on. Billie bit her lower lip and closed her eyes.

Damn. Just when she'd gotten up the nerve to call, he wasn't home.

And then his voice interrupted her thoughts, startling her so much she almost dropped the receiver in her lap.

"Hello?"

"Matt?"

He put the sack of groceries he was carrying down on the counter and leaned against the wall with a sigh of relief.

"Hey, darlin', you don't know how good it is to hear your voice."

Tears welled, and Billie pressed a finger hard against her upper lip, willing herself not to cry. Not yet. Not until she was done.

"Oh Matt, I miss you," she said softly.

Matt groaned, and turned to face the wall. Resting his forehead against a cabinet, he closed his eyes and concentrated on the fact that she'd called and tried to tell himself that everything was all right. But it didn't happen. There was something in the tone of her voice that was scaring the hell out of him.

"So what's going on in L.A.?"

Billie shuddered. *Other than the fact I'm having your baby?* "Not much, just everyone getting ready for Christmas."

Matt heard loneliness in her voice and knew exactly how she was feeling.

"Billie, darlin' . . ."

"What?"

"Are you all right?"

Tell him. Tell him now. And then a memory came back too loud and too clear to be ignored. The memory of the expression on Matt's face when he declared he would have never married Susan if she hadn't been pregnant. It had been so full of regret . . . and lost hope.

"Sure," she said. "I'm fine. But the reason I called . . ."

For some reason, Matt found himself holding his breath.

"I may be out of touch for a while, so I don't want you to worry. But it won't be because . . ."

Matt straightened in shock as he stared out the kitchen window and tried to convince himself he wasn't hearing the death knell of their relationship.

"What the hell does 'out of touch' mean?"

Billie winced. She'd hurt him already. *Oh God, why does this have to be so difficult?*

"Nothing like what you're implying," Billie said, and knew he wouldn't believe her when she didn't even believe herself.

"*I'm* not implying anything, Memphis. *You're* the one who's being vague."

Billie stared down at the floor between her feet and tried to think, but the words wouldn't come. Nothing came but tears.

"I'm not running away," she said, and knew that he could hear her crying.

"Jesus Christ! Don't cry," he groaned, and wished they weren't thousands of miles apart. He couldn't bear to hear her cry.

"I'm sorry," Billie sobbed, and covered her face with her hand. "I'm sorry for everything. I never meant for us to get so mixed up . . . or messed up. All I'm asking you for is time so that I can figure out what to do."

Panic seized him. "About what? Figure out what to do about what? Is it your father? Is he hassling you? If he is, I swear, all you have to do is say the word, and I'll be—"

"No!"

He froze. The shriek in her voice was too shocking to comprehend.

"You can't come out here," she said in between sobs. "I don't want you to come out here. You have to wait. You have to wait until I come to you."

Matt groaned. "Damn you, Billie Jean. Don't do this to us."

"I'm not doing anything to us," she cried. "I just need you to trust me . . . and wait."

"How long?"

She looked down at her belly, imagining that she

could already sense a change in the contour of her body.

"For as long as it takes."

A low curse feathered across the miles and into her ear, but she could hear resignation in its tone.

"Matt?"

"Fine. So we're now officially 'out of touch.' "

"I love you," she said softly.

"That's real good to hear, Memphis. But you have a damned funny way of showing it."

Pain shattered what was left of Billie's resolve.

"Oh Matt . . . don't," she begged.

He sighed. "I love you, too . . . and I'll be waiting."

She disconnected, and when the line went dead in Matt's ear, something inside of him died, too.

"What do you mean, she moved?"

Matt's voice was just shy of a shout as he grabbed hold of the cabinet to steady himself.

"Just what I said," Scott replied, and shifted the phone to his other ear. "I've been trying to call her for two days straight. I wanted to bring her Christmas present by before I left and never could reach her, so I called Stephanie, thinking she might know something I didn't. She hadn't heard from her either. This afternoon, I went by. Someone else answered the door. They had just moved in and were still unpacking their stuff. I checked with the landlord, and he said she'd moved out on Monday. Damn it, Dad, what's going on? Did you two have a fight? Why would she up and run like this?"

A fist of panic curled tight within Matt's belly. "Oh God, oh God." He started to pace. "I didn't think she would take such drastic measures to stay out of touch."

"What?"

"Nothing. It was just something Billie said when she called."

"Then you didn't have an argument?"

"No, hell no!" Matt pinched the bridge of his nose to keep from crying. For the first time in his life, he had lost his sense of direction.

"Look, Dad, don't worry just yet, okay? Maybe we're making a big deal out of nothing. There could be a logical reason for the move, and she just hasn't taken the time to notify everyone yet, right?"

Matt wanted to let himself believe it, but gut instinct told him it wasn't so. Not after the phone conversation they'd had.

"I suppose. If she calls me, I'll let you know. And don't forget to let me know if your flight is delayed tomorrow."

Scott sighed. He'd been looking forward to going home for weeks, but leaving without knowing what was going on with Billie felt wrong.

"Would you rather I stayed here and looked for her?"

As much as Matt wanted to say yes, common sense told him no. He sighed. "We can't save Billie from her ghosts. Only she can do that. All we can do is love her and hope that somewhere inside of herself she remembers that we're here."

"Okay. I'll see you tomorrow. Drive safe."

"I will."

And then something, some sense of urgency, prodded Scott into a need for a reassurance he couldn't name.

He yelled, afraid that his father would disconnect before it could be said. "Hey, Dad!"

"What?"

"I love you."

A lopsided grin broke the pain on Matt's face. "I love you, too, boy."

A small distinct click sounded in his ear. The connection was just as broken as the one he'd had to Billie. With measured movement, he hung up the phone.

"God keep you safe, girl, because right now I can't."

Three weeks into the spring semester, the inevitable happened. Billie turned the corner of the administration building and came face-to-face with Stephanie Hodge.

"Oh my God!" Stephanie shrieked, and dropped her books where she stood.

Before Billie could think to react, Stephanie threw her arms around her and began hugging her over and over.

"We've all been frantic," she squealed, and then stepped back, giving Billie a second look before hugging her all over again. "What on earth made you disappear like that? Scott came back from Christmas break and said his dad has all but gone into mourning. Did you two have a fight? What made you move without telling anyone?"

Just hearing Matt's name made Billie weak with longing. The loneliness of the past couple of months had almost been more than she could bear. She had an overwhelming urge to call, just to hear his voice. But she knew if she did, he'd want answers she wasn't ready to give. She had to be sure that time wouldn't change his feelings for her before she revealed her secret. Only then could she be sure that their marriage would be for all the right reasons.

"Well," Stephanie said. "I'm waiting for an answer . . . and it better be good."

Billie struggled with a smile. She was treading a thin line between fact and fiction as it was. Saying too much to Stephanie could be disastrous.

"It was no big deal. I just needed to move. Tired of being in the same old place, I guess." She glanced down at her watch, gauging the time she still had to get to class. "It was good to see you, Steph, but if I don't hurry, I'm going to be late."

Stephanie couldn't believe this was the same Billie. She was treating her like nothing more than a casual acquaintance.

"You can't leave without giving me your address."

At this point, Billie panicked. "I've got to run," she called, and started across the campus.

"How about a phone number?" Stephanie yelled.

"Later," she called, and broke into a sprint.

Only when Billie was seated inside the classroom did her shattered nerves calm. It was inevitable that she'd see some of her friends during the semester. Even though they were on a different level of study, the location of classes often overlapped.

The professor's lecture went in one ear and out the

other as her mind whirled, locked into the past and the memories of a man she couldn't forget.

Right after she'd moved, she'd struggled for days trying to come to terms with what she'd done. Even now she still believed she was right. She'd made a promise to herself to call Matt sometime in the future, when she was strong enough to say what must be said. It was only fair. This was his child as well as hers, and it had been made with love. Whether the love still remained was yet to be seen.

She fidgeted in her seat, willing the professor to say something that would capture her interest. It didn't happen. Again, her thoughts began to wander.

By graduation she would be nearing her seventh month. She'd already made up her mind that she'd call then. She'd know by the sound of his voice if the love was still there. If it was, then she'd tell him. Until then, the secret was hers to keep.

The decision seemed reasonable. But she hadn't taken fate into consideration.

The letter was from Mel. Billie didn't have to see the return address to recognize the black, backward slash of his handwriting. Clutching it in one hand along with her books, she dug through her purse as she searched for the key to her apartment, wincing when a tiny foot . . . or was it an elbow . . . ricocheted against her rib cage before rolling to a more convenient spot inside her belly.

"Hang on, baby," she muttered as her fingers curled around the familiar ring. Moments later, she jammed the key in the lock and turned it.

A cool blast of air circled around her as she entered. It was a welcome relief from the heat outside. March had come in like a lion and showed no signs of being tamed. Fierce winds blew day and night, fanning everyone's nerves as well as the flames of brushfires that had started days ago, way up the coast.

The sparse furnishings of her new apartment reflected the austerity of her life in general. There was nothing here of Billie. No memento of her life from before except the child that she carried.

She set her books on the table with a thump and dropped into a chair with a relieved sigh, using the coffee table for a footstool to ease her aching feet. Mel Deal's letter was burning her fingers. She ached for news, any news of the outside world. He was the only person who knew where she'd moved to, and she had sworn him to utter secrecy before giving up her new address.

It was the letter that worried her. If he'd needed to talk, why hadn't he called? She shrugged and tore into the letter. She'd find out soon enough.

Dear Billie,

There's no need in beating around the bush with my news. I hate like hell to admit this, but I'm pretty sure Jarrod knows where you live. Gwinny, my secretary of twelve years plus, was in a car wreck. Temporary services sent some pretty young girl who seems to be on the lookout for bigger and better things. It would seem that your father has decided he's it. I didn't know she was seeing him until this morning.

I suspect his interest in her had as much to do with wheedling information out of her regarding your whereabouts as it had to do with lust, although to be fair, she is pretty. At any rate, I didn't want you to be unprepared should he decide to make an unscheduled appearance, although God only knows why he would try. The court proceedings are final, and he knows it. He can't be so vain as to suppose he could actually change your mind.

Once again, I'm sorry I let you down. Take care and call if you need me.

Love, Mel

The letter fell from her fingers and onto the floor. Her first instinct was to panic, and then she reminded herself that even if Jarrod did show up, what on earth could he say or do that she hadn't heard before?

The baby rolled again. At that point, horror struck. The baby! It was an odd sort of terror that should have had no basis for being there. Call it instinct, call it self-preservation, but Billie sensed that if he saw her like this, there'd be trouble.

"Damn you, Jarrod, why don't you get a life and get out of mine?"

She kicked off her shoes before heading to the kitchen. In the middle of a debate between study or sleep, she noticed she had messages on the answering machine and punched the button to listen to the play-back as she dug through the refrigerator.

"No, I don't want any magazines," she muttered, as one caller's message came and went.

It was the next one that got her attention. "Oh my gosh," she said, and turned to check the calendar. "The doctor's appointment! I almost forgot." She patted her tummy and opened a drawer for a fork. "We're going to have our picture taken tomorrow, aren't we, baby. You'll have to smile pretty for the camera, okay?"

Billie grinned at her own wit as she sniffed at a take-out container of cold beef and broccoli stir-fry, then plopped down on the window seat with the box in one hand, her fork in the other, and began to eat.

The ultrasound had been scheduled for weeks. Just thinking about a first glimpse of new life made her weepy. It also made her realize how selfish she was being in shutting Matt out of all this. What if he'd been telling her the truth all along? What if he really did love her? How would he feel when he learned that he'd missed these small milestones? She sighed, her appetite suddenly gone, and dumped the rest of the food down the disposal.

The telephone loomed. All it would take was one call.

"Settle down," she reminded herself. "You've waited this long, at least wait until after the ultrasound tomorrow."

It was a decision that she would live to regret.

Chapter 13

"That's her head . . . and there . . . those are her arms and . . ." He moved the wand farther to the right. "There . . . those are her legs. She's an active little thing." He smiled. "Although I suppose I don't have to tell you that."

Billie laughed through tears. She! It was a girl! *Oh Matt, I didn't know this could be so special. I'm so, so sorry you aren't here.*

The doctor continued to move the wand across her stomach, pointing to the screen as he explained in detail all that was being revealed. Some of it was too complex for Billie to absorb. All she knew and all she could feel were Matt's baby and Matt's love surrounding her, overwhelming her.

"As I said earlier, if this little lady is punctual, you'll be having yourself a firecracker baby."

Billie's mind raced. A July baby. What fabulous birthday parties she would have. Celebrating a birthday along with the birth of a nation would be such fun. Picnics, swimming parties, fireworks. The need to call Matt was too strong to ignore.

"Are we almost through?"

"Just about. Nurse will finish up here. Don't forget to stop by the desk and pick up a copy of the ultrasound. It will be her first in a long line of home movies, right?"

"You mean what I just saw is on a tape? I can take it home and look at it anytime I want?"

He laughed. "Anytime you want."

A bit of her guilt lifted. Matt wasn't here, but he wouldn't miss it after all.

The trip home was euphoric. After months of nerve-wracking indecision and lonely, sleepless nights longing for Matt's voice, for his arms around her to chase her fears away, her joy had overcome her worst fears.

She pulled her car into the parking lot and exited on the run, clutching the videotape tightly in her hand as she headed for her apartment.

The sun was hot on Billie's head, but her white knit shorts and the loose-fitting top were cool antidotes to the weather. Lawn sprinklers jetted in unison between walkways bordered by flowering ground cover rich with color. Tiny purple blossoms clung close to dark verdant leaves, while other varieties bore white and yellow blooms to mingle with the rest.

As she turned the corner of the sidewalk, a sprinkler suddenly swung her way. She squealed and leaped out of the way just before it passed.

Her step was buoyant, her expression serene as she entered the building and headed for the elevator. Even the OUT OF ORDER sign on the door couldn't ruin her mood. The stairwell was just to her left, and she hit the door with the flat of her hand and started up the floors, mentally preparing herself for what she would say when she talked to Matt.

How did one impart this kind of news? Hello Matt, I missed you, I'm pregnant . . . or, forgive me for not calling, but I'm going to have your baby? She smiled. She was just being silly. When she heard his voice, she knew what she was going to say. *I love you.* After that, everything else should come easy.

Only slightly winded as she reached the fourth floor, she exited the stairwell with keys in hand.

During the past few months, she'd prepared herself for everything possible except the man who was waiting for her outside her door.

From his casual grace to his cold, handsome face, he hadn't changed a bit. The white summer slacks and pale blue shirt that he wore accentuated his thick graying hair and his dark summer tan. Even though the bottomless source of his income had been cut off, it would seem his tastes still ran toward the expensive.

She'd almost forgotten Mel's letter and the warning he'd given her. Almost . . . until now. Years ago she would have given anything for her father to show up for an unexpected visit. Now, when it no longer mattered, Jarrod Walker was here. With hardly a pause in her step, she lifted her chin, clutched her video a little tighter, and headed for her door.

His gaze went from her face to her belly and back again. His shock was evident, and she could almost see the machinations of his devious mind trying to figure out how he could use this to his greatest advantage.

Billie paused, unwilling to unlock the door and let

him in. Letting him into her home would sully what refuge she had left. Whatever he had to say, he would say it out here in the hall.

"Jarrod, to what do I owe this pleasure?"

His eyes narrowed. He'd planned to throw himself on her mercy and claim that her absence had brought him to his senses, but it would seem that she hadn't been as overwrought and lonely as he'd hoped. Someone had obviously been keeping her company . . . close company.

"Billie, are my eyes deceiving me, or are you about to make me a grandfather?"

She felt a surge of nausea. In all these months that she'd carried this baby alone, the only debate she'd been coming to terms with was sharing it with Matt. Not once had she considered that becoming a mother meant she'd be giving Jarrod Walker a grandchild. Her lips thinned in determination. She didn't intend to give him another damn thing . . . ever.

"I'm pregnant, if that's what you're getting at. However, you do not fit in my future. So what are you doing here?"

"I came to see you. To apologize for what happened between us. All I can say is after Phoebe left me, for a time I must have lost my mind."

Phoebe? Oh yes, number six. For a minute she'd forgotten her name.

She leaned against the door, pretending a casualness she didn't feel. An inner instinct was telling her to run, although she felt silly in thinking it. The man was a heel, but he *was* her father, for Pete's sake. What could he possibly do that would be any worse than what she'd already endured?

"I accept your apology. Thank you for coming."

His well-hidden anger began to seethe. Jarrod bit back a sharp retort and took a deep breath instead. After what had come and gone between them, he'd known this wouldn't be easy.

"Now, Billie, surely you won't send me away so abruptly. I've come all this way. I thought we might go out to dinner. See a show, do something together."

Billie's chuckle came out without warning. It wasn't really her fault. After all, he'd ignored her for so long, she couldn't be blamed for appreciating the irony of his timing.

"I've lived out here, alone I might add, for the better part of seven years. Not once in that entire time have you set foot in this state, never mind come to see me. Why now, Jarrod? Why now when it's too late to care? Surely you don't think I'm this stupid?"

Son of a bitch, this isn't going to work after all. What the hell will I do now? Defeat reared its ugly head, and he found himself glaring at her belly as a sneer spread across his face.

"I don't know . . . you look pretty stupid to me. One would have thought in this day and age of preaching safe sex that you would have had better sense than to get yourself knocked up."

A swift flush of anger stained her cheeks, but she would not bicker with him. He liked it too much for her to give him the satisfaction.

"I suppose you're right. But, what's done is done. Actually, I'm looking forward to being a mother."

"Why? So you can go out the same way yours did?"

Her anger shot to the surface so quickly she didn't have time to retract it.

"Damn you! Damn you, Jarrod, go away. You're mean and lazy and your good looks are fading. It must be hell living in your skin knowing that one of these days the pretty little girls that you like aren't going to give you the time of day."

He hadn't prepared himself to hate. Not at this level.

He tried to talk, but nothing came out except spit. It hung at the corners of his mouth as a red haze colored his vision. His hands curled into fists, and his voice was shaking as he spewed forth his venomous declaration.

"The day she told me she was having a baby, I should have dropped the both of you off a bridge."

Billie covered her own stomach with the flat of her hand and took a step backward against the wall.

"How do you do it, Jarrod? How do you rationalize hating your own child?"

There was a wild, almost-crazy gleam in his eyes as he leaned forward. Billie tried not to panic, but when the heat from his breath seared her eyelids, she wanted to run.

"You still don't get it, do you? That's just it, you little witch! You're not mine! You're not my child, and I've known it from the start! She cheated on me, and the guilt ate her alive. That's why she killed herself. Not because she hated me, but because he didn't love her enough to take her away."

The walls in the hallway started to tilt. Every point of reference Billie had ever known fell away. As suddenly as it had gone, focus returned, and when it did, reality came with it. She looked up at him with a mixture of disgust and relief.

"Thank God!"

He stared at her. This hadn't been the reaction he'd expected.

"Thank God? That she's dead?"

"No, Jarrod. Thank God that not one drop of your blood runs in my veins. Thank God that I will not bear a child that can call you grandfather." Her voice was shaking as she took a step forward, pointing a finger straight into his face. "And thank God that when you die, your miserable seed will die with you."

Jarrod inhaled slowly, shocked by the hatred in her words. He couldn't take his eyes away from her face, or from the light that burned behind her dark brown eyes as she said aloud the thing that he feared most.

It was true. When he died there would be no one left to mourn his passing. He didn't see that it was all his fault. He wouldn't face his guilt in raising a child who'd learned distrust at his knee. By his own actions, he'd taught her hate and shown her greed, and now it was coming back on him a hundredfold.

And while Jarrod was facing some truths of his own, Billie was coming down from the adrenaline rush. Sick from the revelation, as well as the years of unresolved rage that hung between them, she couldn't find the impetus to speak—until the baby's sudden movement brought her back to her senses. With a mother's instinct, she realized that her emotions were somehow affecting her child. She had to end this, and end it now.

"Go away! Go away now before I call the police and have you arrested for harassment."

Jarrod's head jerked as if she'd coldcocked him. His eyes blazed but, oddly enough, he did as she ordered. He pivoted on his heel and headed for the elevator.

"It's out of order, remember?" she said, and stalked past him toward the stairwell. She pushed the door wide, then stepped aside, holding it open with her body. "Use the stairs. It will give you time to contemplate your next petty little scheme."

In all of Jarrod's years of wrongful doings, for the first time in his life, what happened next was truly an accident. It didn't stop the event from happening, but the regret was there all the same.

Blind with anger, he shoved his way through the door, intent on getting out of her sight and out of the state.

When she realized that he was not slowing down, that he would barrel right past her, instinct made her turn sideways to keep from being bumped. She never knew what connected first, his shoulder to her back or his foot to her heel. Whatever it was, it was enough to unbalance her. She staggered forward, only to find herself teetering at the top of the landing, her arms waving in a frantic effort to regain her footing. But the baby made her top-heavy, and the angle was too much to correct. With a high-pitched wail, she fell head over heels down the stairs.

To his credit, Jarrod actually grabbed for her, but he

missed. He stood transfixed at the top of the stairs, watching in horror as she bumped and rolled, then came to a stop, crumpled in a heap on the landing. As he watched, a pool of red began to seep onto the floor beneath her.

"Oh no!" He started down the stairs, taking them two at a time. A couple coming up the stairs, who'd seen her fall, came running up as he knelt at her side. "Help! Help! Call an ambulance! Call 911! Tell them she fell. Tell them she's pregnant!"

A familiar drawl raised Matt's ire.

If you're tryin' to kill yourself, you'd be better off usin' a rope.

He threw his pen across the room and unplugged his answering machine with a yank. Damn Daisy Bedford, she was going to drive him crazy, yet. He wasn't trying to kill anything, but if he did, she could very well be on the top of the list.

From her latest cryptic message it would seem that she'd seen him take a fall on the dirt bike this morning. It hadn't amounted to much. He'd hurt himself worse falling from a standing horse, and he'd been sixteen years old and stone drunk at the time. If he remembered right, that was exactly two weeks before he'd taken Susan out to Sutter's pond and had his own sweet way with her body.

He sighed. He hoped when he got old he didn't go through any sort of second childhood like some he knew. His first one had been tough enough.

He stared back at the phone, debating with himself

about leaving the machine unplugged and knew he
didn't have the guts to chance it. With a sigh of defeat,
he retrieved the pen from the corner of the room where
he'd thrown it, then walked back to the cabinet and
picked up the cord, calmly popping the phone jack
back in place. There was old anger and an ever-present
pain in his voice as he looked up at the calendar above
the phone.

With a hard slash, he raked the pen across the date,
marking one more day that she hadn't called.

"Damn you, Memphis. You've turned me inside out.
It's been two months and seventeen days since I heard
your voice. If you want to hear me bleed, just call. I'll
gladly oblige."

With a slump to his shoulders no one would have believed of the usually robust man, Matt turned and
walked out of the house, unable to bear the emptiness
of the rooms alone.

A brisk wind circled the yard, lifting bits of newly
mown grass from one spot and scattering them in another. He walked without seeing the daffodils on the
verge of blossom, didn't notice that the honeysuckle
climbing the pump house wall was heavy with buds
about to burst, didn't care that the same pair of robins
were back, making a new nest in the old birdhouse
Scott had made in a high school woodworking shop
class his sophomore year.

It was spring. A time of rebirth. Of new beginnings.
And his life was on hold, waiting to see if the woman
he loved had the guts to love him back. A pickup truck
topped the hill and started down the lane toward the

house. He paused, adjusting his Stetson a little lower across his face as he waited with his hands on his hips.

He recognized the vehicle. It was Nate Givens, and Charlie Todd would be along shortly. His part-time hired hands were arriving for the day's work. Nate waved as he drove past, heading for the barn area where he always parked. Matt started to follow when he thought of the message he'd found on his machine and stopped and turned. Well aware that Daisy Bedford probably had her damned telescope trained on him at this moment, he doffed his hat and blew her a kiss, then jammed it back on his head and headed for the barn. To hell with Daisy. To hell with women everywhere.

Thunder rumbled across the rolling Texas hills, followed by intermittent shafts of cloud to ground lightning that constantly cracked like the echo of a repeating rifle against a high canyon wall. Matt winced and resisted the urge to duck as he ran from the pickup to the house. Ducking would serve no purpose. If it hit him head high or down near his heels, he would still be fried. Getting out of it altogether was what he had in mind.

"Have mercy," he muttered as he cleared both back steps in one leap and entered the house on a run.

Water ran from his hat and down the back of his shirt. His jeans were soaked and plastered to his legs. It wasn't often that he got caught without rain gear, but this was one of those days.

The storm had come up without warning. One

minute it had been hot and sultry, the next thing he'd noticed was a cool wind blowing down his neck and black clouds rolling in, moving to the northeast at a deadly pace.

The chill in the house only added to the misery of wearing wet clothing. He shivered as he looked down at the puddle he was making and started peeling off clothes, one wet layer at a time.

When he was down to his briefs, he dumped the sodden pile of clothing on the washer and started through the house to get something dry. The message light was blinking as he walked past the phone. Knowing that the power could go off at any time and that it would be hours before he heard it, he punched the button and paused to listen.

When he heard Scott's voice, he grinned, but it faded as he listened to the panic in his voice.

Dad! It's me! For God's sake, call me. It's an emergency! I found Billie!

The message had ended, but Matt stared at the phone without moving. Emergencies and the woman he loved did not go together well in his mind. His hands were shaking as he started to dial, then realized he couldn't remember Scott's number.

He took a deep breath and tried it again. This time instinct carried him through until he heard his son's voice. Bracing himself for something he might not want to hear, he started to talk.

"Scott?"

Scott went limp. He'd been sitting by the phone for the better part of two hours, praying as he'd never prayed before. On the one hand, he wanted to be with Billie, and on the other, the news he had to tell could not have been left on an answering machine.

"Dad! Thank God!"

"Where is she?"

Scott winced. There was so much longing and fear in his father's voice that he wanted to cry. Instead, he started to talk and, because he was so upset, everything came out all at once and backwards.

"It was a miracle that we even found out. One of Stephanie's friends works as a volunteer at the hospital, and she saw them bring Billie in. She said she remembered Stephanie talking about Billie's odd disappearance and thought we'd want to know."

Matt's heart lurched. "Hospital? She's in a hospital? What happened? Was she in an accident?"

There was no easy way to say what had to be said, and he knew that keeping anything—even the tiniest bit of truth—from his father was impossible.

"Someone said she fell down some stairs. Julie, that's Stephanie's friend, said there was an older man with her when they brought her in. She thought it was her father, but she wasn't sure."

"Oh God, how far did she fall? Was she hurt bad? Is she conscious?" And then what Scott said suddenly clicked. "Her father? My God, they don't even speak anymore. What the hell was he doing there?" His mind raced, sorting through the possible scenarios without drawing any conclusion.

"Uh, Dad . . ."

Suddenly, Matt realized there was more, something

else he hadn't been told. Fear made him weak as he turned and leaned against the wall for support.

"What, goddammit! I'm hundreds of miles away and going out of my mind! Don't play with me, son! Spit it out!"

"She was pregnant, Dad. Billie was going to have a baby, and she lost it."

This time leaning against the wall didn't help. Matt staggered, then went to his knees. A loss he couldn't name, a devastation he had yet to comprehend, was driving all thought from his mind. All he could do was remember the feel of Billie coming apart in his arms and not knowing that they'd made more than love. They'd shared so much. Why, why hadn't she shared this with him as well?

"Dad? Are you all right?"

Too blinded to cry, too hurt to say more, all he could do was nod, and then he realized Scott could not see. When he took a deep breath and tried to talk, it came out as a moan.

Tears that Scott had been holding back started to fall. He'd known this news would hurt his father, but he hadn't been prepared for the level of devastation.

"Dad, are you going to be all right?"

Matt took another deep breath, then covered his face with his hand. "I'll be out on the next flight. Don't bother to pick me up. I'll take a cab. Which hospital is she in?"

With dogged determination, he made himself remember the directions Scott gave him, then crawled to his feet and hung up the phone. He immediately called to book a flight. After all the visits he'd made to California, he knew the number to the ticket counter at the Dallas/Fort Worth airport by heart.

Lightning ripped across the sky, cracking sharply through the line and popping the connection loudly in his ear as he waited for someone to answer his call. When they did, he was brief and to the point.

"This is Matt Holt. I need a ticket on the next flight to L.A."

"I'm sorry, sir, but flights are grounded for the time being."

"I don't care when it takes off, I just want a ticket on the next flight." And then he took a deep breath to still his shaking voice. "It's a family emergency, okay? Please. When is the next flight scheduled to leave?"

Sympathy replaced the clerk's normal tone of voice. In a few short minutes Matt had his ticket. Now all he had to do was get to the airport and pray that the storm would soon pass.

Matt stared blindly at the bright lights of the city framed by a thick cloak of darkness, trying to fathom which light marked the spot where his lady had lived, where their baby had died, where she was at this moment, alone in the dark and grieving for a child she'd never got to hold.

He drew a deep, shuddering breath, blocking out all but the task at hand. He had to find Billie. After that, things would be all right. They'd have to be.

Yet later, when he exited the hospital elevator, his duffel bag slung over his shoulder and his black Stetson jammed low across his forehead, he got a familiar whiff of hospital disinfectant and the odor of illness that lingers long after the patient has gone and he wondered if he'd been fooling himself. In a place like this, nothing was ever all right.

His boots made a short, clipped sound on the white-tiled floor. The duffel bag bounced and swayed with the rhythm of his walk as he followed the sound of voices toward what he assumed would be the nurses' station.

"Billie Walker's room, please."

The duty nurse looked up, as did two others standing nearby.

"I'm sorry, sir, but it's past midnight. Visiting hours were over long ago. You shouldn't even be on the floor."

"What room is she in?"

She rose from her seat. "I'm sorry, but you'll have to come back tomorrow. Visiting hours are over."

"You don't understand, I can't. Not until I see her."

"Sir. I said, you'll have to come back tomorrow. If you're not willing to follow the rules, I'm afraid I'll have to call security."

Matt leaned across the desk, pinning the nurse with a hard, blue glare, but his voice was shaking when he started to talk.

"I've been looking for my lady for months. Today I learned she fell and miscarried our baby . . . a baby I didn't even know existed." He took a deep breath as he struggled to continue. "I flew out of Dallas on the heels of a tornado and then had to sit between a man who snored and a woman who still hadn't stopped talking when the damned plane landed." Matt's voice broke as he pleaded. "Don't tell me I can't see her. Please. I won't make a sound. I won't even touch her. Just let me inside her room."

"Well," the nurse began, struggling with her own composure. His plea had been too moving to ignore, and she knew that the woman in question *had* suffered a miscarriage.

"Well now, I shouldn't."

Matt waited. He would have waited all night if need be.

Finally, she sighed. "Okay, come with me, but so help me, mister, if you don't do as you promised, I'll call security. Her welfare is what counts."

Matt followed her up the hall. When she paused and entered a room to their left, it took all his nerve to follow her inside.

Billie was alone in the room. Curled up on her side, one hand tucked beneath her chin, the other outflung, unable to bend because of the IV fastened to the back of her hand. Long, unruly tangles of the dark hair he so loved to touch were strewn across her face, as well as the pillow askew beneath her head.

He dropped his bag near the door and walked past the nurse to stop at the head of her bed. With a soft, gentle touch, he lifted the hair from her eyes, looking hard and long at the bruises and scrapes on her arms and face, at the drying tracks of tears on her face, at the tiny drops of blood on the pillow near her lip.

He lowered his head. "Billie, sweetheart, what have you done?"

"Sir, you can—"

He'd forgotten the nurse was still there. He turned, his eyes swimming with unshed tears. "Matt. My name is Matt Holt."

Her touch was gentle as she pointed to a chair in the corner. "Okay, Matt. You can pull this chair closer to the bed if you like, but please don't disturb her rest. She's sedated and needs to recover all her strength. She lost more than a baby today. She came close to losing her life. We had to transfuse her."

Matt's jaw tilted, taking the truth on the chin just as he'd taken every hard blow life had dealt.

"But she's going to make it . . . isn't she?"

She nodded and gave his arm a quick pat.

"Doctor says she's on the road to recovery. Barring any unforeseen complications, she should be fine." Her voice was low as she gazed back down at her patient upon the bed. "It's a tragedy that will take time to heal."

Matt blinked. He knew about tragedies. And he had the time. For Billie, he had all the time in the world.

"There will be other babies," she said softly.

Matt ached in too many places to count. "The baby . . . ?"

"A girl. She lost a little girl."

He turned, looking down at her poor injured face and remembering a time when it had been full of life and laughter, when they'd shared so much joy and so much love.

A baby girl.

Pain shattered within him. Tears that had been hanging on the edge of control pooled and spilled, flowing down his cheeks in silent misery. When he could think to move, he went for the chair, carried it as near to her bed as he could get, and quietly lowered himself into it. When the nurse was confident that the man was going to do as he promised, she slipped out of the room and went back to her duties. She'd broken one small rule this night, but from all that she'd seen, it was nothing compared to the lives that fate had just mangled.

✿✿✿ *Chapter 14*

The hospital shift was changing. Voices that had become familiar to Matt during the night were no longer around. He heard different people and more laughter than the soft, occasional chuckle he'd heard up the halls during the night. But it was daylight. There were rounds to be made. Baths to be given. Food to be fed. Life did go on, even when one was not inclined to let it.

True to his word, Matt had kept his distance from Billie although he'd heard every sigh, every moan, every tear that she'd shed in her semiconscious state. And he'd hurt and bled and cried along with her, but only in his heart. Not by word or deed had he let anyone see his pain, especially Billie. One of them had to be strong, and it was obviously not going to be her.

The chair in which he'd spent the night was back in the corner of the room where it belonged. He stood at the window, looking out at the new day.

Sunlight glittered across the roofs of the buildings, while a faint haze hovered just above the horizon. He knew from experience that as the day grew, the haze would thicken. While he watched, a helicopter lifted off from the hospital rooftop and circled in the air before aiming for some unknown destination.

Pedestrians down on the street were dodging traffic as they hurried to jobs, while down in a courtyard a gardener stood with hose in hand, watering various pots overflowing with colorful blooms. Bright, vivid colors that made him think of a child's paint box.

A child.

Sudden knowledge pierced him as he bowed his head and groaned. His baby would never see sunlight, or flowers, or run barefoot in the brown Texas earth. She'd never laugh, or talk, or run screaming through the house just from the joy of being alive. Yesterday her brief chance at life had ended.

Why, God, why? It just wasn't fair.

A soft, nearly nonexistent sigh sounded behind him. He spun. Silhouetted by the bright light coming through the window, he was nothing but a dark, looming shadow to the woman who lay on the bed.

Billie stared without blinking, looked without seeing, breathed without being alive. Sounds receded, leaving her somewhere deep within herself, where the pain couldn't find her, where the emptiness in her belly no longer existed.

Matt held his breath, waiting for her to speak, or at least in some way acknowledge his presence. When she did neither, he couldn't stand it anymore. He moved to her bedside and cupped her face with the palm of his hand. The touch was gentle, almost reverent, yet she didn't seem to know that he was there.

"Billie, sweetheart?"

It wasn't so much the silence that struck him as what he saw when he tilted her face to the sunlight and looked into her eyes. The dark, chocolate brown seemed dull, almost lifeless. An odd panicky feeling skipped along his nerves, warning him that things weren't all that they seemed. Her eyes were open, but he would have sworn she could not see.

"Billie?"

Still no answer.

"I love you, sweetheart. We'll get through this together, okay?"

Her eyelids started to fall shut, slowly, like curtains being pulled across a window. He thought that she was falling asleep until he realized that was only a blink. When they opened again, revealing the same blank stare, he shuddered, then took a step back.

"Oh God, Billie Jean, where have you gone?"

"Good morning. How are we doing?"

Matt looked up and glared at the nurse who entered the room. Where the hell did all that cheer come from when everything he'd loved in life seemed suddenly lost?

"What's wrong with her?"

His abrupt question startled the nurse into hastening to Billie's side. Vitals were taken and noted without comment.

"She hasn't spoken. She looks, but I don't think she sees me. Why? Did she hurt her head in the fall? Is her hearing impaired? Can she see?"

"You'll need to talk to doctor," the nurse said. "He's on the floor making rounds. I shouldn't think it will be too long before he arrives. After examining Miss Walker, I'm sure he'll be able to tell you more."

But when the doctor came in, Matt had to leave the room with his questions unanswered. He stood just outside the door, refusing to budge until the doctor came out. He was so focused on waiting for it to open that he didn't know Scott was there until he spoke.

"Dad."

Matt turned, and the look on his face made Scott sick.

"Dad, what's wrong? Is she worse?"

"The doctor's in with her now. I'm waiting to talk to him."

"What did she say when you got here last night?"

"Nothing. She was asleep."

"But she's awake now, what did she . . ." Scott stopped in midquestion and took a deep breath. His father was too quiet. Too still. Something was wrong. "Dad . . . she did wake up . . . didn't she?"

"Her eyes are open, but I don't think she's home."

The odd phrasing might have puzzled some, but not Scott. He'd heard that remark all of his life, and the connotation was not promising.

"You mean she's . . ."

"I don't know what I mean," Matt said. "All I know is when she opened her eyes, she wasn't *seeing* what was before her. Hell, she didn't even blink when she looked into the sunlight."

Scott felt sick. He couldn't imagine the Billie they'd known going through life in darkness. "Oh man, what if the fall damaged her sight?"

"I don't care," Matt said shortly. "I don't care if she never sees again. I just want her to get well. We'll deal with whatever else comes, but we'll do it together." And then his voice broke, and he looked away, unwilling to let anyone see him cry. "I just don't understand why she kept this from me. She knew I loved her. I told her so damned many times, in so many ways."

There was nothing else to be said for the truth, so they waited, and as they did, another man exited the elevator and walked rapidly toward Billie's room.

When Jarrod saw the doctor coming out of the door, he hastened his step, preempting Matt's questions.

"Doctor! You've been in to see my daughter! How is she?"

Matt forgot what he'd been about to ask Billie's doctor as he absorbed the fact that the man behind him had to be Jarrod Walker.

He turned slowly, letting his gaze rake across the cool, almost-indifferent expression on the big man's face while the doctor reacted to the question.

"Mr. Walker, isn't it? I remember you from yesterday."

They shook hands cordially while Matt stood to one side, waiting to hear what the doctor was about to say and see how the man who called himself Billie's father would take it.

"She's awake," the doctor said. "And that's good. Her vital signs are stronger. The transfusion helped that, of course."

Jarrod maintained a calm expression while his belly flopped. Awake! Oh God, then that meant she could talk. He needed to talk to her. To assure her that he'd never meant for her to fall. Sweat beaded beneath his armpits and on the palms of his hands, but it wasn't heat, it was panic. He could envision himself being arrested on the spot.

"That's good, that's good," he muttered. "But when can I see her? I need to talk to her, to explain."

That was an odd thing to say. Without giving himself time to reconsider, Matt stepped into the conversation without introduction.

"Explain what?"

The growl in the big cowboy's voice surprised Jarrod. He'd seen him standing there, but had assumed he'd been waiting to talk to the doctor about something else.

He hadn't considered that he might be there on Billie's behalf until he'd heard the anger in his voice.

"Who are you? And what business is it of yours why I need to talk to my own daughter?"

Matt took another step forward just as Scott grabbed for his arm.

"Dad . . . easy does it, okay?"

"You were with her when she fell, weren't you? What I want to know is how it happened."

Jarrod blanched. He was too late. Billie must have already said something for them to be so suspicious.

"It wasn't my fault. We'd been arguing, you know how parents and children can fuss. It didn't amount to anything, not really."

Matt's hands curled into fists. "What wasn't your fault?"

"Why, that she fell. We sort of collided on the stairwell. She staggered, and I grabbed for her. I never meant for her to fall."

"You son of a bitch."

Before Scott could react, Matt's fist connected with the side of Jarrod's jaw. He went down like a pole-axed steer. One minute Jarrod was looking into the wild, blue eyes of a pissed-off man, and the next thing he saw was the ceiling. Staggering to his feet, he grabbed his jaw, ready to dodge the next blow, but the doctor jumped between them.

"I'll have none of this on my floor. If you two have a disagreement, you'll take it outside, or I'll call security."

Matt was so mad he was shaking. "Call them. While you're at it, call the police. It sounds to me like this man might have some explaining to do."

Jarrod paled even more. "This is none of your damned business," he grumbled, and then winced as his jaw began to feel as if it had just come unhinged.

"That's where you're wrong. It's *all* my business. That's the woman I love lying in there on that bed. That was my child she lost. I warned you once to leave her alone, remember? You should have taken my advice."

Nausea rolled through Jarrod, taking what was left of his nerve with it. This had to be the cowboy from Texas!

"We'll just see about that," he said. "I want to talk to my daughter, now."

Again, the doctor intervened. "That's what I've been

trying to tell you. At this point, talking to her is impossible. She seems to have suffered more than physical trauma from this accident. I've already called Dr. Seifert in for a consultation. We'll know more after he's seen her."

"Who's Dr. Seifert?" Matt asked. "What more is there to know?"

"He's a psychiatrist. From my initial exam I'd say that Miss Walker is suffering an emotional withdrawal of some kind. She's cognizant of some things, but others . . . it's as if she's chosen to shut part of her life out." He frowned, and pushed both men farther apart. "Now, settle your differences somewhere else. I have rounds to make."

While Matt's hopes took a new nosedive, Jarrod was counting his blessings. In spite of everything, he saw a way out.

"Doctor, wait please! This is terrible, just terrible," he said quickly. "Know that you have my permission to do whatever it takes for her treatment, and I'd appreciate it if you would recommend some sort of care facility for her after she's released. I'm assuming she'll need around-the-clock care and, if she's declared incompetent, I'll need to go to court and get a power of attorney . . . on her behalf, you understand."

This time, Scott caught his father before it was too late. "Don't, Dad. Don't hit him again . . . at least not here."

Matt was livid. Billie had been right all along. All this man wanted was an avenue to her money. And talk of having her committed was more than he could bear. His voice was barely above a whisper as he shrugged out of Scott's arms and jabbed a finger into Jarrod's chest.

"No one's sending her anywhere. When she's ready to be released, I'm taking her home with me. If she needs around-the-clock care, I'll see that she gets it, and I don't need her damned money to do it. She took you to court once to get you out of her life, and you can bet your last dollar that I won't let you back into her life again. Now, I'd recommend you get out of my sight before I call the police myself and let them sort through what is left of her life."

"Gentlemen . . . do I call security?"

The doctor's question hung in the air between them, but Matt stood his ground. He didn't care if they called the National Guard. He wasn't leaving Billie's side.

The tension grew as Jarrod stared, gauging the cowboy's warning against all that he knew. The man stared back, unwavering, unblinking, until Jarrod finally snapped.

"Fine, and to hell with you both. It doesn't matter anyway, she's all yours. She's not really my child. I told her yesterday she wasn't, and I'm saying it again. Her mother was a weak, lying whore who didn't have the guts to stay around for the fight. You can have her. I don't care. She'll wind up just like her mother . . . you'll see."

With that, he turned and walked off, leaving Matt speechless, unable to believe what he'd just heard.

Scott tried to imagine how Billie had reacted, hearing that kind of news. "Oh man, Dad, they must have had one hell of a fight."

The doctor sighed. "It takes all kinds, and I'd better make a note of this latest development. It could help Dr. Seifert make some sense of this. If Miss Walker suffered some sort of personal shock or revelation right before she lost the baby, that might account for her unwillingness to communicate now."

The doctor left, but Matt refused to move until Jarrod Walker had disappeared from sight.

Scott stepped up beside him, hesitating to break the silence between them. He'd never seen his father this mad and out of control.

"Dad, are you all right?"

The anger showing in Matt's eyes was as close to white-hot as an emotion could be.

"No, but I will be." And then he turned toward Billie's room, looking beyond the doorway to the woman who lay so still upon the bed. "And if I have anything to say about it, so will she."

It was the plane ride from hell. The only saving grace was that the flight was direct, and that Matt only had to negotiate Billie through two airports instead of three. By the time they landed in Dallas, his stomach was in knots, while Billie seemed oblivious to all that went on around her.

He'd endured snide remarks and sidelong glances of sympathy on her behalf until he was ready to fight snakes barefoot. When the plane finally landed, he held her hand and waited until everyone else had disembarked. A stewardess who'd helped Billie in and out of the bathroom twice during the flight came back to their seats to offer her assistance as Matt began the time-consuming job of getting her to move of her own accord.

"Is there anything I can do?"

He felt like crying, but managed a slight smile instead.

"Maybe say a prayer for her?"

She touched Billie lightly on the arm.

"She's very pretty."

And so damned lost. But Matt didn't say it. Instead, he smiled again and thanked her.

With the help of a redcap and airport security, he managed to retrieve their luggage and his truck. Only when he had her safely buckled inside the cab and out of the airport did he breathe a slight sigh of relief. One hurdle down, only God knew how many left to go.

He resisted the urge to pull her closer. Buckled in beside him in the middle of the seat, she was as close as he could get her.

Her head bobbed with the bounce of the truck as it moved along the highway. She stared forward with no particular intent, neither focusing nor blinking with any degree of regularity. Only now and then did he see her look, really look at something. But it was so brief, and always at something inanimate. It wasn't anything from which he could take hope.

"Billie . . . sweetheart?"

He waited for her to respond, although he'd already accepted that it wasn't going to happen. At least not yet. When she remained silent, he pretended that she'd somehow answered.

"Are you as hungry as I am?" He kept talking as he drove, carefully maneuvering his way through the busy traffic. "Don't you think we'd better stop and get something to eat before we get home? I've been gone nearly two weeks. Whatever was in the refrigerator is bound to have spoiled."

Finally he stopped talking, more from despair than from lack of anything to say. Half an hour later he turned off the highway and onto an access road, aiming for a McDonald's just ahead. He ordered for two, wondering if he was going to have to eat both, and then breathed a small sigh of relief when he handed Billie her hamburger and she lifted it to her mouth.

"Well, thank God for small favors," he muttered, watching in amazement as she bit and chewed until the food was all gone. At least somewhere inside she was willing to function on a life-sustaining level.

When she was finished, her hands dropped to her lap, as if they'd run out of anything else to do.

"Here, baby," he said softly, and slipped a straw into her mouth. "You must be thirsty after all of that."

It took a moment, but she reacted once again, only not to him, but to the sustenance that was being offered. As she drank, Matt knew that she would have accepted the same thing from her father had he offered . . . and she hated his guts.

"Do you need to go to the bathroom?"

He waited. Before when he'd asked, she'd moved of her own accord. This time, when she didn't react, he took it as a firm no.

"Okay, then, we're off. I don't know about you, but

I can't wait to get home. I'm sick and tired of sleeping in someone else's bed."

He dumped their trash in a curbside barrel and pulled back onto the highway.

Okay, God, you've been with me this far. I'm counting on you for the rest of the ride. Just let me get her home. After that, I think I can handle about anything.

Like Billie, God didn't answer, but Matt felt better for having asked. And when he topped the hill that led toward home, a knot of tension in the back of his neck began to unwind. He glanced at his silent passenger and managed a slight grin.

"Hey, Memphis, look down there. We're home."

The pickup truck hit a rut, bouncing Billie off to one side. Before Matt could think to react, she reached out, grabbing onto his leg and righting herself in the seat.

It wasn't much as incidents go, but for Matt it was damn near a miracle. He didn't care whether she even knew that it was him she'd grabbed on to. What mattered was she'd reached for help. One day, she'd do it again, and he was going to be there waiting when it happened.

"That's my girl," he said softly, and patted her on the knee. "You hang in there, baby. When you're ready to come back, I'll be waiting."

He hadn't seen the videocassette until unpacking her clothes while getting her ready for bed. Even then he hadn't wondered what it might be, or even why it was in her things. Not even Jarrod had been aware of the significance of the cassette that the paramedics had found at her side and transported with her to the ER. It had been with her when she was admitted to and released from the hospital, as well as making its way through baggage checks.

He'd tossed it aside to help her into a nightgown and robe. Only after he'd taken her by the hand and led her back down the hall to the living room did he drop it by the VCR.

"Let's watch a little television while I brush your hair, okay, honey?"

Billie neither agreed nor disagreed. She simply stood, waiting for him to make her next move.

"Here, darlin', sit down on this cushion while I go get your brush."

With little more than a nudge, Billie dropped crosslegged onto the cushion, staring glassy-eyed at the picture that had come on the screen.

Matt ran from the room and was back in seconds. When he returned, he realized he'd been holding his breath, fearful that when he left she would somehow disappear. He sighed, then leaned against the doorway, wiping a weary hand across his face. If he survived this, he could survive anything.

With little more than lamplight by which to see, he sat on the couch behind her, then pulled her between his legs, using his knees as braces against her shoulders. With more gentleness than one could have imagined from a man of the land, he took down her hair.

At first the brush felt cool in his hands, but the longer he held it, the warmer the handle became. Carefully, so as not to catch any tangles, he began to pull it through her hair. Over and over in long, easy strokes, he brushed. One side, then the other. Minutes turned into a half hour and then an hour, and when he felt her relax, he knew she was responding to him on some level.

"That feels good, doesn't it, darlin'?"

And he kept on brushing.

There was a huge, gaping hole in her heart. She knew it was so because, when she drew breath, she imagined she could hear an eerie wail where love used to be. She was beyond physical pain, responding only to the stimuli that she needed to survive. She ate without tasting. Drank without knowing relief. Tended to her bodily functions automatically. Only once had an awareness of where she was intruded, but it had happened so quickly that she'd not had time to prepare.

It was the sudden movement of falling to one side. The same sensation she'd had just before tumbling down the stairs. Back then, she'd reached out, but no one had been there to right her. Today had been different. Today when she felt herself falling she'd reached out and connected with reality. That it was the hard, muscled thigh of Matt Holt didn't register in her mind. All she'd known was that this time something had saved her from pain.

And now there was a strange sort of peace surrounding her, easing the lost, panicked feeling that seemed to keep her at bay. She didn't know that she rested between the strength of his legs, or that his broad, gentle hands were soothing her in the only way he knew how. For now, being safe was enough.

When her hair was sleek as silk and sliding between his fingers without pause, he knew that he'd done all he could. Tossing the brush aside, he swung a leg over her head and shoved himself up from the couch to get the remote control. He didn't know about her, but he was in no mood for sitcoms.

His attention returned to the videocassette that he'd set aside earlier and, once again, he wondered why she would have an unlabeled tape in her possession.

"There's only one way to find out." He shoved it into the VCR before going back to the couch. "Come here, darlin'." He lifted her from the cushion and into his arms. "We're going to the movies, okay? You pretend this is a drive-in . . ." His composure shattered as he gathered her close, whispering softly in her ear. "And I'll pretend that you care."

With only half an eye on the television screen, he went about the business of securing her safely within his arms. Making a lap for her, he angled her long legs off the floor and onto the couch, until it almost looked as if she'd crawled in his lap and simply gone to sleep. Her head was on his shoulder, her arms lying limply in her lap.

"Just rest. I've got you safe, and no one's ever going to hurt you again."

Then he focused on the screen, and there was no one present to witness his shock or the overwhelming pain that spread across his face.

*   *   *

Daisy Bedford was past angry and too close to panic for someone her age. She'd left so many nervous messages on Matt Holt's machine that it was a wonder he hadn't driven by and set her house afire out of pure spite. It wasn't until a few days ago that she realized he wasn't even home, and that was because Nate Givens had had the misfortune of having a flat right in front of her house and knocked on her door to use the phone because he didn't have a spare. He'd told her Matt had gone to L.A. for a few days.

Today she'd breathed a huge sigh of relief when she'd seen that familiar truck come flying over the hill and past her house. She'd had an overwhelming urge to run out and flag him down just to hear him cuss. But she'd resisted it and had settled instead for a perch by her upstairs window with spyglass in hand, peering through first one eye and then the other for a sign that would tell her all was well.

It didn't come.

She knew Matt better than nearly anyone alive. He'd been gone for the better part of two weeks. She'd seen him unload his guest and the baggage. He hadn't come back out again. That was another thing that didn't sit right.

No rancher worth his salt would walk into a house and then stay inside after a two-week absence without running out to check his stock and property, unless he'd gone and gotten himself married . . . or something was wrong.

She knew it was Billie Walker he'd brought back.

She recognized that head of dark hair and those long legs. What didn't seem right was the stiff set to her posture and the way she seemed to stumble against him as he'd helped her inside.

By the time darkness settled, Daisy was leaning toward the theory that trouble was afoot. She stared through her telescope, waiting for a small sign of life that didn't come, until she refused to wait anymore.

With the determination of a woman half her age, she grabbed her hat and headed outdoors with flashlight in hand.

"All he can do is tell me to mind my own damned business. At least I'll sleep better knowing I'm wrong." Having settled her reason for being nosy firmly in mind, she started her truck, turned on the lights, and drove to the ranch house far down the road.

Chapter 15

Now that Daisy was at the ranch, the idea didn't seem as brilliant as it had when she'd left home. Twice she started to knock and hesitated. She could just imagine what Matt might do or say if she interrupted a honeymoon session in progress. But every time she thought about leaving, something held her back. She'd been operating on gut instinct for too many years to ignore it all now.

Although the house was dark, a faint glow from a single burning lamp spilled out from the window and onto the porch—a faded yellow square of illumination on the weathered flooring, like melting butter on slightly burned toast.

Daisy went to the window, angling her head to the part in the curtains until she could see into the room. He was there, sitting on the couch with that girl in his arms. She should have been satisfied with what she saw, but she wasn't. There was something terribly wrong with this picture. No newlywed she knew sat holding his bride while he cried.

The last time she'd seen him this devastated was on

the day of Susan's funeral. It was that memory alone that gave her the nerve to intrude.

She knocked. Briefly. Lightly.

No footsteps sounded across the floor. No door opened to admit her. She knocked once more. This time more firmly, with more authority.

She moved back to the window. He was still there, unmoving. And the tears still fell.

Panic preceded every thought as she dashed back to the door. She opened the screen, wincing as it squeaked on its hinges. Her fingers curled around the doorknob as she gripped, then turned. It gave without effort, and Daisy found herself standing just inside the door.

The air was still, the room silent. The television played with no sound, while Matt sat staring at strange images undulating across the screen in a mystical, black-and-white ballet. Billie lay motionless in his arms, looking blankly toward the darkened hallway leading toward the bedrooms as if she was expecting to see a ghost suddenly appear. On the surface, the scene was almost idyllic, and yet there was an underlying sense of despair.

"Matt."

He didn't respond. In fact, she didn't think he even knew she was there.

"It's me, Daisy. Is everything all right?"

He blinked, then drew a long, shuddering breath, his head moving in slow motion as he finally turned to look at her.

"Daisy?"

She closed the door, and only after she started toward him did she realize she was walking on tiptoes.

"I was worried."

The tape ran to the end. Like a robot, Matt hit the rewind button. While Daisy was trying to make sense of it all, Billie suddenly took a deep breath. As she did, it seemed that everything came to a stop.

The tape clicked. Matt froze and stared down at Billie with a desperate, waiting expression on his face. When she finally exhaled, then relaxed, he closed his eyes briefly in some nameless, voiceless pain. Only when Daisy spoke again did he remember that she was even there.

"Is she sick?"

He dropped the remote to brush wayward strands of hair from Billie's face. The motion was so light, so gentle. Daisy had never seen a man behave in this way, especially Matt Holt.

"Damn it, boy, you're starting to scare me," she muttered. "You can tell me it's none of my business, but I need to know what's going on just the same."

He looked down at the clear, perfect features on Billie's face. If he squinted just right, he could make himself believe that she was in a dozing, dreamy state. But he wasn't the kind of person to live in a make-believe world, and neither, he knew, was Daisy.

He picked up the remote and hit the play button. With eyes fixed on the graphic images that suddenly appeared, he started to talk, and Daisy had to lean close to catch all he said through the catches in his voice.

"See her?"

Daisy stared first at the screen, then down at Billie, trying to make sense of what he'd just said.

"See Billie? Yes, boy, I see her, but what's that got to do with what's on the tape?"

"No, her." He pointed toward the television. "That's the only picture I'll ever have of our daughter." His mouth curved in a sad, lost grin. "Just look at her roll. Ah, damn. Wouldn't she have played heck on this ranch? All this wide-open space to grow up in."

Daisy dropped into the chair behind her, gripping the arms with her arthritic fingers to keep from falling on her face as shock swept over her. Baby?

"How did you get such a thing?" she muttered, staring in disbelief at the vague, distorted images on the screen.

Matt took a deep breath, gauging his pain around the words that must be said. "Modern medicine is a miracle, isn't it? That's an ultrasound of the baby Billie was carrying. It takes a while to figure out what you're seeing, and then when you do . . ." His voice trailed off as his attention locked once again on the mobile little image.

Daisy slumped. *Was* their baby? She looked down at Billie's flat belly and sighed. Oh my. This was worse than she'd thought.

"Why isn't she talking? Is she all right? Was she in an accident?" Then she realized she was whispering.

Matt tightened his grip as he looked into Daisy' eyes.

"No, Daisy, she's not all right. This was the way

found her when I got to L.A." Once again, his voice broke, and he leaned down and kissed Billie's forehead near her hairline. "She fell down a flight of stairs and lost the baby."

Daisy pursed her lips as she struggled not to make this sound like an accusation. "I didn't know you were going to be a father."

"I didn't know it either."

A new tear tracked its way after the one drying on his face. There was a bitterness in his voice of which he wasn't aware, but Daisy heard and saw and knew that Billie Walker wasn't the only one suffering from this tragedy.

"Well now. I guess she had her reasons." She glanced at Billie. "Only I don't suppose she's said much about them yet, has she?"

Matt shook his head. "The doctors call this stress-induced trauma. It's affected her emotionally rather than physically. Personally, I think she's just lost. One of these days she'll remember I'm here, and then she'll come back to me. I believe that because I can't live thinking any other way."

Fear made her angry. Daisy hated to be afraid, and he was talking crazy. The very idea. People being lost inside themselves. Not being able to live without her.

"You listen here, Matt Holt. You can do anything you set your mind to, and you know it. This isn't the first time you've had yourself a setback, and if life's what I think it is, it won't be the last. If you want her to get better, then you can't be draggin' your ass around like some whipped dog. You've got to behave as if nothin' is wrong, or she's gonna be afraid to give life another try. You hear me?"

When he didn't answer, she yanked the remote control from his hand and pointed toward the screen.

"How long you been watchin' this?"

"I don't know."

She turned it off. "However long it was, it's enough for today. That's not to say you can't ever watch it again, but I don't think you ought to just now. Not when the loss is so new. And don't tell me I don't know what I'm talkin' about, 'cause I do. I buried two babies and my man before I was thirty-five years old. You can't dwell on the past, boy, or it will eat you alive."

When Matt didn't answer, she got down in his face. "You hear me, Matt Holt?"

He blinked, then slowly looked up. For a long, silent moment, neither spoke. Finally, he was the one to break the glare.

"Yes, ma'am. I believe that I do."

Daisy let out a pent-up sigh. "Well! Then that's that. I'll just let myself out. You get up and get yourselves to bed. Tomorrow will be a busy day. You've been gone nearly two weeks, you know. Amory's bull has been bellowing at the northeast corner of the pasture for days, and you need to check that fence and make sure it's not down. Also, I heard in town the other day that one of the Bailer boys bought some cows at auction and the darn things come down with shipping fever. Their pasture joins one of your lease lands, right? And . . ."

Matt grabbed Daisy's hand. The grip was firm but gentle. "I get the picture."

He looked back at Billie, realizing for the first time since his declaration to bring her home that he should have gone about the business of hiring a nurse to look after her when he had to be out working.

Daisy was already ahead of him.

"If you think you can manage at night, I'll be here bright and early every morning. I don't do a thing but sit in that drafty old house by myself anyhow. May as well be doin' somethin' useful."

For once, he was speechless. "Daisy, I can't ask you to—"

"You didn't. I offered. Now that's that. Get yourself some sleep and do like I said."

He caught her off guard when he pulled her toward him. Before she knew it, he'd kissed her on the cheek.

"Look here," she spluttered. "I'll have none of that. This is a hands-off offer. If you're wantin' to fool around, you're gonna have to look elsewhere."

Matt laughed. As far as laughter goes, it wasn't much. But it was the first time he'd felt like it in a very long while.

"Daisy Bedford, if you were younger or I was older, I'd give you a run for your money."

Her mouth pursed as she yanked herself out of his grasp. "No you wouldn't, you good-lookin' liar. You've already got the love of your life right there in your arms. What we've got to do is get her well."

"Yes, ma'am, that we do."

Daisy's tears came swiftly and unexpectedly, blurring what she saw of Matt's face as well as the room around her. With a huff, she hustled to the door before she did something silly, like cry.

"Lock this door when I leave. Just anyone could walk right in, you know."

The door shut with a thump, and moments later he heard the sound of her truck driving away.

He looked down at Billie, then picked up her hand, threading their fingers together until it looked as if they were clasped. So slim, so fragile. Just like the hold she had on life.

"Are you getting sleepy, sweetheart?"

She blinked slowly, and then, to Matt's surprise, a single tear appeared in the corner of one eye and rolled down her cheek. He hid his face against her hair and took a slow, deep breath, calming himself before he could speak.

"Me too, Memphis. Me too."

There was little else he could say to let her know how deeply he mourned their shared loss. Carefully, he shifted her on his lap, then stood up with her in his arms.

"You might not know it, and you don't have to care, but I can't find the strength to let you out of my arms. We might not communicate on one level, but we can on another. When we sleep, it will be together or not at all. Got that?"

Shadows loomed as he started down the long hallway toward the bedrooms at the far end of the house. A light burned in the bathroom that adjoined them. When they entered the room he put her down. For a moment she stood, as if orienting herself with being upright instead of reclining.

When it seemed that she had, she turned and walked into the bathroom without shutting the door. He sighed. The least he could do was give her privacy. Remembering Daisy's orders to lock up, he went back through the house to the front door. When he reentered the room, she was sitting on the edge of the bed, staring at her hands.

Matt gritted his teeth, unwilling to let the futility of it all overwhelm him. Talking quietly but calmly, he took off her robe before gently scooting her to the inside of the bed, then he undressed and crawled in beside her. She moved restlessly as he straightened the covers, aware on some level that she was in a strange place.

"Come here, sweetheart."

He held her close, offering his chest as a pillow. When her struggles ceased, he felt deliverance from at least one small worry. If it gave her any measure of comfort, he was happy to oblige.

He didn't expect to get much sleep, but when he next opened his eyes, it was morning.

In that first tiny glimmer of cognizance before full awakening comes, before past events become memories, he held her while she slept and knew an overwhelming sense of peace that all was right with his world. And then reason dawned and old aches came rushing back. The lost feeling of loving someone and not knowing where they were. The emptiness that comes from love not being enough, and the shattering pain of death with which the living must come to terms.

It was a new day, and already his throat was tightening and his eyes burned, reminding him of how many tears he'd shed. Just when he was about to give in to a new wave of despair, he realized something was different than it had been when they'd gone to bed.

Last night when he'd pulled Billie into his arms, she'd come without objection but with no cooperation. His breathing stilled as he lifted his head and looked down at the way she was lying.

She'd thrown her leg across the lower half of his body, almost pinning him into place. One of her hands was tucked beneath her chin, while her forehead rested against his shoulder. She'd slung her other arm across his belly and, even in sleep, was clutching at him in mute desperation.

"Ah, Billie, trust your instincts, darlin', they're trying to tell you something."

Joy filled him as he gathered her close, and it lasted until her eyelids quivered and the rhythm of her breathing began to change. He could feel her waking up . . . and withdrawing . . . and he tried not to care.

That's all right. One of these days you're going to forget yourself, woman, and when you do, I'll snatch you back from that hell you crawled into and never let you go.

True to her word, Daisy Bedford was on the front porch before he had finished dressing. When he opened the door, she pretended to frown at his bare chest and elbowed her way in the house, holding a foil-wrapped pan before her like a queen bearing gifts.

Matt grinned. "Hope that's not sweet potatoes. I like them just fine, but not for breakfast."

"Go put on your clothes before the biscuits get cold."

He leaned over the pan, lifting the edge of the foil and sniffing deeply in appreciation. "Mmm, Daisy Mae, you're too good to be true."

She glared. "My name is not Mae, and I'm gonna give you what for if you don't do as you're told."

He followed her into the kitchen.

Daisy noted the empty sink and the tidy cabinet tops—a sure sign that, as yet, no one had been fed. "Where's the girl?"

"In my room. I haven't had a chance to get her dressed yet."

"Then first things first," Daisy said, and led the way to his room. "I'll help her while you finish dressing. Then while you two eat . . ." She paused to look at Billie with a long, considering stare. "Does she feed herself?"

"Yes, ma'am."

"Okay then. While you eat, you can tell me what needs to be done."

He knew she was going to fuss, but he couldn't help but hug her all the same. He wrapped his arms around her, cuddling her close against his bare chest and feeling the withered, fragile bones of a woman who'd outlived nearly everyone she loved.

"I love you, Daisy Bedford." Then he kissed her before he set her free. "In a friendly sort of way, you understand."

She flushed, then grimaced, deepening the wrinkles in her face.

"You're a worthless sort, but I suppose I care for you, too." And then she grinned. "Like I might some stray pup."

Billie sighed and rolled over on the bed, then onto her feet, pulling off her nightgown as she walked into the bathroom. Once again, she seemed not to notice that the door was ajar or that company had arrived.

"Well I never," Daisy spluttered as more and more of Billie's bare limbs were revealed.

Matt smiled gently, then reached out and closed the door.

"I don't think she realizes that we're here. Somehow she's shut out everything except what she's able to deal with, and that isn't much."

"We'll find a way," Daisy said. "Together, boy, we'll find a way."

Mel Deal's long, bony legs dangled from the tailgate of Matt's pickup as he sat nursing a beer. The invitation to come to the ranch and visit Billie had been a surprise, although he and Matt had been in touch almost from the onset of her condition.

The hospital had found Mel's name in her purse as next of kin, and per hospital policy, promptly notified him of her condition. He'd arrived only hours after Jarrod Walker's exit and found himself in the position of becoming moral backup for the man Billie had obviously loved.

A preconceived judgment he'd made of Matt Holt made a swift about-face when he'd realized that not only had Billie kept her whereabouts a secret from Matt, but she'd hidden the fact that she was pregnant with his child.

This weekend visit had been cathartic for both men. Mel had a chance to see firsthand that Billie was healing in body, if not in mind, and that she was not just being cared for, but was, quite literally, being coddled.

Mel had never seen anyone hover as Matt did around Billie. The man's love for her was obvious in everything he said and did, but worry was taking its toll on him. The clean, handsome lines of his face were sharper, more defined. He'd lost weight since Mel had first met him in L.A., and from the shadows in Matt's eyes, also sleep.

Mel glanced at the man sitting beside him and tried not to let his concern for Matt show, choosing to focus on a topic on which they'd both agree.

Billie wandered about the courtyard in front of the house. The white, gauzy dress she had on hung from her body like a curtain, only now and then revealing the outline of what was beneath. She wore it because it was cool, because it was easy to put on, and because Matt had dressed her in it when he got up.

Mel's hands tightened around the brown long-neck. "She looks good, doesn't she?"

Matt nodded. "She likes the garden. Daisy even caught her watering something the other day. I took it as a good sign." His eyes crinkled until there was nothing but mere slits of blue showing through. "You know . . . as a kind of a nurturing thing."

Tears burned the back of Mel's throat, and he tilted the brown long-neck and swallowed beer and tears alike. "Yes, I know what you mean. It's just so damned hard seeing her like this."

Billie knelt, momentarily moving out of Matt's line of sight, and he stiffened and frowned. When she stood, he relaxed. "Something makes her happy, even if it's not me. Look at the way she smiles."

Sunlight fell on the child's head, burnishing the soft curls and warming her bare shoulders as she toddled through the flowers in the front yard. A butterfly fitted across her line of vision. As she turned to follow its ascent, the bright, wide-eyed look she gave Billie made her laugh with delight.

"Look, baby! It's a butterfly. Can you say butterfly?"

Baby smiled a wide, happy smile and went after the bright-winged insect in hot pursuit. Billie followed the child with her mind, never letting her out of her sight. Her breath caught as she watched the child's progress. How like Matt she was. All that thick black hair, and those piercing blue eyes. Oh my, she was going to be such a charmer. She'd drive all the boys . . . and her daddy . . . just wild.

Billie smiled, then waved. "Come back, baby. You've gone far enough."

Baby stopped, the pursuit of the butterfly forgotten as she grabbed for a fistful of flowers instead.

Billie laughed and ran for her, bending down just in time to save the blossoms from being beheaded.

"Oh, no you don't. I know you. You weren't going to smell them, you were going to eat them."

Her arms encircled the child's tiny body, savoring the sweet baby smell and the sensation of little arms wrapping around her neck.

"I love you so much," Billie murmured, and nuzzled her nose in the head full of curls. "Yes, I do. Mama loves you and your daddy more than anyone else in this world."

She walked back to the front porch, bouncing the child in her arms. Baby wiggled, then snuggled, slowly relaxing as Billie dropped into an old cane rocker Matt kept in the shade. Settling the child in her arms, she pushed off with her toe. Back and forth, back and forth they rocked. And time passed while Billie's arms and her heart were full.

Mel squinted the distance. "She sure likes that rocker, doesn't she?"

Matt nodded.

"I'm going to have to be leaving soon. I'm due back in court tomorrow."

Matt glanced up at the porch, watching the woman in white who sat rocking to her heart's content. "You may not believe me, but she knows that you came. She's been real easy this weekend. Sometimes she's not, you know."

Mel swallowed the last of his beer and set the empty behind him in the truck bed. There was something he needed to say, and he didn't want to make a fool of himself when he said it.

"Uh . . . Matt?"

His gaze moved from Billie to Mel, and he waited for what would be said.

"There's something I've been needing to say to you ever since we met in L.A."

Matt stiffened, expecting judgment.

Mel cleared his throat. "You're a real good man, Matt Holt. Not many would have done what you've done."

He frowned and looked away, slightly embarrassed. He knew Billie viewed Mel and his wife, Adelene, as the parents she never had, but it felt good to know that they hadn't judged him and found him wanting.

"I didn't do anything special except fall in love with your girl."

"That's not so. I don't know many men who would have undertaken what you've done. And the fact that you don't resent what happened to her makes it even better." Then he grinned, trying to lighten the seriousness of the conversation. "The only thing I regret out of this whole damned mess is that I missed seeing you deck Jarrod Walker."

Matt grinned slightly. "Who told you about that?"

"Your son. The doctor. Several nurses. You pulled a real Hollywood hero stunt, didn't you?"

Matt still believed that Jarrod Walker had somehow been responsible for the baby's death, and the thought made him sick.

"Hell no," he muttered. "I was too close to murder for that."

Mel nodded. "I know what you mean. I've been at that point with him a few times myself over the years, just never had the guts to do it."

Matt grinned a little broader. "Well now, if you ask Daisy, guts are not my shortcoming, but brains are. I don't know if maybe you weren't the wiser. I made myself a real enemy in Jarrod Walker. I just hope to hell he stays out of her life."

Mel slapped his knee. "That reminds me, I meant to tell you. The bastard seems to have lucked out again. He actually found himself a woman with money, which is what he's spent his life trying to attain. Last I heard, they were on their way to Acapulco to get married." Then he grinned. "I hope her purse strings are tight, and the noose around his neck that much tighter. I hope he has to dance to her tunes for the rest of his miserable life."

"Amen," Matt said, then abruptly slid off the tailgate as Billie wandered around to the back of the house. "I don't know where Daisy is. I'd better . . ."

At that moment, Daisy appeared, holding Billie's hand and talking to her a mile a minute. Billie didn't seem to be bothered that her destination had been altered without her consent, and Daisy hadn't bothered to ask.

"You're real lucky to have her, you know," Mel said.

Matt silently watched both women, one old that life had not been able to break, one young and trying to heal. In his mind, he knew Mel was referring to Daisy, but somehow the two had become intertwined. His luck was that both women had entered his life when he'd needed them most. It was only fair that he return the favor.

Mel offered his hand. "I'd better get going. Again, I can't thank you enough for the invitation." He glanced back up at the house. "Guess I better say my good-byes to her, too, even though it'll go in one ear and out the other."

Matt watched Billie as she strolled across the yard with Daisy riding shotgun. "She knows. Don't think for a minute she doesn't. I'm convinced that one of these days she's going to turn around and give me hell for something I just said or did. And when it happens it'll be because I let her hang out with Daisy too long." A lonely expression drifted across his face, then away so quickly that one could almost imagine it had never been. "So help me God, I can't wait."

He watched as Mel walked toward the house, then looked away when Billie froze in his arms. It was always the same. Something was making her happy, but whatever it was, contact with another human being always drove it away.

A shadow suddenly crossed Billie's line of vision and she lost momentary contact with the baby. Fear for the child drove everything else from her mind as she froze in place.

"Baby, baby, come back!"

Her heart raced as she tried to get past the fear. Just past the shadows she could hear the baby's laughter, see the flowers as they bent upon impact of her passing, but she couldn't see her anywhere.

"Baby! Stay here with Mama or you're going to get lost . . . get lost . . . get lost."

The echo hurt. Billie closed her eyes against the pain and turned inward upon herself.

Even though Mel felt her pulling away, he had to say it. "Take care, honey. Aunt Addie and I love you and miss you. You hurry up and come back to us, you hear?"

With one last hug and a swift, parting kiss, he went to his car, suddenly anxious to get back to Memphis. He made himself a mental note to pick up some flowers after he landed. He couldn't remember the last time he'd bought Adelene flowers, or told her he loved her . . . really told her, not the halfhearted byword he tossed over his shoulder on the way out the door.

Yes, when he got home tonight, he was going to make up for lost time before something could steal his last chance.

✿ ✿ ✿ Chapter 16

"Matt! Help . . . help me!"

He sat straight up in bed, his heart slamming itself against the wall of his chest as he struggled to find the lamp switch. When a wash of white light flooded the room, he turned in silent confusion. He had to have been dreaming because he heard Billie speak.

A sheet was twisted around her waist and the braid that he'd made of her hair was coming apart. Long black strands were escaping as her head thrashed upon the pillow while she frantically grabbed at the air above the bed.

Matt grasped both hands, wanting her to know he was here.

"Billie . . . sweetheart . . . you talked!"

His voice was shaking as he scooped her from the bed and cradled her across his lap, rocking her as he used to rock Scott when he'd suffered bad dreams. Pressing his lips to her temple, he whispered softly against her ear.

"I'm here, darlin', I'm here. Just follow the sound of my voice back home."

She struggled within his embrace, fighting with

some demon only she could see, and then, to Matt's dismay, the agitation was over as suddenly as it had begun. She went limp in his arms.

Tears ran from beneath dark lashes while her lips moved in some silent recitation. He leaned closer, holding his breath and listening, praying that this was the breakthrough they'd been waiting for.

"Gone . . . before you could see. So perfect. So small." He felt her shudder, then heard her sigh. "Should have told you before. Too late. Too late."

A wave of tenderness washed over him. There was so much guilt in her voice, so much pain on her face. He needed her to understand that no matter what had happened, they still had each other.

"I love you, Billie. Do you hear me, sweetheart? I love you."

Like a window closing against the tempest of a storm, her features stilled, her breathing slowed, and while he watched, she came slowly awake.

Matt held his breath as she opened her eyes. There, in the space of a heartbeat, he saw recognition—right before the shutters fell back on her world.

"No!" he groaned, and held her even closer. "No, damn you! It's not too late. Tell me now, Billie. Help me understand. Don't do this to me! Don't you do this to me again!"

She lay there without moving, letting his pain wash over her like excess water spilling out of a dam.

Like a man possessed, he dumped her back on the bed and grabbed for his Levi's, jamming one foot and then the other into the long, boot-cut legs. Barefoot and shirtless, he dragged her from the bed and to her feet before leading her through the darkened rooms and out of the house.

Billie struggled to yank free from an unrelenting grasp. It was dark, so dark, and she couldn't find baby anywhere. The more she called, the more panicked she became.

Baby! Where are you, baby?

But there was no answer, only the soft, flapping sounds of a night moth as it flew against her face and then off into the night. The rough-hewn planks of the front porch were uneven beneath her bare feet. The sultry night air made the blood in her veins feel heavy, too thick to flow. The pressure upon her wrist stayed constant, an earthbound anchor that she bitterly resented.

Why? Why didn't they let her go? Didn't they understand? She needed to find the baby.

Matt took the steps at a frantic pace, hauling her firmly behind him with no hesitation as they stepped onto the grass. It stretched out before them all the way to the road, a cool jade carpet of substance and shadow.

Tiny brilliants scattered themselves through the heavens while the glow from a three-quarter moon washed the earth below. The night was still, the air heavy with the humidity of a dew waiting to fall.

Overwhelmed by an anger tinged with desperation, he grabbed both of Billie's hands and jerked her toward a flowering bush beside the porch.

"Feel this, damn it! It's real! It's alive." He grabbed at a thick clump of the tiny white blossoms running the length of each dangling spray, then yanked. They came away in his hand as he crushed them between his fingers and shoved them beneath her nose. "Smell these? They bloomed for you, Billie Jean, only you refuse to see!"

When she stared at a point in space just over his shoulder, he ground the tiny blooms between his fingers, then dropped them to the ground at their feet as he pulled her across the lawn. A few short strides later they reached the fence that separated yard from driveway. With a sharp tug, he slapped the flat of her hand against the smooth, treated cedar.

"It's the fence. The white cedar fence. Feel how smooth . . . how strong. Remember laughing at Mike when he tried to jump over it? Do you?"

By now he was shouting, praying for a sign that she heard him, almost wishing she would flinch from the sound, or turn on him in anger for raising his voice. All she did was sway in place like a broken doll trying to balance on worn-out legs. He took her by the shoulders, pulling her close until they were eye to eye, and he could feel the slow, plodding draw of each breath that she took.

"God damn you, Memphis! I saw you look! You saw me! Don't turn away from me again. You're in there somewhere. You have to be . . . I just know it!"

And then, as swiftly as the anger had come, it dissipated, leaving him weak and heartsick, ashamed for having treated her this way. A thin film of perspiration trickled down the middle of his back as he lifted her hands to his lips and, with a groan, gently kissed the tip of each finger in quiet regret. When he had finished, he pulled them to his chest, forcing them flat against his skin, splaying her fingers across the beat of his heart.

"Feel that? It's my heart, Billie Jean, and it's breaking. Please darlin'." His voice broke as he dropped his head. "I'm not strong enough to stand losing you *and* the baby. I love you, Billie. Help me to help you."

Instead of an answer, she shuddered, then moaned before dropping to her knees. With head bowed, she wrapped her arms around her middle and started to rock in a mindless, hopeless motion.

Matt stared, stunned by the fragile curve of her neck and the thick, dark braid hanging down her back. Her shoulders were slumped and shaking, as if the weight of the world was too fierce to uphold, while the hem of her gown was staining with the dew that was beginning to collect.

With a low, aching groan, he reached down and pulled her to her feet.

"I'm sorry, sweetheart. I'm so, so sorry." When he picked her up in his arms, she went unresisting. For a long, quiet moment he held her, his forehead resting against the crown of her hair. "I'd better get you back inside and into something dry. You're gown is all wet, and so are your feet."

His steps were slow and measured as he walked back into the house, taking great care not to bump or bounce her any further. As he entered the bedroom, the stark confusion on her face made him sick with remorse.

When he set her down on the bed and stripped off her gown, she offered no resistance, but when he took a clean T-shirt out of his drawer and pulled it back over her head, he thought he heard her sigh.

Pulling a towel from the rack, he went to his knees before her, gently drying one foot and then the other before tucking her back into bed. Before he stood up, he cupped her face with his hand, feathering a soft, reverent kiss near the edge of her mouth as he turned out the light.

"Go back to sleep, sweetheart. Maybe there you can find peace." His lips twisted bitterly as she settled in place. "If I knew how to get there, I'd join you," he said, then turned and walked out of the room.

A dog lying in wait in the road ditch bolted up and out, barking in a wild, frantic yelp at Daisy Bedford's tires as she sped down the road. With a curse and a frown, she swerved, hoping that she'd missed the damn thing. She'd hate like hell to have to tell Elvis Petrie that she'd run over one of his dogs.

A glance in the rearview mirror relieved her mind. She and the dog had lucked out this time. The wretched cur was already trotting back to the ditch with tail wagging and tongue hanging, readying itself to lie in wait for the next unsuspecting driver to happen that way.

Thank goodness. She was already late.

This fact accounted for her state of mind as well as the frantic pace at which she was driving. For the first time in longer than she could remember, she'd slept past seven o'clock. When the driveway leading to the Holt ranch appeared, she breathed a sigh of relief.

Moments later the brakes locked, and the wheels skidded across loose gravel as she brought her truck to a sliding halt at the front gate. She got out and trotted up the walk, the frazzled gray bun on her head bouncing with her rocking gait.

Appearance was the last thing on Daisy's mind. She'd given no thought to the ancient blue jeans and short-sleeved plaid shirt that she'd yanked from her closet. If it covered her person, then the purpose was served. She didn't care that her legs were more than slightly bowed or that her shoulders had slumped with age. Her spirit was still strong and willing.

Then she looked up. Matt was sitting on the top step, looking down at the ground while resting his elbows on his knees. He wore nothing except for Levi's and boots. No shirt. No hat. Not even a belt.

"Mornin', Matthew, isn't this a little early for sunbathing?"

He lifted his head, and the look in his eyes stopped her right where she stood. *Oh my. Oh no.* She was afraid to ask what was wrong.

"You have no idea," he drawled, and got to his feet. "She's still asleep."

Daisy stared as he came toward her. When he passed her, heading out of the yard, she turned, then yelled.

"Hey! You haven't eaten breakfast, have you? Are you sick? What happened here last night?" When she got no answer, she yelled even louder. "Matthew Wade Holt, where do you think you're going?"

He paused, then turned. The full force of early morning sunshine was right on his face. Worry niggled in the back of her mind as she stared. She would have sworn she could see tears in his eyes. She hadn't seen him cry since the day he'd brought Billie home.

"Matthew? Where *are* you going?"

"To hell, Daisy. To hell."

With that, he resumed his trek toward the barn. Twice Daisy thought about going after him, and each time she remembered the girl who would be left alone in the house. But when a familiar engine roar revved, then echoed within the confines of the tool shed, she spluttered, then cursed, then started after him. It was too late.

Matt burst out of the shed on the dirt bike, flying through a narrow opening between fences and jumping a cattle guard with no regard for safety. The bike fishtailed as it landed, then he quickly disappeared over a hill beyond the corrals.

"Oh good grief," Daisy muttered as she watched dust trying to settle in his wake. "That's just all I need. If you don't break your damn neck, Matthew Holt, I might do it for you."

With that, she hobbled into the house, slamming the door shut behind her.

Scott drove without a thought for the scenery, his mind fixed upon getting to the ranch. The phone calls from his dad had been few and far between, and when they'd come, Scott learned more of what was happening from what Matt didn't say than what he did.

Because of that, for the first time in his life, he dreaded coming home. Not so much for what he'd find when he got there, as for what might still be missing.

There was also the thing about the summer job he'd been offered. Granted it was only in Dallas, but too far away to commute. His dad had lived for the summers when he could come home, and Scott knew it. How was he going to react when he learned he had taken a job, and an apartment, away from home?

He glanced at his watch, noting both day and time. Exactly three days ago he'd taken his last final. On June 5 he was to start work. If the job panned out, it would be offered to him permanently after he finished his last semester.

With a determination that would have made Matt proud, Scott jutted his chin and stomped on the gas. He had exactly two days to find a way to say what had to be said.

Matt grunted as he leaned over the hood, tightening the last nut on the rebuilt carburetor that he'd just installed. The flatbed truck was old and had definitely seen better days, but it served its purpose very well. It had been missing part of the floorboard as well as one sideview mirror for years and would never have passed inspection. He hadn't bought insurance for it in over five years; he didn't consider it necessary since he never drove it off the ranch. It went from hay field to barn and back again, and when haying season was over, was parked in a shed.

Last year one of the barn cats had her litter on the seat, and he hadn't had the heart to disturb her until she moved them out on her own. By chance, he'd sold the first cutting of hay and hired men to haul the second one into the sheds. After that, an unexpected dry spell had ruined the last cutting of hay, so the cat had had a year of undisturbed tenancy.

But this year was another story. He'd kept the windows rolled up and patched the hole in the floor. In disgust, the cat had opted for the barn loft to drop her latest litter, leaving Matt to hammer and patch all he chose.

The last few weeks had played hell with his mind. The woman he loved was still caught in a place he couldn't see, couldn't hear, couldn't find. At night she slept in his arms, talking, sometimes even crying in a way she would not . . . maybe could not, do while awake.

The psychiatrist he'd consulted hadn't been any help. Even when Matt had explained that she'd started talking in her sleep, which was in his opinion a breakthrough, the man had been cautiously optimistic, recommending only two options. Matt could have her committed and let the professionals deal with her in their own ways, or wait and hope time could heal a broken spirit. For better or worse, Matt's choice was already made. He had let her leave once against his better judgment. It would never happen again.

With a grunt, he levered himself from underneath the hood and was reaching for a grease rag when a familiar Jeep came over the hill. It was Scott!

A brief smile broke the sharp angles of his face as he

wiped off his hands, dropped the rag on the tool box, and started toward the house.

Scott stood beside the Jeep for a moment, absorbing the familiarity of home as he took a deep breath and stretched, releasing tension from travel-weary muscles. Even though he longed for a good night's sleep, just being on Texas soil felt good.

"Hey, boy."

At the sound of Matt's voice, Scott turned, a wide grin upon his face. But when he saw his dad he was thankful that the Jeep stood between them. It gave him something to hold on to to steady the shock. He couldn't believe the change in his father's appearance. The upper body bulk of him that always strained at his shirts was absent, as was the solid band of muscle around his waist. He had the gaunt, wiry look of a man on the run.

Oh, man. Oh, Dad. What have you had to go through?

He circled the Jeep slowly, and when they came face-to-face, Scott was the first one to offer the hug. To his undying relief, Matt's grip was as strong and steady as ever, maybe even more so. His bulk was gone, but not his strength. Like Matt, it seemed unwavering.

"Been wondering when you'd show up."

Scott grinned. "I drove like hell to get here."

Matt nodded. Enough said. They knew each other well enough to read between the lines to the underlying wealth of love that father and son shared.

"Get your bags, and let's go inside. It's hot enough to fry tortillas on a hubcap out here."

"Dad?"

"Yeah?"

"How's Billie?"

He shrugged. "Come see for yourself"

It wasn't what Scott wanted to hear. Matt kicked the door shut behind him as he dropped his Stetson on a hook by the door.

"Hey, Daisy. Look who came home."

The old woman stuck her nose out of the kitchen long enough to arch her eyebrows and swipe at a hank of loose hair dangling near her ear. She grinned at Scott, then glanced at the suitcases both men were carrying.

"If that stuff's not all clean, don't expect me to do your laundry."

"Now I know I'm home," Scott drawled. "The only difference is I'm hearing that voice in person instead of on the answering machine."

She glared, waving a long wooden spoon dripping some kind of sauce. "Impudent pup. You keep your fancy California smart talk to yourself, boy. You're back in Texas, now, you hear?"

Matt eyed the drips and tried not to grin. "If I'd known we were eating off the floor tonight, I would have mopped it this morning before leaving the house."

"That does it! One's no better than the other! See what I have to put up with!" She glared at both men before swiping at the drips with a dish towel.

"Daisy, where's Billie?"

The old woman's expression softened perceptibly.

"On the back porch. Can't you hear that damn swing squeakin' on its chains?"

The baby squatted in a patch of sunlight, poking a short, chubby finger at a beetle that had made its way up the back steps.

"Careful, sweetheart. It might bite," Billie warned, and then, while she watched, the beetle took a sudden turn toward the baby's finger, startling her so that she fell backward onto her diapered bottom. Just as her face was screwing up for one heck of a wail, Billie scooped her into her arms.

"See, Mama told you to be careful." She sat down in the porch swing, settling the little girl upon her shoulder. Tiny sniffles sounded near her ear as she patted her on the back, cuddling her close to her heart. "You're okay. You're okay. You're not really hurt, are you? No, you're not. Mama's baby is a big girl, yes you are."

As they swung, Billie rested her cheek against the child's soft curls, relishing the love and unwavering trust of a child.

"Such a brave little girl. You're going to be just like your daddy, aren't you? Never afraid of anything." She took a deep breath, letting it out on a sigh. "And you'll grow up too fast, won't you, baby?" Instinctively she tightened her hold. "But that's not for a while, right? It will be a long, long time before Mama has to let you go."

The screen door creaked on its hinges as Scott exited the house. Fooled by the sweet smile on Billie's face, he went straight up to her and took her by the hand.

"Hey, B.J., long time no see."

Billie jerked as the baby slipped out of her arms and toddled off the porch and out into the yard.

Baby . . . don't go too far or Mama won't be able to see you.

To Scott's dismay, Billie's smile disappeared, replaced by a vague, unsettled expression and a blank, dull stare. Scott turned her hand loose and looked up at Matt.

"Uh, Dad, did I do something wrong?"

Matt scooted into the swing beside her. Sliding his arm across the back of the swing, he pulled her close, giving her a quick hug and kiss.

"No. She reacts to Daisy and me the same way." He ruffled her hair in a light, teasing manner. "She just likes what's up here"—he pecked the top of her head with his finger—"better than what's out here."

Tears blurred Scott's vision. Embarrassed, he looked away, but not before Matt saw.

"Don't be ashamed to show your feelings, son. God knows I've done enough of that in the last few months to last me a lifetime."

A sudden understanding of the devastation his father had been enduring just dawned. Scott turned, his face filled with sympathy, for Matt—and for Billie.

"God . . . I'm so sorry."

"For what? None of this is your fault." And then he sighed. "Hell, for that matter, very little of it is mine. I lay full blame at the feet of that bastard who called himself her father. He's the one who ruined her trust in men. He's the one who taught her that failure was her heritage." Old anger deepened his voice. "And although we may never know for sure, I think he's the one who caused her to fall."

Without pausing to care whether she liked it or not, Matt pulled Billie from her seat and into his arms, letting her legs dangle off the edge of the swing as he tucked the hem of her sundress carefully around her knees.

Her resistance was slight, but it was there just the same. For Matt, it was more than she'd shown at first. He pushed off with the toe of his boot, then kept the swing rocking as she settled within his embrace.

"She likes to swing and rock. Whatever she wants, she gets. I just wish to God she'd turn around one day and tell me to leave her the hell alone." His voice was wistful as he looked back at Scott. "That's what I wish."

Once again, Scott turned away, staring out at the wide-open spaces beyond the backyard and wishing he hadn't come home. He felt like an intruder at a funeral, although no one was dead. When he looked back at Billie he wondered if it was wrong. There was nothing left of the B.J. he'd known. Like the baby she'd lost, maybe she was already dead and she just didn't know it.

Scott came in the back door on the run. Grease streaked his T-shirt and the edge of his jaw. When he reached for the phone, Daisy glared at the stains on his hands. With a nervous grin, he paused, then headed for the bathroom. A few minutes later he came back a wiser and cleaner man than when he'd gone in.

He held up his hands for her review. "Better?"

She shrugged, muttering to herself as she walked out of the room. "Don't much matter to me how you look. It's not my house."

He rolled his eyes and picked up the receiver, punching in the numbers he now knew by heart.

"Mr. Masterson? It's Scott Holt. I just wanted to let you know that I'd be reporting for work on Monday as we'd planned." He listened, memorizing the instructions that he was being given, then nodded as his soon-to-be-boss finished. "Yes sir," he added. "I won't let you down."

He was still smiling when he turned around. Matt was leaning against the door with a cocky grin curving the corner of his mouth.

"Uh, Dad, I was going to tell you . . ."

Matt interrupted. "I hope that's about a job. I'd hate to think I wasted four good years of my hard-earned money just so you could come home and dodge cow manure."

Scott went weak with relief. "It's a good job, Dad—with a Fortune 500 company that's really going places. The best part is, if I do well this summer, they've promised me a position after I graduate."

Matt smiled. "Congratulations, Son. I'm really proud of you."

"There's only one catch. It looks as if there will be lots of long hours with little extra pay. I was also told that I will be on call should a crisis arise."

"So?"

"So . . . I figured I'd better live in Dallas this summer rather than try to commute."

From the very first moment that Matt had held his son in his arms, he'd known this day was coming. As inevitable as it was, it was still tough to accept, but he'd be damned if he'd let Scott know it. Instead of bemoaning it, he grinned.

"Think you're ready to be a real swinging bachelor, huh?"

Scott almost blushed. "Lord, Dad. I've more or less been living on my own for years now. I'm not exactly wet behind the ears."

"Oh, I didn't say you were wet. I just want to make sure you aren't still a little bit damp."

A quick surge of fear almost made Scott retract his own words. It was done! His dad knew and didn't object. All of a sudden he felt as lost and useless as a newly weaned calf with a wide-open meadow before him. There were so many places to go, and yet the only place that seemed safe was right back where he'd been.

"I'll probably come home most weekends."

Matt grinned. "How much do you want to bet?"

They both laughed.

"You know what, Dad?"

Matt waited.

"Being a college graduate isn't so much. I hope one day I learn to be as smart as you."

The grin slid off Matt's face, replaced by a sharp, almost-angry look. "Just try not to make as many mistakes as I did in the process."

Chapter 17

Scott had come and gone so swiftly that after a while it seemed he'd never been there. Although his phone calls home were more frequent than when he'd been in college, they were also briefer. Matt could sense him pulling away. In one respect he was glad, because that meant Scott was learning how to be his own man, not just Matt Holt's son. But on the other hand, it only intensified Matt's loneliness.

June moved into July and then beyond, taking Scott back to California to finish his last semester. Hot days melted one into the other, moving Matt and Billie into a phase where the oddity of their lives almost seemed normal.

A straight south wind was blasting through Texas. It had been blowing steadily for the better part of two days and taking Matt's patience with it. Cattle had drifted into bunches and were standing with their heads down, their rumps to the wind. If anything was loose, it was either flapping and popping or blowing across some prairie, forcing Matt to go about his chores with a hammer and nails at close hand.

In spite of one of Daisy's dire warnings, he'd even climbed on top of the barn and refastened loose nails in the sheet-metal roof. She'd watched from the porch with her heart in her mouth as he'd traversed the angles and peaks of the roof upright, expecting him to be blown off at any moment. When he'd finally come down, satisfied that everything was firmly in place, she'd breathed a quiet sigh of relief and gone back into the house.

Even Billie seemed restless. The wind howled beneath the eaves and whistled through unseen cracks, giving a lost, eerie whine to an already-unnerving sound. Matt brought the cane rocker in from the front porch, placing it before the living room windows, where she sat and rocked in a frantic rhythm, as if trying to keep pace with the wind. It seemed as if all of Texas was blowing north, one layer of earth at a time.

By midafternoon of the third day, Matt had taken refuge inside the barn to do some odd jobs. Even though it was sweltering inside the small tack room, he chose it over the blast furnace of sand in the air outside. Although he'd sold their last horse over a year ago, he worked for more than an hour on the tack, repairing bridles, soaping saddles, mending and replacing girths. Anything to keep himself busy.

After a while, there was nothing left there to do. With a weary sigh, he took the bandanna out of his hip pocket and wiped at the sweat running down his face before returning what he'd been using to the shelves. His hands were full of bottles and jars when a strong gust of wind blew something straight through the only window in the room.

It sounded like a gunshot and happened so quickly that Matt didn't have time to do more than throw up his hands to protect his face and eyes from the shattering glass.

A quick, burning sensation seared his right arm, and the palms of his hands suddenly felt as if they were on fire.

"Son of a—"

He staggered backward as wind began tunneling through the new opening, blowing bits and pieces of whatever was loose, mixing that with the broken glass and the blood dripping from the ends of his fingers.

For a moment he just stood, staring in confusion at the bright red spots congealing with the dust on the tack room floor. Then a wave of dizziness hit him, and he shook his head, trying to clear his vision. The weakness shocked him almost as much as it scared him. He'd been hurt a thousand times in his life, and he'd never reacted like this.

Then he looked at his shirtsleeve and, in spite of the heat, felt cold. From just above the elbow it was soaked with blood and sticking to his skin all the way to his wrist. Brushing away the glass fragments from the palms of his hands, he stuck his finger in the rip on his sleeve and pulled.

At that point panic set in. A bright red spray instantly patterned itself on his shirtfront.

"Oh hell," he muttered. An artery had been cut. Instinctively, he reached to staunch the flow. But when he started to squeeze, pain shattered his resolve. In shock, he yanked his hand away and stared at the palm.

He could see gashes between the wide streaks of blood and suspected that pieces of glass must still be inside. The more pressure he put on his arm, the deeper the bits gouged into him. But for Matt, his choices were already gone. He gritted his teeth, ignored the pain, and grabbed at his arm.

Within seconds he was out of the door and running toward the house, holding his arm as tightly as he could bear.

The wind lifted the Stetson right off his head. It sailed with the currents like a flat, black sail and disappeared into a dust cloud. He didn't care. He'd been meaning to buy a new one for years.

Grit pummeled his face as he ducked his head, trying to protect his eyes from the worst of the punishment. Once he looked up, judging the distance he had yet to go and, for the first time since the accident, faced the possibility that he could actually bleed to death within yards of his own home. The house seemed miles away, and his vision was starting to waver. And then he saw Billie looking out the window. He couldn't die. What would happen to her if he did?

With renewed determination, he kept moving, one foot in front of the other. When his boot hit a step, a wave of profound relief nearly sent him to his knees. If he could just get inside, Daisy would help.

He grabbed for the doorknob, but his fingers slid around it as if it had been greased. He looked down. His hand was slick with blood.

With desperation in every movement, he swiped his hand on his jeans, then reached for it again.

"Damn it, turn!"

And it did.

He was shouting Daisy's name as he staggered through the doorway and kicked the door shut behind him. After the perpetual roar from outside, the muted sounds within the house seemed ominously silent.

He leaned against the wall, clutching his arm as tightly as he could bear, while a fresh wave of dizziness came over him.

Oh God, I can't pass out. I'll bleed to death before she even finds me. He took a deep breath and shouted.

"Daisy! Daisy! Help me! I need help!"

But no one answered, and no one came running. The only sound was the constant, repetitive squeak of Billie's rocker.

Billie! She *could* help . . . if only she would.

He staggered toward her chair, coming to a stop between her and the view. Maybe if he could get her attention—

He leaned down, and his blood began dripping in perfect red circles upon her hands, her arms, and the front of her skirt.

"Billie? Sweetheart? Where's Daisy?"

Her nostrils flared as she jerked back, almost in shock. Matt had no way of knowing that he'd walked right between her and the image of their baby that lived inside her head.

"Damn it to hell, Billie Jean! It's me, Matt. Help me." His blood was now splattering her hands and running between her fingers. "Please wake up and help me." And then his voice broke as he straightened and swayed. "Sweet Jesus, I must be worse off than I thought if I'm asking you for help."

He staggered toward the kitchen area, determined that he could make it that far. Daisy had to be there. No one left Billie alone.

Baby was restless. Billie didn't blame her. The wind had been blowing hard for days, too hard for her to go out to play. Today was even worse. Although it was way past her nap time, no matter how hard Billie rocked, she wasn't able to get her to sleep.

"Ssh, baby, Mama's here . . . right here."

The baby snuffled against her neck. Billie smiled as she rocked. Dear God but she loved this child. Even her tears were precious.

She kept the chair moving with the toe of her shoe, back and forth, back and forth, patting the child's bottom in rhythm to the motion. And finally, she felt the baby relax and knew that she'd fallen asleep.

She shifted her hold now, cradling the little girl in her arms, savoring the quiet time when she could gaze her fill at the child she and Matt had made with their love.

Even asleep their baby looked like Matt. Thick dark hair lay in tangles all over her head, and eyelashes so black they looked like shadows lay motionless upon her soft cheeks. Billie ran her finger down the curve of her cheek and smiled. When she was pouting, she even jutted her chin and pursed her tiny mouth just like him.

"I love you, little girl. So, so much."

And then a shadow fell across Billie's lap and she frowned. That awful wind. It had blocked out the sun. She hated it when that happened. Baby liked the sunshine, even when she slept.

The shadow darkened as the wind began to wail. From out of nowhere, an overwhelming sadness gripped Billie's soul. A band of real pain tightened around her heart, and she panicked, clutching the baby even closer to her breast. When she did, the baby awoke, looking up at Billie in sleepy, blue-eyed confusion.

"I'm sorry, darling, did Mama wake you?"

To her dismay, the baby started to cry. But not the loud, wailing sound of an unhappy child. Instead, they were the quiet, constant tears of an earthbound angel longing for home, running from the corners of tiny blue eyes and onto Billie's arms.

Fear made Billie mute. All she could do was stare, then watch in horror as the child's image slowly disappeared.

"No! God, no!"

The wail came up from the depths, from the heart, from the soul of a mother who'd been left behind. Billie jerked as a painful awareness came to her. It was the gut-wrenching knowledge that all she had left of the baby were tears.

She blinked, and blinked again. Sounds became louder inside her head. The room grew lighter, then even lighter still. She looked up and out through the window to the dust blowing past, to the trees bending low, to the flower bed only partially sheltered from the ongoing blast. She clutched at the arms of the rocker, then quickly jerked her hands back in disgust as she became aware of something sticky all over her skin.

She looked down. Instead of tears she saw blood. All over her hands, her arms, even the front of her dress. Stunned, she tried to remember if she'd hurt herself, if she'd taken a fall. But she was here in the rocker, safe from the wind, and she felt no pain.

She stood up in a daze and then turned. More blood! There on the rug, then the floor and down the hall. A mysterious red trail that disappeared through a door farther down.

Without thought, she followed the drops. With a pounding heart, she walked into the kitchen and into an ongoing nightmare.

He was leaning against the cabinet trying to dial the phone. His features were twisted from pain, and his skin was so pale. Too pale. With near-silent steps, she moved across the room. When she was right behind him, she touched his arm with her hand, and he reacted as if he'd been shot.

"Matt?"

He turned, and the look on his face just before he passed out was one of utter joy.

Billie dropped to her knees and instinctively tried to staunch the flow of blood.

"Matt?"

He didn't respond. An overpowering rage made her shake, made her weak. Still clutching at the wound on his arm, she screamed his name over and over into the quiet of the room.

Daisy came up and out of the storm cellar on the peak of a scream. The sound stopped her in her tracks. Someone was screaming Matt's name.

"Oh Lord," she muttered, and made a dash for the door, moving faster than she'd moved in years.

She came in on the run. Taking one look at the man on the floor and the woman trying unsuccessfully to staunch a life-threatening flow of blood, she reached for the phone.

"Is he going to be okay? Please, Scott, tell me the truth?"

Scott's arm tightened on Billie's shoulders as she stood beside Matt's bed, staring with red-rimmed eyes at the unconscious man she loved more than life.

"I swear, honey. The doctor said he'll be weak for a while, but that he's going to be fine. You and Daisy saved his life."

"Why doesn't he wake up? It's been hours."

Scott shrugged, then frowned. He couldn't help but worry a little himself, but if the truth be told, one of them had to stay calm, and the way things had been going, he was it. Even Daisy had lost her composure. Right after the ambulance had taken Matt away, she'd called Scott in tears, trying to explain about Billie's awakening and his father's accident, all in one breath.

But that was yesterday, and this was today, and he was trying to follow some of his father's old advice and not dwell on the past. Matt had lived by an axiom that eating the same food twice was impossible, so swallow what you bit into and get on with it. The way things had gone, it was damned good advice. He just wanted his dad to wake up and raise a little hell. It would make things seem a whole lot more normal.

And then, while they were watching, Matt started to move. Only a little at first. A couple of fingers twitched, then his eyelids fluttered. Scott even thought he heard a soft moan.

Billie gasped, then clutched at Scott's sleeve. *Oh, thank you, God.*

"Scott, look! I think he's waking up."

Scott leaned down. "Dad? It's me, Scott. Can you hear me?"

Matt opened his eyes. Confusion mixed with pain as he fought his way back to cognizance.

"Scott?" He started to move, then winced and looked down at his arm. His voice was thick, his movements groggy.

"What happened?"

"You cut your arm, but you're okay."

"Cut my arm? How? When did it—?" And then everything came back all at once. The memory of flying glass, of trying to get to the house, and of Billie calling his name.

"Billie . . . where's Billie?"

With a pounding heart and more regret than she knew how to voice, she moved from behind Scott and into his line of sight.

"I'm here."

He closed his eyes in a momentary prayer of thanksgiving. *I didn't imagine this after all.* When he looked up, he held out his hand.

Her fingers curled into fists as she hesitated. As much as she wanted to touch him, there was something she had to say first.

"There's something I need to tell you."

The room tilted, and Matt took a deep breath, willing himself not to go out just yet. "No, darlin', you don't need to—"

Scott gave Billie a long look, gauging her newfound strength of mind against what she was about to face. Satisfied with what he saw, he gave her a quick hug.

"I'll be right outside if you need me," he assured her, then walked out of the room.

Billie took a slow, deep breath. How does one put pain into words? And then she looked into Matt's eyes and saw deliverance. There was love, and trust, and something she hadn't expected. She saw pride. After all the wrong choices that she'd made, how could he feel this way?

Her chin trembled, and tears filled her eyes.

"Oh, Matt, we were going to have a baby. The most beautiful little girl in the world." Her voice broke, and she took a deep breath, trying to say the unthinkable. "I'm so sorry. I didn't mean to lose her."

He tried to smile. In spite of what he'd just endured, she was somehow still the more fragile.

"Come here, darlin'. Come let me hold you."

Her eyes widened, spilling more tears as she stared at the bandages and the IV.

"I'm afraid I'll hurt you."

His smile broke, then tilted downward, and it was all he could do not to cry himself.

"On the contrary, Memphis. You're going to hurt me if you don't."

With a shudder, she took a step forward, then slowly leaned over, letting her head rest just below his chin.

"I love you, Matt Holt."

His hand fisted in the thickness of her hair, then loosened as quickly. He'd learned the hard way that to keep someone you love, you have to let go.

"Ah, God, darlin', I love you, too, but I was beginning to think I'd never hear you say that again."

She lifted her head. Unable to bear the distance between them, she reached for his arm, running her fingers lightly against the surface of his skin.

"I left you, didn't I?"

He nodded, then blinked as the room started to spin. Damn this weakness. He needed to think, not to pass out. He tried another smile and reached for her hand.

"But you didn't go far. When it was time, you came back, just like I always knew that you could."

A swift memory of where she had been made her weak. Had it all been a dream? Or had God really given her a glimpse into heaven after all?

"I wish you could have seen her."

Matt's heart was breaking in so many pieces. For him . . . for Billie . . . and for the baby daughter that he'd never hold.

"I do, too, sweetheart. I do, too."

And then he moved her hand to his face, cherishing

the softness of her skin against the stubble of day-old whiskers. "Billie?"

She moved closer.

"Do you love me?"

She managed a smile. "Yes."

"Enough to marry me?"

Her breath caught on a sob. "Yes, oh, yes."

Matt closed his eyes, letting a fresh wave of vertigo pass. "Then that's that," he mumbled, trying to remember if he'd left anything out.

"You need to rest," she whispered, and cradled his hand in her own, feeling the strength and remembering the tenderness.

He nodded, and still she couldn't bring herself to walk away. Maybe she'd stay just a little while longer . . . at least until he was asleep. She didn't want him to have to fall asleep alone. He might get nervous. Even afraid. She couldn't bear it if he was afraid.

Scott poked his head inside the door, saw that his dad was asleep, then whispered that he was going down the hall and would bring them back something to eat. Billie nodded, relieved that he wasn't going to insist that she leave. At least not just yet.

Matt's breathing eased into a more normal rhythm, and she knew that he was drifting. With a tender touch, she brushed the short, dark strands of hair from his forehead, then glanced down at the thick brush of his lashes making shadows on his cheeks. A picture flashed in her mind as she watched him sleep, a picture of a little girl with dark curls and bright eyes who'd run through flowers after butterflies too swift to catch.

"Oh, Matt, I want to have another baby with you. I will take such good care of it, I promise."

Right on the edge of a dream, he heard her whisper. He struggled, trying to wake up enough to tell her yes, that she could have a houseful of babies if she wanted. As long as she loved him, it would be all right.

But he was too tired, and she was too quiet, and he fell the rest of the way asleep.

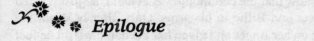 **Epilogue**

It was snowing outside the church. Little bitty persistent flakes that did nothing more than mess up a windshield, but it was nevertheless a snow. Matt didn't care. In fact, it seemed fitting. They'd met in a blizzard. The least they could do was get married in the snow.

The sanctuary was full. Friends and acquaintances had gathered and were waiting to witness the union of Billie Jean Walker and Matthew Wade Holt. Some swore they couldn't believe it was happening, others claimed it had been inevitable.

Mel and Adelene Deal were on the bride's side of the church in the pew where parents should sit. In Billie's eyes, they were all the family she had.

Daisy Bedford sat straight and proud, claiming the same right for the groom. Her wild tangle of flying gray hair was neatly wound up in a twist, and she'd even forgone her usual attire of blue jeans and boots for a tea-length chiffon dress of soft baby blue. She might have passed for a sweet little old lady except for the glitter in her eye. It was all the warning she was willing to give that clothes did not make the man . . . or woman.

Matt fidgeted as he peeked through the door toward the altar. He'd waited all of his life to marry for love, and now that the ceremony was at hand, he just wanted it over and Billie in his arms. Only after he'd put the ring on her finger and given her his name would he feel safe. They'd given up so much to get to this day. Surely nothing would happen to ruin it. Not now. Not when they were so close.

"Look out, Dad. You're leaning on the decorations."

At Scott's warning he looked down, then stepped back, relieved that he hadn't ruined the flower arrangements, although it would hardly have been noticed.

Bright crimson poinsettias were everywhere. Dozens and dozens of pots had been placed along the floor in front of the altar, as well as on every pedestal, then massed in a pyramid shape directly behind where the preacher would stand. The true Christmas red honored the holiday and highlighted the brightly lit tree sitting off to one side.

Instead of the usual greenery one expected at weddings, dark pine wreaths hung from hooks on the walls, each decorated by a single, dangling red bow. The air inside the church was warm, bringing out the clean scent of fresh-cut evergreens.

Scott thumped his dad on the shoulder as a big grin spread across his face.

"You know, Dad, you're real smart. Getting married on New Year's Eve is a sure way never to forget your anniversary."

Matt didn't even smile. "I couldn't forget marrying Billie if I tried."

Silenced by the solemnity with which his father was taking this day, Scott could only nod in agreement. Out of all of this he'd learned one hard-and-fast truth about himself. He didn't ever intend to get married until he loved a woman the way his dad loved Billie. And God willing, she would love him right back.

The preacher opened the door and leaned inside. "Gentlemen, it's time."

Matt's heart skipped a beat as he followed the preacher into the sanctuary. As he took his place at the foot of the altar and Scott moved in behind him, he realized that, in a twist of irony, Scott was going to be at the altar at both of his father's weddings. Granted Scott hadn't been born for the first, but he'd been there just the same. It only seemed fair that he serve as best man at the last. He was the best man Matt knew.

The organist struck a chord. The familiar strains of "Silent Night" suddenly filled the air as Stephanie Hodge entered the room. As Billie's only attendant, she came down the aisle with a smile on her face, clutching a nosegay of fresh holly and pine. The hem of her green velvet gown lightly brushed the floor as she swept past the pews. When she got to the altar, she winked at Matt. To her delight, he winked back. Blond curls bounced as she stifled a giggle. She should have known she was out of her league in trying to tease a man like Matt Holt.

While they were still smiling, the organist paused. A quick silence filled the church. Matt turned, then held his breath. As he looked up the aisle, a swell of music brought everyone to their feet.

And then she was standing in the doorway, and he didn't think he'd ever seen a more beautiful sight. If he squinted his eyes and pretended a bit, he could have believed that an ice fairy had walked in from the cold. She was dressed all in white, from the top of her veil to the toes of her shoes.

And she'd chosen it not for the virginal color, but in commemoration of the day that they'd met. The full, gathered skirt floated around her like snow, and the veil that covered her face drifted as she started to move.

Billie blinked, peering through tears and tulle, trying to clear her vision enough to chance starting down the aisle. Her heart tugged as the music engulfed her. On the happiest day of her life it seemed she couldn't stop crying.

Oh God. This is so hard to do alone. Please don't let me make a fool of myself.

Because she had no close friends with small children, she'd chosen not to have a flower girl. But when she started down the aisle, the strangest thing happened. As she took her first steps, she could almost see the image of a small, dark-haired girl with curls bouncing, scattering fistfuls of flowers that she'd yanked from their beds. The image was so real that she almost missed a step.

Don't, Billie. Don't do this to Matt—or to yourself.

She paused and took a deep breath, focusing on the love of her life, who waited at the end of the aisle. He was waiting for her to catch up, just as he'd been from the first day they'd met. All she had to do was take the next step, and the next, and she would be in his arms. She lifted her head, fixed her eyes on the end of the aisle, and started toward him.

Matt's gaze was locked upon her passage, so when she stumbled, it was more than he could bear. Her whole life had been so solitary. Rules and manners be damned—he wasn't going to let her take another step alone. His chin jutted as he stepped out of his place and went up the aisle to meet her.

When Billie saw him coming, she started to smile. And when they were face-to-face, he winked, then stepped to one side, offering his arm. She took what he offered, then held on tight.

It would later be said by all the women who'd witnessed the stunt that it was the most romantic thing they'd ever seen. The men had another view of Matt Holt. They claimed he'd always walked a path not taken, so why should he change his ways now?

Unaware of the whispers flying about the room, they had eyes only for each other as they stood at the altar, waiting for a man of God to bind them forever. One had only to look to see the calm on their faces and the peace in their hearts to know that this was right. Whatever happened from this day forward, they would face it the same way they'd come down the aisle.

Together.